AF497254

A NEW
HISTORY OF DOVER,

AND OF

DOVER CASTLE,

DURING THE

ROMAN, SAXON, AND NORMAN GOVERNMENTS,

With a short Account of

THE CINQUE PORTS,

Compiled from Ancient Records,

AND CONTINUED TO THE PRESENT TIME;

BY

W. BATCHELLER,

Embellished with four Plates, & illustrated by four Plans.

TO WHICH IS ADDED

A NEW DOVER GUIDE,

And a Description of the

VILLAGES NEAR DOVER.

Dover:

PRINTED AND PUBLISHED BY WILLIAM BATCHELLER,

KING'S ARMS LIBRARY.

1828.

PREFACE.

In this concise history it is intended to comprise, within a narrow compass, whatever may be found most interesting relative to the Town and Port of Dover, to its venerable Castle, or to its romantic and picturesque neighbourhood. Although our limits have rendered it necessary to omit some particulars, and concisely to treat of others; and although the present treatise forms an abridgement of a larger work* intended for publication, (should a sufficient number of subscribers be obtained for that purpose,) yet we hope to present to our readers the leading features of Dover history, so far as such an abridgement will admit.

Great care has been taken to arrange the different subjects in a regular and successive order; and, by means of a general statement of contents, and a copious index, to render it perfectly easy to refer to any particular object or event.

In our account of the castle, it has been our aim to give a general description of that ancient fortress; and to trace the various changes that have

---

* See the prospectus, at the end of this volume.

taken place from the remote period, when the lofty
eminence on which it is seated, wore the livery of
its native green, and was ascended only by the
solitary hunter in his pursuit of the wild deer,
down to the present moment, when we see it
studded with forts and crowned with battlements;
and to view in succession, the sodded encampment of the haughty Roman, the massy walls and
towers of the fierce Saxon, and the more finished
and regular fortifications of the polished Norman,
displaying, within a short distance of each other,
specimens of ancient masonry, through a long
succession of past ages.

The grand and beautiful views, presented to the
eye of an observer, placed on these towering battlements, have been carefully noticed; and the
present state of the fortress, the modern defences,
and the appearance of this majestic pile, when
viewed at a distance, have been attentively considered.

In describing the various buildings and entrenchments, we have found it necessary to introduce
some technical particulars, which, however interesting to the antiquarian, we fear may not be
so agreeable to every class of readers. Had our
limits been more extended, it would have been our
object to have diverted the tediousness of such
details, by introducing a greater number of events
and circumstances, illustrative of the manners and
habits of the times to which they belong.

To point out the more confined camp of the
Romans, the extended works of the Saxons, and

the exterior walls and forts of the Normans, we have introduced four wood cuts, which delineate the ground plans of the works constructed by each race of these warriors. We should have been more gratified to have substituted copper plates; but the expense would have been too great for this small treatise.

In our review of the cinque ports, among which Dover has ever held a conspicuous rank, our limits have confined us to a general notice of their heroic and brilliant deeds of arms, which are recorded in our ancient histories.

The history of the town and port is traced from a remote antiquity, when the hardy and painted natives, issuing from their woods and wilds, formed their warlike ranks on the declivities of the mountains, which at that time enclosed the port, and viewed, with hostile eye, the Roman navy approach the haven, which then covered the bed of the valley. The Romans triumph; the sea recedes; and this enterprising people fill the vacant space with walls, baths, battlements, and towers, which, in succeeding ages, are mutilated and despoiled by the fierce Saxon. The Norman rebuilds the ruinated heaps, and extends the fortifications; and, in the course of another century, the town is adorned with stately buildings and majestic edifices. These fell a prey much less to the ravages of time, than to the desolating spirit of avarice and oppression, which, in the reign of Henry the Eighth, scattered their baneful influence over the whole kingdom. The tyranny of the monarch is imitated by his representatives, the leading men in the principal towns, the privileges and immunities of which being wrested or bartered away, a long night of declining prosperity ensues, and this place, among others, is visited by comparative indigence. The narrow policy and avaricious spirit that darkened the minds of the rulers, paralyzed the sinews of industry; and, blinded by self interest, they could not perceive that their own prosperity rested on the general welfare of their fellow towsmen, and that both must ultimately stand or fall together. The narrow and crooked streets, which at the present day deform many parts of the town, are strong evidences of such a perverted policy and of such indigence; and though improvements are rapidly advancing, many years will be necessary to remedy the defect.

In our account of the churches and religious houses, we have endeavoured to give a picture of past ages, and to avoid every thing like censure in mentioning the rites and ceremonies that have given place to a more enlightened devotion. And though we are not ashamed to be called Christians, or to acknowledge that religion justly claims our first and chief attention; and though we think not lightly of the numerous divisions that have unhappily taken place among us, yet we hope it may not be discovered in our narrative, whether we be Roman catholics, members of the established church, or seceders from it. The dissenters now form a large and respectable portion of society; and the ingenuous reader will candidly confess that their places of worship have a fair claim to our notice: and, in searching for their origin, we have been able more clearly to elucidate the social history of the town, during the last two centuries.

Ground plans would have been very desirable in our description of the harbour, and we were desirous of introducing them; but the expense would have greatly enhanced the price of the work. We have, however, so far as any records can be found, endeavoured to point out, in as clear a manner as possible, the various changes that have taken place in this once famous haven, since the time when it left its ancient bed in the valley.

In delineating the civil jurisdiction of the town, we have found considerable difficulty; and though we confine ourselves to a simple relation of facts, without adventuring remarks of our own, we are fearful it may seem to convey a reflection on the present bench of magistrates. Nothing, however, can be farther from our intention; and we give place to no man, in reverence to their office, in a ready obedience to their authority, or in fervent wishes that their government may be an honor to themselves, and it must then prove a blessing to those who live under it. And we cannot conceive it possible that any one should suppose, that the magistrates of the present day, can be accountable for any unworthy transactions of their predecessors.

We beg to express our gratitude for the kind assistance we have received from many worthy friends, whose names we do not consider ourselves at liberty to mention.

The difficulty and expense in collecting materials for this work, have been much greater than was anticipated; and the numerous references that have been made to ancient and modern authors, have required much time and attention: and though brevity has been studied, so far as could be consistent with perspicuity, the size of the book, has exceeded our first calculation.

We conclude our preface by soliciting the indulgence of the public to this first attempt; and should any errors have been inadvertently admitted, we should feel obliged to any one, who would have the kindness to apprise us of them.

CONTENTS.

CONTENTS.

DOVER CASTLE.

HISTORY OF DOVER.

—»»●●●««—

THE CASTLE.

THE earliest accounts respecting this majestic
castle, occur in the writings of our ancient historians, and some few scattered remains, in those
of other countries. The enquirer, on referring
to them, will soon find cause to regret that, instead of the result of actual investigation, he
meets with little more than a repetition of legen-
dary traditions. It is not surprising, then, that
the stream of its history, arising from such a
source, should flow on turbid and confused,
involving the origin of this venerable pile,

  ——— " scarce less strangely
" Than those more massy and mysterious giants
" Of Architecture, those Titanian fabrics
" Which point, in Egypt's plains, to times that have
" No other record."

A castle, in its general sense, is a place or
strong hold, fortified by nature or art, and may
include the various methods of encampment; but

in its stricter meaning, it is usually applied to buildings walled with stone, and intended for residence, as well as defence.

Early fortifications appear to have been little more than mere entrenchments of earth, situated chiefly on the tops of natural hills: and the dens in the mountains and the thickets of Scripture, have been considered as strong holds or hill fortresses of a similar description. That their high places were used, in the earliest ages, for warlike purposes there can be no question; for we find that the Israelites assembled to make their stand upon Mount Tabor, in consequence of an exhortation from Deborah the prophetess, when their land was invaded by Jabin, the king of Canaan. Also, when Samson had made a great slaughter of the Philistines, he went and dwelt on the top of the rock Elam, where we find afterwards three thousand men of Israel went up to confer with him. Many specimens of this rude kind of entrenchment, remain at the present day in this island, and it is very probable that the first erections on the hill near Dover, were of a similar kind.

Seated on the summit of a high cliff, on the north-east of the town,

" A noble wreck in ruinous perfection,"

the Romantic Castle of Dover has often invited the pencil of the artist, and arrested the attention of the traveller. It is no less renowned in history; and our early writers speak of it as being the key of the whole kingdom, and represent it as a fortress of the first importance, both in regard to its great strength, and as forming the principal point of defence opposite the coast of France. Almost inaccessible from its natural position, endeavours have been made to render it impregnable by the military constructions of successive ages. It offers, in consequence, to the eye a confusion of style in its several parts; the more ancient of which have been suffered to moulder into ruins, while the later additions have a manifest reference to the altered system of warfare. Since the bow and the battle-axe have been laid aside for the cannon and the mortar, the commanding hills in the neighbourhood, formerly of little avail, now present a formidable means of attack, and lessen the importance of this fortification.

The numerous and diversified combination of works and buildings here presenting themselves, is calculated to render this one of the most interesting castles in the kingdom; since it is capable of affording ample gratification to the admirer of antiquity, in its specimens of Roman, Saxon, and Norman masonry; and both pleasure and instruction to every spectator, where an opportunity is offered of contemplating the ancient and modern systems of warfare on the same spot.   B 2

THE ROMAN FORTIFICATIONS.

Of the Roman military works in this country, the greater part were temporary; many, however, were stationary posts; and some few, to which the greatest importance was attached, became walled encampments. Those which at present occupy the hill adjoining Dover, are bounded by the surrounding ditch,[1] and it will be unavailing to seek for additional traces of their labour in the castle beyond it.

The octagon building, the parapet, the peculiar form of the camp and ditch, all demonstrate the skilful hand of the Roman architect and engineer. Indeed, it was the constant practice of this brave and enterprising people, where the extent of the ground would permit, to raise their camp in the form of a parallelogram, with curved angles, resembling an oval,[2] and to secure the same by the aid of a high parapet and deep ditch. Such appears to have been the original design of the Roman camp on this eminence, before it underwent any alteration by the Saxons or the Normans.

It seems to have escaped the attention of the historians who have ascribed the erection of this work to Julius Cæsar, on his expeditions to this country, that the place of his landing, the

---

¹ Plate i.   ² Plate i.

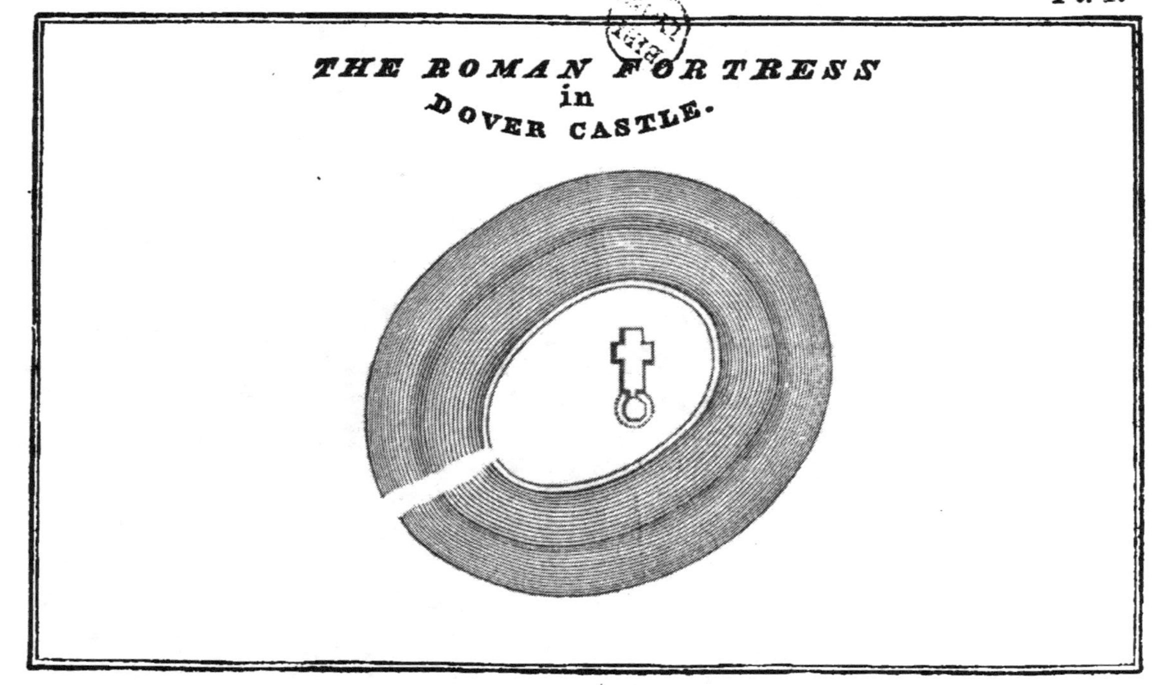

THE ROMAN FORTRESS
in
DOVER CASTLE.
Pl. I.

period he remained here, the damage he sustained in his fleet by a storm, and the difficulties he had to encounter from the heroic opposition of the natives,[3] are circumstances, when minutely considered, entirely at variance with the employment of his time in that undertaking.

A considerable interval elapsed between the final departure of Julius Cæsar from our island, and the re-appearance of the Romans in order to subdue its inhabitants. We cannot, therefore, date any part of the Roman buildings earlier than their next visit, (A. D. 43,) in the time of Claudius Cæsar. This emperor, either prompted by motives of inordinate ambition, or by a determination to resist an injury, resolved, in the third year of his reign, to attempt the conquest of Britain. For that purpose he despatched hither Aulus Plautius, of consular dignity, who, according to Tacitus, attended by an army of supernumerary forces, subjugated a portion of the country, converted it into a province of the Roman empire, and placed over it a body of veterans to secure its tranquillity.

It was in this expedition of the Roman commander, that, by the direction of his guide, he first overtook and defeated the celebrated British chief, Caractacus, one of the noblest defenders of our ancient liberty. This victory was acknowledged, even by the conquerors of the world,

---

3 See History of the Town.

to have been one of the utmost importance for the
reduction of this island, that had ever been
obtained. The spirit of this illustrious chief,
however, was not to be subdued at once; and
though in the progress of the Roman arms,
immediately subsequent to this transaction, we
hear but little of Caractacus, it is not to be
supposed that he was negligent in his endeavours
to inspire his countrymen with thoughts of vengeance. The greater part of his dominions fell
under the power of Aulus Plautius, who, four
years after this, was recalled. The affairs of the
island were left in the hands of the legates or
commanders of the legions; and in the interval
which occurred, until the appointment of another
governor, the Britons were enabled to gain some
advantages.

Successful in his first expedition, Claudius
was encouraged to persevere in his designs, and
he accordingly, (A. D. 43,) ordered Publius Ostorius Scapula to Britain. On his arrival, this
distinguished general found the natives in a state
of tumult and insurrection; and he immediately
disarmed those whom he suspected of revolu-
tionary intentions, and erected forts and castles
to intimidate the rest. This is the first authentic
account of the existence of Roman masonry in
the kingdom.. It is natural to conclude that
Scapula would fortify this principal point of defence, opposite the coast of Gaul, before he

built forts in the interior parts of the country ; and we think it probable that the first masonry on the castle hill may be dated between the years A. D. 43 and 49. That they had some kind of encampment here, prior to this period, can hardly be doubted. Such a commanding situation, from whence they could annoy their enemies, and which was always open, either to receive succours from abroad, or to secure a retreat to their own vessels, must have engaged their early attention.

The Romans, having determined to unite Britain to the provinces of the empire, were obliged to encounter the perils of the ocean in passing to their new possessions. These voyages were dangerous, in the night-time, without the assistance of light-houses. To remedy this defect, the octagon building or watch-tower[4] was erected during the governments of Aulus Plautius and Publius Ostorius Scapula. Another of these buildings was erected on the opposite coast, near Boulogne.

The foundations of this pharos or watch-tower, are laid in a bed of clay, which was a usual practice with the Roman masons, and is considered as a criterion of their labours. Its exterior shape is an octagon, and the interior a square, the sides of which are each about

---

[4] Plate ii, fig. 2.

fourteen feet, and the thickness of the walls, to the first floor, ten feet. The lapse of time has so materially impaired this edifice that it is now impossible to determine its original height, which, at present, is about forty feet. It was built with a stalactical composition, instead of stone, and intermixed with courses of Roman tiles; seven courses of the composition, and then three courses of the tiles alternately. The composition was formed under water, and cut into blocks, about a foot in length and seven inches deep,

The Roman tiles are of their usual depth, and many of them were cast in a peculiar mould, having grooves and projections corresponding with, and falling into each other, like a half dovetail, which rendered them close and compact.

Notwithstanding our want of evidence that the Romans or Saxons had recourse to this tower as a fortification, it was certainly applied to a defensive purpose by the Normans. The introduction of their architecture, in effecting the necessary alterations, conduced greatly to its present appearance, the masonry on each side of the apertures, internally, differing extremely from the original style; and the openings or windows, at the base, being considerably wider than those at the top. These openings, formerly intended to admit light, were afterwards converted into loop-holes, and the exterior arches contracted to a narrow slip, to which they ascended by steps cut in the wall. The arch over the original entrance, which is about six feet wide, is still perfect, while the other arches owe their ruinous condition to the idle curiosity of those who detach fragments of the composition, to acertain its hardness.

Mr. Lyon says, that this structure was repaired and cased with flint, in 1259. This casing is now falling off in several places, and the original masonry is again exposed to the influence of the elements.

A peal of bells was hung in this building when it became useles, as a place of defence. These bells, by the influence of Sir George Rooke, were afterwards removed to Portsmouth, from which borough he then held a seat in the house of commons.

After this, the board of ordnance disposed of the lead that covered this ancient structure, and left one of the first specimens of Roman architecture in this island, to moulder and decay, exposed to the violence of every winter storm.

The body and tower of the church are the only remaining buildings within the Roman fortification.[5] Though of a more recent date than the pharos above described, they still retain obvious traits of ancient workmanship. Historians and

---

[5] Plate ii, fig. 3.

antiquarians all unite in the opinion, that this sacred edifice was either founded by a Roman architect, or constructed with the materials of some dilapidated building, left by that people when they retired from our island. This latter conjecture is certainly much at variance with the general current of experience, and we can hardly suppose that a structure, raised by Roman architects, would have fallen into ruins in the course of two or three centuries.

Some of our ancient historical records attribute the origin of this church to Lucius, a British king by Roman courtesy, whose dominions extended over the eastern parts of Kent, and who was converted to Christianity A. D. 172. It does not appear chimerical that a monarch in those times, on renouncing the idolatrous superstitions of Pagan worship, and embracing the Christian faith, should feel induced, in commemoration of such an event, to erect a place of devotion to the honor and service of his adopted religion. Whatever credibility may be attached to this legend of our ancestors, it may not be unsatisfactory to enquire, whether the Britons were then sufficiently acquainted with the useful arts, to design a work of this description. Their intercourse with the Romans had now subsisted more than two centuries, and many of their chiefs and great men had visited Rome and foreign countries, while numbers of their youth were incorporated in the Roman armies and served abroad. By these means they had an opportunity of acquiring such a knowledge of the arts, as might be requisite for an undertaking of this kind.

Roman tiles appear in every part of the building, and a hasty survey might lead an observer to imagine, that no regularity was pursued in its construction. The result of an attentive observation, on the contrary, will prove that, in whatever age the masonry was raised, one uniform design was implicitly followed, although there are certainly no means of accurately deciding, whether it be the production of a British, Roman, or Saxon artist.

A general rule among these artificers, consisted in securing the angles of their edifice with square blocks of stone, when their walls were raised with flints and such other hard substances, as were available on the spot. In the present instance, the common Roman tiles were principally used for that purpose; from which we may infer that the architect could not avail himself of a sufficient quantity of stone, which would have prevented the necessity of burning tiles. In digging on the north side of the Roman fortress, in 1796, the workmen, found a place resembling a kiln, where the tiles were probably manufactured.

The angles appear to have been carried up

with an irregular intermixture of stones and tiles.
This confusion of style is not coeval with the era
of foundation, but has been caused by the subsequent hands of those, who, in repairing the
structure from time to time, have filled up the
dilapidations, proceeding from the destroying
arm of violence and the storms of ages, with
other materials than those originally used.

In addition to the inovations of succeeding
ages, in the angles, there are other places in this
edifice which evince ample traces of after execution. If, for instance, we minutely examine
the walls, we shall discover, from the interior,
that they once contained apertures intended for
windows, now entirely occupied with masonry,
and bricks may also be seen in various directions; particularly in the chancels.

This church is in the form of a cross. The
tower is supported by four lofty arches, the
pilasters on the north and south sides consisting
of squared stone, with a bead embracing the
front of an eliptic arch. This work is modern
in comparison with the other two arches, which,
including their pilasters, are formed with tiles
after the method of the Romans. The sides of
the tower are square, each measuring twenty-
eight feet, while the extent of the body of the
building is sixty feet.

Few places of worship have undergone greater
alterations. The first roof was extremely flat,

and when that failed, another was raised considerably higher, and larger windows, higher up, were put in the body of the church. After this, a third roof, higher than the first, and more horizontal than the second, was constructed, and their various heights may still be traced by the marks of each which remain on the south-west side of the tower.

The triple columns in the angles of the tower, and the voussoirs spreading from their capitals, appear to denote that a portion of the work has been added since the introduction of Saracenic or Gothic architecture into Britain. Although early writers affect to trace its origin to the remotest ages of Christianity, yet the numerous styles of architecture, to be observed in the ruins, involve the period of its foundation in considerable obscurity; nor is the uncertainty of its history removed until the arrival of St. Augustine, A. D. 596.

In that year Gregory the Roman pontiff, having made enquiry into the state of religion in this island, became exceedingly desirous of converting its inhabitants from the errors of idolatry, and to disseminate among them the blessings of the Gospel. For this purpose he despatched hither one of his monks, named Augustine, to communicate the glad tidings of salvation to Ethelbert, king of Kent, and to his subjects. After several conferences with this ambassador

of peace, they were induced to receive his doctrine, and to embrace his faith. Christianity
being thus established, we are informed that
Ethelbert, in return for the spiritual favours
conferred on him by Augustine, and admiring
that prelate's unaffected zeal and integrity in
the cause of his Divine Master, granted permission to him and his attendants to remain
in the kingdom, and gave them the church
within Dover castle, for the celebration of the
offices of religion.   This edifice having been
profaned by the services of superstition,[6] it was
re-consecrated by St. Augustine, and dedicated
to the Virgin Mary, mass having been publicly
performed in it.

Eadbald, however, succeeding to his father, retarded the progress of Christianity, by relapsing
into paganism : but on his conversion afterwards,
as an atonement for his offences, he founded a
college in the castle for twenty-four ecclesiastics,
and annexed it to the church.

The canons placed here retained possession
until A. D. 696, when Withred, king of Kent,
judiciously deciding that religious pursuits should
be unconnected with the profession of arms,
erected a building for them in the town, and
removed them and all their immunities from the
castle.   The college of Eadbald, it is presumed,

---

6 Darrell's MSS.

was constructed with less durable materials than those of the church or pharos, or was raised only for a temporary purpose. Not a vestige of it remains at the present day, to elucidate either its site or the skill of its architect.

Three chaplains, attired as prebends by virtue of the dignity and antiquity of the institution, were formerly allotted to this church. A certain routine of duty was assigned to them, by which each was obliged to rise at an appointed time, in rotation, to sing matins privately, before the long peal preceded the performance of the same rite in the chapel. The first chaplain repeated mass to the governor at the high altar; the second, to the marshalmen and officers, at ten o'clock, at the altar of the Virgin Mary; and the third, to the soldiers, at nine o'clock, at the altar of relicks. If, at the conclusion of these ceremonies, the priests wished to leave the castle, permission was granted, on the condition that they would be present at the celebration of high mass; but they were strictly prohibited all absence which might cause neglect of duty, and were not suffered to interfere with the avocations of each other. Several other regulation were observed which cannot be noticed in this short history.

At the period of the reformation, the three chaplains were reduced to one, who remained the officiating minister for the garrison and the inhabitants of the castle, until the year 1690, when the service ceased, but the stipend is continued.

Several individuals of distinction have been interred within the walls of this church. In that part which contained the grand altar, the remains of Sir Robert Asheton, who held the office of chamberlain under Edward III, were deposited. The stone which contained his effigy, with the inscription and the grooves of the brass work, remained a few years since, but is now demolished. He presented the great bell to this church.

Henry Howard, earl of Northampton, and lord warden of the Cinque Ports, in the reign of James I, was buried on the right hand side of the south chapel, in 1614. Of this nobleman it was said, That among the nobility he was the most learned, and among the learned the most noble. A monument, which cost £500, was erected to his memory by Stone, the famous statuary. His body and monument were removed to the chapel belonging to the hospital of East Greenwich, in this county, in 1696, on account of the ruinous state of the church. A tablet, to record this, remained in the wall, but is now demolished.

Records remain of several other great names, which cannot find a place in a work of this kind. Their ashes are now mouldering in these dilapidated ruins, where the noble and the slave embrace each other in the same peaceful silence.

The ground on the south side of the church, has been appropriated for the interment of the garrison soldiers. Of a few, their memoirs are recorded on the spot, and

"Their names, their years, spelt by th' unletter'd muse,
" The place of fame and elegy supply."

Time has left us here no other memorial of those who have fought our battles or guarded our shores; and these raised heaps of sod, no less than the monumental arch that crumbles over them, present to the observer a melancholy picture of mortality.

Another spot of ground, on the north side of the castle, without the walls, has lately been consecrated for a place of burial, and the garrison use it occasionally for that purpose.

There was formerly a well within this fortress, which is now nearly filled up with rubbish, and the top covered with an arch.

SAXON FORTIFICATIONS.

The Romans, obliged to withdraw their forces from the distant provinces to check the progress of the northern barbarians, retired from the British isles: and the natives, divided among themselves, and strangers to the common interest that should unite them, became an unresisting prey to their neighbours, the Picts and Scots, who took advantage of the departure of their late protectors, by repeated acts of aggression.

C

In this emergency Vortigern, the British leader, had recourse to the Saxons, and invited that powerful people to his assistance. Two Saxon chiefs, Hengist and Horsa, arrived on the Isle of Thanet, with a few followers, in the year 449. After receiving several reinforcements they completely defeated the Picts and Scots, and restored peace to Vortigern and his subjects. Hengist, however, conscious of the essential services he had rendered, and of the importance of his presence among those who owed their existence to the timely aid of his prowess, perceived that he could as easily dictate laws to the succoured, as to the vanquished.

Accordingly, on the arrival of more numerous forces, he assumed a high tone of authority, and leading his troops to glory and conquest, at length founded the first independent kingdom in Kent. The unhappy divisions, previously subsisting among the inhabitants, had greatly retarded the progress of masonry, and the ensuing wars occasioned a rapid declension of the useful arts in this island.

When in possession of Kent, the Saxons were too well acquainted with the utility of beacons or watch-towers, on desirable elevations, to destroy the Roman works which we have attempted to describe. They appear to have extended the ground-work, by adding to the original fortress all the spare ground that could be levelled with

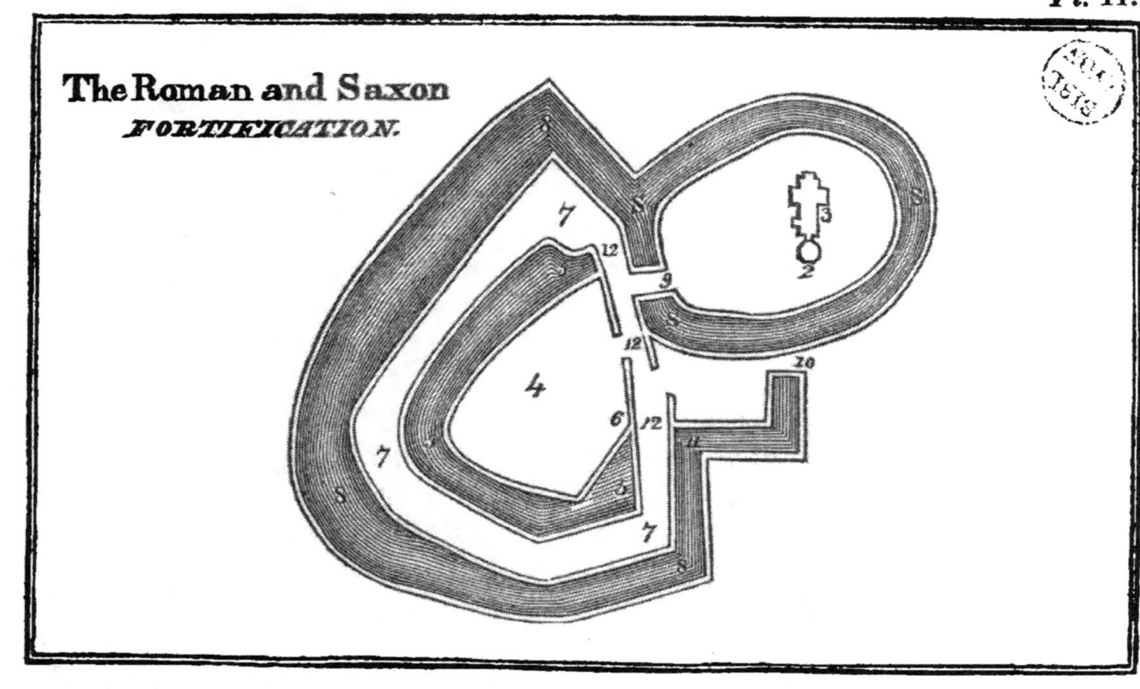

The Roman and Saxon
FORTIFICATION.

it. These additions, characteristic of a rude and barbarous age, were, however, designed with judgment, and adapted to the limited space they were intended to occupy. The fortress raised by the first Saxons, differing materially from that of the Romans, consisted merely of perpendicular sides, without parapets, surrounded by deep ditches. Their principal object was to secure the ground-work, disregarding entirely those accommodations for residence, considered in after time to be indispensable. The hut covered with turf, or a cave in the rock, was deemed a sufficient shelter for these sons of simplicity. In the year 1800, one of their excavations, nine feet in width and fifty in length, was discovered leading under the Roman work.

. The interior part of their fortress, called the keep,[7] was even with the edge[8] of the perpendicular ditch, and raised twenty feet above its surrounding vallum.[9] The keep was formed with the chalk dug out of the interior ditch, and the vallum was levelled with what was cast out of the exterior one.[10]

The narrow ridge of the hill on the north-west side of their fortress, was the most assailable point; and this work was evidently intended to protect the entrance[11] into the Roman fortress, by extending the means of accommodation for

---

7 Pl. ii. fig. 4. 8 Pl. ii. fig. 5,5,5. 9 Pl. ii. 7,7,7. 10 Pl. ii. fig. 8,8,8
11 Plate ii. fig. 9.

a greater number of men to use their arms in defending this pass.

On the south-west side of the Roman fortress, and on the exterior bank, was the original entrance[12] into the Saxon fortification. This bank was reduced to a narrow path, where the ascent of the hill was most difficult, by a recess[13] cut in the rock, and to force that passage would have been a rash attempt of a besieging enemy. The sentinel, on being driven from the first, would have found a second, and even a third[14] post to defend, and might have annoyed the assailants severely before they could have gained possession of the fortress.

Prior to the reign of Alfred the Great, which commenced in 872, the hostile Danes had spread war and desolation over the fertile plains of Britain. In order to secure the sea coast from their exterminating arm, Alfred fortified the towns and castles with walls and towers; and the fortress on the hill at Dover, must have been considered of the first importance.

Repeated rains and frosts, through a course of years, had thrown down the perpendicular sides of the ditches, that had been cut in the chalk rock, and the place became defenceless. To remedy this defect, and to render such an important station by art impregnable, the original

---

[12] Pl. ii fig. 10.   [13] Pl. ii. fig. 11.   [14] Pl. ii. fig. 12.

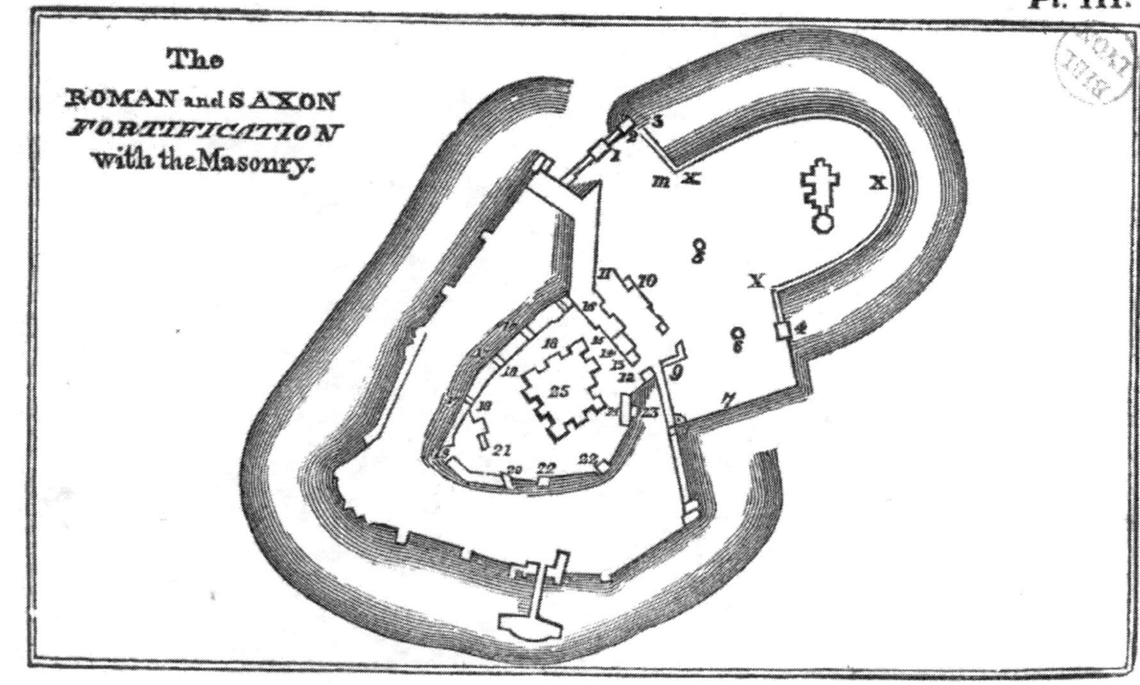

The
ROMAN and SAXON
FORTIFICATION
with the Masonry.

ground plan, which extended to the north-west of the Roman fortress, was surrounded with masonry. The passes leading to the keep, the vallum, and to the Roman works, were defended with gates and towers, and a fortified bridge thrown over each of the ditches. Several other towers were built at irregular distances in the wall, which we shall endeavour to describe as we proceed. The first that presents itself is

Godwin's Tower.[15]—Godwin was appointed earl of Kent about the year 1057, in the reign of Edward the Confessor, and part of the revenue of Dover was assigned to him on becoming guardian of the Cinque Ports. The manor of Goodnestone was also presented to him, by the same monarch, on condition that he should cause additional works to be erected in this castle. He extended the entrance into the Roman fortress,[16] by removing the old ramparts between Colton[17] and Arthur's[18] gates. On the side opposite, he made a vallum across the Roman ditch, and reared the wall,[19] within the parapet, from the angle near Colton gate, round the ancient works of the Romans. This he continued across his new vallum to a gateway[20] adjoining the wall, in which he built his tower.

This edifice was situated in the centre of the wall, between the new gateway and the first

---

[15] Pl. iii. fig. 1.　　[16] Pl. iii. *m n.*　　[17] Pl. iii. fig. 4.
[18] Pl. iii. fig. 11.　　[19] Pl. iii. *x, x, x.*　　[20] Pl. iii. fig. 8.

angle of the Saxon masonry. Underneath it was a sally-port for cavalry, communicating with the interior parts of the castle. When this fortress was besieged by the Dauphin of France, in the reign of king John, it was through this sally-port that Stephen Pincester entered with four hundred horse, to the relief of Hubert de Burgh, who, by this assistance, was enabled to oblige the French prince to raise the siege.

After the Norman conquest, apartments were built over the passage to the sally-port, to contain the king's wardrobe, when he visited the castle, and as a residence for his suite. Time has, however, long since destroyed the buildings and choaked up the passage with their rubbish, when the gate was closed up.

On the outside of the Norman wall, the arch leading to the souterrain, may still be seen; but within, all traces of the old works are buried, and the connecting parts of the Roman and Saxon plans completely destroyed.

Clinton Tower[21].—Three towers were erected on the exterior bank of the Roman trench, prior to the numerous additions in the latter years of William the First. One of them was intended to defend Colton gate; and a second, to protect the entrance to Godwin's tower. The third, called Clinton's tower, was built near the vallum made

---

21 Pl. iv. fig. 66.

by Godwin across the ditch. This tower was square, but how long it existed as a place of defence, or at what time it was destroyed, is uncertain; nor was the site of it precisely ascertained until the workmen, in the year 1794, dug up the last remains of the foundation, while sinking the ground for a new road.

Jeffery Clinton, who formerly had the command of this tower, derived his surname from Clinton in Oxfordshire. While one derives his descent from Wevia, sister of Gunora, a Norman duchess, another, who was a contemporary, asserts that he was elevated, by royal favor, from an obscure origin. He was by profession a soldier; and, together with several other honorable and lucrative offices, was chamberlain and treasurer to Henry the First, and chief justice of England. Turning to the right, we arrive at

Valence Tower.[22]—This edifice was circular, and stood on the S. E. side of the Roman fortress. William Valence formerly commanded in it, from whom it obtained the name. He was son of Hugh le Brun, by Isabella his wife, and widow of king John, and derived his surname from the place of his nativity in France. Nearly allied to Henry the Third, he was invited to England, constituted governor of Goderic castle, knighted, and, among other proofs of royal

---

22 Pl. iv. fig. 67.

attachment, obtained a grant of the castle and honor of Hartford.

The following anecdote, however, is a proof that all these honors only contributed to produce, in the favorite, acts of unwarrantable violence. Having one day, without permission, hunted in the park of the bishop of Ely, and being in want of refreshment, he and his companions went, self-invited, into the manor-house; where, because ordinary beer was set before them, they broke open the cellars; and, after drinking as they pleased of the best blood of the grape, "Flown with insolence and wine," they pulled the spigots from the casks, and left the remainder to run waste.

He was slain at the battle of Bayonne, and a noble monument was erected to his memory in Westminster abbey.

At a very early period this tower was applied to the purpose of grinding corn for the garrison, and thence called Mill tower. It was destroyed during the American war. In the bank of the Roman fortress, near the site of the tower, is a bomb-proof casemate.

Mortimer's Tower[23].—This quadrangular defence was raised to protect the entrance through Colton gate. Parts of the foundation, which was sunk several feet in the solid rock, are still

---

23 Pl. iv. fig. 68.

remaining under ground. Next Colton gate, in an angle of the wall, is a stone door frame, which probably led through a souterrain into the Saxon works.

Ralph de Mortimer was the commander in this tower. He was the son of Roger de Mortimer, who was allied to William the Conqueror, and had been a general in his army before he came to England. Edric, earl of Shrewsbury, refusing to submit to the Norman yoke, was defeated by Mortimer, who, for his valour, was rewarded with the earl's forfeited lands, and his castle of Wigmore, which was afterwards his principal residence.

Colton Gate and Square Tower. [24]—These structures were built over the original entrance of the Saxon work, and were probably much altered at the Norman conquest. The custody of them was at that time committed to Fulbert de Dover, who appointed an officer to keep guard, and granted lands for that purpose in his lordship of Chilham. Lord Burgherst had the command of this tower in the reign of Edward the Third, and his arms, *a lion rampant, double tailed, or*, still remain in front, on a stone shield. In 1772, part of the wall [25] that surrounded the Roman fortress, and connected it with this tower, was taken down.

---

24 Pl. iv. fig. 4.　　25 Pl. iii. *n.*

The college of the first canons, according to tradition, was seated in the quadrangle, enclosed by a wall from Colton to Harcourt towers.[26]

Harcourt Tower.[27]—This tower was erected over a passage enclosed by two parallel walls, leading from Peverell's tower.[28] The sides were supported by arches opening a way to the Souterrain gate,[29] from whence a flight of stone steps led to the gateway of Suffolk's tower.[30] Through slips in the wall of the caponnier, the archers could command the vallum opposite the apartments of the governor, and also the side of the hill towards the town and cliff.

This tower, Souterrain gate, and the wall that connected them with Well tower,[31] are entirely destroyed; and all traces of the ancient foundations, were obliterated in the year 1797.

Harcourt tower took its name either from the manor of Harcourt, in Oxfordshire, which was given for maintaining ward here, by William the First, or from William de Harcourt who was appointed the commander by Robert de Arsick, and whose father accompanied the Conqueror to England.

Well Tower and Gate.[32]—This tower derived its name from a well contained in it, which is

---

[26] Pl. lii. fig. 7, 8.   [27] Pl. iii. fig. 8.   [28] Pl. iv. fig. 36.
[29] The precise site of this gate appears to be uncertain.
[30] Pl. iii. fig. 12, 13.   [31] Pl. iii. fig. 9.   [32] Pl. iii. fig. 9.

about three hundred and eighty feet deep, but whose origin is uncertain. As it is not within the Roman fortress, it cannot claim so high a date. Besides this, and the well mentioned in our account of the Roman fortifications, and that which will be noticed in describing the keep, there is a fourth near Colton gate,[33] which is now mostly used by the garrison. It was secured in 1800 by a work of bomb-proof masonry. Other wells have been discovered in different parts of the castle.

The Armourers' Tower.[34]—The arms for the use of the garrison, were manufactured and repaired in this tower. In making the alterations in these parts of the castle, during the years 1795 and 1796, the last remains of this tower were erased from the foundation.

King Arthur's, or North Gate.[35]—This gate led through the area before Palace gate, into the Roman fortress. There was also a passage to the Roman works, and to earl Godwin's sally-port, that passed between two parallel walls. All the connecting parts of the ancient works, are here demolished, the foundations dug up, and part of the Roman fortress levelled with the quadrangle.

Duke of Suffolk's Tower, and Palace Gate.[36]— The entrance into the Saxon keep, at this gate,

---

[33] Pl. iii. fig. 6.   [34] Pl. iii. fig. 10.   [35] Pl. iii. fig. 11.
[36] Pl. iii. fig. 12, 13.

facing the Roman camp, was once secured with a port-cullis ; and the grooves are still remaining in the stone work.   It was formerly called Palace gate, because it led to the entrance of the palace, now called the keep.   Some have supposed that it was also called Subterranean gate, from a concealed passage that led from it to Peverell's tower ; but Mr. Lyon affirms that this gate is entirely destroyed.

Suffolk tower was formerly a recess in the wall, until it was converted into a stately mansion, by Edward the Fourth, for his brother-in-law, the duke of Suffolk.   It was the father of this duke who, being accused of treason, and endeavouring to depart the kingdom, was beheaded, by a common seaman, in Dover roads.   After a sham trial, they obliged him to lay his head over the side of the vessel, and, with a rusty sword, severed it from his body, which was afterwards brought on shore, and laid on the sand.   Report says that his head was placed on a pole near it. The body was taken to the collegiate church of Wingfield, in Suffolk, and interred in the chancel, but it appears to have remained uncertain what became of the head.   Some few years since, in sinking ground for a cellar, near the Antwerp Inn, a head was found, enclosed in a stone receptacle.   As this ground formerly belonged to St. Martin's church, it was conjectured that this was the duke's head, and that it was buried here.

The Old Arsenal.[37]—This tower, from a very remote period, had been a receptacle for the arms and machines, used for the defence of the castle. Tradition had assigned them a Roman origin ; but Darell, who had seen them and admired their workmanship, has transferred their date to the reign of king John, or that of Henry the Third.

The King's Kitchen and Offices.[38]—These were probably fitted up in the time of Edward the First, who frequently visited the castle. They originally occupied the whole space between the old magazine, and the eastern angle of the Saxon keep. Barracks were built upon the site of these offices in 1745.

King Arthur's Hall.[39]—As the origin of this building is not developed in history, it will be useless to enter into a discussion as to the probability that king Arthur was the founder of it. It was situated on the north-east side of the keep, in the front of three towers,[40] and the space is now occupied by a mess room, kitchen, and barracks.

The King's Gate and Bridge.[41]—This entrance was defended by a strong outwork, which enclosed a small area before the great gates. Some of its ruins still remain. There does not

---

[37] Pl. iii. fig. 14. [38] Pl. iii. fig. 15,16. [39] Pl. iii. fig. 18,18,18. [40] Pl. iii. fig. 17,17,17. [41] Pl. iii. fig. 19.

appear to have been any port-cullis at the outer gate, and it is probable they had only a draw-bridge to secure the passage.   The inner gates,[42] however, which opened from the area into the keep were not only defended with a port-cullis, but with a tower on each side, from whence the archers could defend the whole vallum.

Towers in the interior wall, on the south-west side of the Keep, called Magminot's Towers.[43]— When marshal of the castle, Magminot might occasionally place archers in these towers; but the lands he held were for building and guarding towers in the exterior walls.

Gore's Tower.[44]—In the reign of Henry the Eighth, this building in the curtain, was called Gore's tower.   Nothing more is known of it.

Arthur's Lesser Hall, or Guaonobour's Chamber.[45]—This apartment was anciently called Arthur's Private Hall, or his Queen's Bedchamber, and is placed between Gore's tower and Palace gate.   Henry the Eighth, when residing in the castle with Anna Boleyn, made it a store-room for his provisions.

The Keep.[46]—We now come to the principal building in the castle, called the keep, from its occupying the centre of the quadrangle already mentioned, which the Saxons had distinguished

---

42. Pl. iii. fig. 20, 21.   43 Pl. iii. fig. 20, 22, 22.   44 Pl. iii. fig. 23.
45 Pl. iii. fig. 24.   46 Pl. fig. 25.

by that name. It is a large and massy square edifice, the sides varying from 103 to 123 feet; and so lofty that, from every point, the eye naturally turns towards it, and perceives it to be the chief point from which to assail a besieging army, and a secure strong hold for the besieged.

The north turret of the keep is about 95 feet above the ground, which is 373 feet above the level of the sea. The view from it is grand and beautiful, including the North Foreland, Ramsgate Pier, the Isle of Thanet, Reculver church, Sandwich, and the intermediate country; the town of Calais, and the French coast from Boulogne to Gravelines.

The foundation of this tower, generally 24 feet thick, and in some parts considerably more, was, according to an ancient chronicle, laid about the year 1153, by Henry, son of Henry I. not long before he ascended the throne, when he came from Normandy, to the relief of Wallingford castle. In its construction the architect has followed the plan of Gundulph, bishop of Rochester. Erected in turbulent times, when refinement and luxury were little advanced, it is not surprising that convenience and accommodation were less consulted, than strength and security. We know not whether to characterize this building as a solid mass of masonry, with occasional cavities left in it; or as a few rooms and passages separated by thick walls, and these enclosed by thicker ones. The only avenues by which light and air could be admitted, were long apertures or loopholes, extremely narrow on the outside, but gradually widening as they enter deeper into the wall. Some of these holes were constructed in a very peculiar manner. The opening within side was about eight feet wide, and of a considerable height. The bottom tended upwards in a flight of steps, and the sides continued to draw nearer to each other, while the top was finished in a circular arch. The opening was thus contracted, as it arrived at the outside, to a narrow slip. From hence the archers, ascending the steps, could take their aim, and direct their arrows on the enemy in the quadrangle below, who could neither see their assailants, nor return their missiles with any chance of success; since it would be difficult to hit the loophole; and if they should, the ascending arrow would strike the arched roof of the window, without effect.

The keep is divided into three stories, which communicate with each other by means of circular staircases, in the north and south angles.

The ancient entrance was by means of a flight of steps, parallel to the south-east side of the building. These steps, about fourteen feet above the quadrangle, led to a noble vestibule, which ascended on the north-east side, and opened into the second story, near the north angle. In these

outer steps and vestibules the military architects
of the feudal age, exerted all their skill; and
formerly, a draw-bridge, gate, and portcullis,
besides concealed galleries or passages in the
wall, defended this important pass.

The method of warfare being much altered,
the building has, by degrees, laid aside its stern
and gloomy aspect: comfort has been sought
after; loopholes have widened into windows;
and light and air are permitted to cheer and
refresh this once sombre edifice.

But we will return, for a moment, to its
ancient state: and, in so doing, particularize
the three stories.

Ground Floor. In the centre of this floor is
a space of fifty feet square, divided by a partition
wall, in which are three arches. Here the stores
were deposited, and from hence was a communication with the stairs in the angle of the
tower. Two loop-holes, on the north-west side,
commanded the quadrangle and the entrance
from King's gate; and two others, the space
between Palace gate and the stairs leading to
the vestibule. On the south-west side was a
gallery or passage, fifty-two feet long and twelve
feet wide: this has, for some years past, been
used as a magazine. Near the east angle are two
rooms, one about thirty feet, the other thirty-
eight feet long; in each of which was a small
aperture in the wall, for the admission of light

and air. These were formerly used as prisons.

. *Second Story*. The strongly guarded vestibule, which has been mentioned, led into this story, which is divided by a wall into two nearly equal sections, with two large rooms, in the centre, on each side. They were both intended for defence, and had each a window on the north-west. Ascending the vestibule, on the right, and in the centre of the north-east side, is a small room, intended to defend the passage. It was appropriated to the knight or officer on guard, at such times as the king, or any person of distinction, resided in the keep, or in case of siege. Opposite to this guard room was a handsome chapel, richly ornamented with arches in the Saxon style, and it is still in a good state of preservation. This was intended for the use of the king, or, in his absence, for that of the governor.

A noble flight of steps, leading from the east part of this second story to the royal apartments on the third, was very strongly defended. At the foot of the stair case was a large arch-way to receive a gate. Should the enemy force this gate, there was another, higher up, which was defended with a port-cullis. In the walls, on each side of the stairs, and on the landing places, were concealed galleries for the archers, who, although invisible to the assailants, could have made dreadful havoc among them. The stairs on the south side, leading from this to the story below, have long since been closed up. In the wall, on the south-west side, are two large galleries, with an enlarged window between them. There are recesses in the galleries, in one of which is a fire place ; but the workmanship appears to be of so late a date, as the time of Elizabeth. The original design of them was probably to carry from one story to another, within the tower, the beams for the catapultæ, and other warlike instruments, instead of exposing the beseiged to the enemy, by raising them on the outside of the wall. In each of these galleries were two loop-holes ; and two other galleries, with loop-holes, commanded the whole quadrangle on the south-east

Third Story. This story, like the former ones, is divided into rooms and galleries, which communicate with each other at the angles. The principal rooms were royal appartments. Some of the galleries were much confined, with room for only a few men to use their arms. In the thick wall, on the north angle, and between the top of the stairs and the entrance to the royal apartments, is the famous well which has been ascribed to Julius Cæsar; but which was probably dug by the Saxons long before the building of the keep. This is the well which the duke of Normandy required Harold, on his oath, to deliver up to him, on the death of king Edward.

In 1800, bomb-proof arches were constructed over the top of the building, and the castellated battlements mounted with cannon of 68lb. caliber.

NORMAN FORTIFICATIONS.

Towards the end of the reign of Edward the Confessor, earl Godwin, the father of Harold, having raised a commotion in the kingdom, was obliged to take refuge on the continent. To counteract the rebellious power of this haughty earl and his sons, assistance had been solicited of William duke of Normandy; and he arrived in this kingdom during their banishment. Edward received him very graciously, and with a courtesy suitable to his high rank, and to the exalted reputation he had acquired.

Some time after, Godwin, being restored to royal favour, returned to England, and was reinstated in all his honours. The visit of the Norman, however, excited in the breast of that nobleman a jealousy not to be extinguished by his death, but which descended with increased virulence to his son and successor, Harold. This aspiring spirit, prompted by an insatiable thirst for empire, omitted no means of increasing his popularity, and thereby paving the way for his future advancement, on the first vacancy that presented itself; an event which the age and infirmities of the Confessor induced him to place at no very distant period.

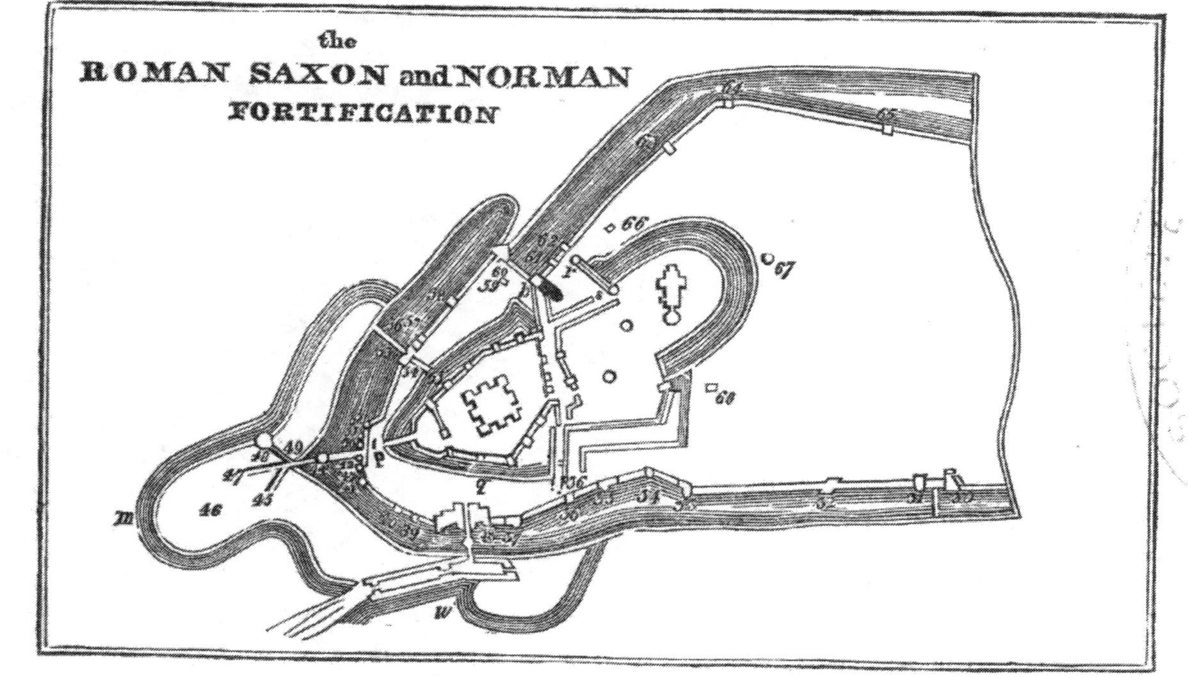

Pl. IV.

On the restoration of his father to power and fortune, certain relatives had been required as hostages for his fidelity; and Edward, for the greater security, had consigned them to the custody of the duke of Normandy. Harold was greatly mortified that persons so nearly allied to himself, by the ties of consanguinity, should remain prisoners in a foreign country; and he succeeded in obtaining the king's consent to their release, by artfully representing his own powerful and popular influence.

To accomplish this purpose, Harold, with a numerous retinue, immediately embarked at Bosham, in Sussex, but was driven by tempests on the coasts of Ponthieu. Here he was made prisoner by Guy, the count of that territory, who demanded an enormous sum for his ransom. Harold soon contrived to send intelligence of his situation to duke William, who instantly demanded his liberation; and the circumstance appeared most propitious to his views.

In the Norman court the earl was treated with munificence; but the tokens of insatiable ambition, so visible in his character and conduct, could not escape the penetrating eye of William, who felt alarm, lest he also might cherish hopes of one day wielding the British sceptre.

Harold, though caressed, enjoyed but the semblance of liberty, and was compelled by the necessity of his situation, to do homage for his lands and honours in England, and thus acknowledged William, as the apparent successor of king Edward. But the jealousy of the Norman required more than the mere ceremony of homage. Before an assembly of his chief barons, Harold was constrained to swear that he would promote the accession of William to the English crown, that he would guard his interest in the court of Edward, and that he would deliver up the well in Dover castle, and admit a Norman garrison into the fortress.[1]

At length, loaded with presents but distressed in mind, he was permitted to leave the court of his rival. He obtained the release of Haco, one of the hostages; but Wulfnoth, the other, was detained by the policy of the Norman.

When, in cooler moments, Harold reflected on the concessions he had made, he persuaded himself, that on oath extorted by fear, might be violated without any infringement of justice, and it appears to have had but little influence on his future conduct.

At the time he returned to England, the Northumbrians were in a state of insurrection; and he conducted himself with great prudence and moderation, in redressing their grievances, and, by these means, disposed them to obedience.

---

[1] See these details in William of Poitou, who received the particulars of the oath from persons who were present. Gul. Pict. 79, 80, 85.

On the death of Edward he was proclaimed king, in an assembly of the citizens of London, and the southern counties cheerfully acquiesced in his succession. He then hastened to the north, and conciliated the affection and allegiance of the Northumbrians. By marrying Editha, the daughter of Alfgar, he secured to his interest her two brothers, the potent earls, Morcar and Edwin; and his power appeared to stand on a firm and secure basis among his subjects.

Neither Harold nor William had any legitimate title to the crown. William founded his claim on the appointment of king Edward. Harold made the same pretence, and also rested his title on the choice of the people. The undoubted heir was Edward Atheling; but his imbecility of mind rendered him unfit to govern.

The news of Edward's death, and the coronation of Harold, soon reached the ears of William, who lost no time in assembling his vassals and allies, to assert his pretended right to the English crown. Harold prepared to oppose him; and the inhabitants on each side of the channel, were astonished at the immense preparations that were making to decide this mighty quarrel.

While Harold was encamped on the coast of Sussex, awaiting the arrival of the Normans, news was brought him that his own brother Tostig, and the king of Norway, had invaded Northumberland, and were cruelly ravaging the country.   He flies to oppose them; and, after a severe contest, they are totally defeated.

After several months had passed in making preparations, William lands at Pevensey. Harold was then at **York**; but soon arrives at the Norman camp. Senlac, nine miles from Hastings, was the spot chosen by Harold for this important contest. Here he posted his forces, on the declivity of the hill, in one solid and compact body. In the centre waved the royal standard: by its side stood Harold and his two brothers, Gurth and Leofwin; and around them the rest of the army, every man on foot.

On the opposite hill William was marshalling his troops. About nine in the morning his squadrons began to move, passed the interval between the two hills, and slowly ascended the eminence on which the English were posted. The Normans began the contest; the shock was dreadful; but the English, at every point, opposed a daring and impenetrable front. By repeated attacts the confidence of the Normans melted away at their heavy loss, and at the bold countenances of their opponents. Disappointed and perplexed, they had recourse to stratagem, and numbers of the English fell: but the main body remained firm and immoveable. William fought like a lion, and had three horses killed under him, while one quarter of his heroes lay lifeless on the ground, or breathing out their

souls in the agonies of death. Harold was no
less dauntless, and displayed a courage worthy
the crown for which he was fighting. His brothers were both slain; and a little before sunset
an arrow, shot at a venture, pierced his eye.
He instantly fell, and the knowledge of his fall
relaxed the efforts of the English. At dusk
they broke up and dispersed through the woods,
and left the Normans masters of the field. The
body of Harold was found among the slain, and
deposited at Waltham abbey, founded by him in
1062. In the reign of Elizabeth, his coffin was
found, covered with a grave stone, and with no
other inscription than INFELIX HAROLD.

After this decisive battle, William expected
that the natives would offer him the crown. In
this he was disappointed. London was put in a
state of defence, and Edgar Atheling placed on
the throne. The inhabitants of Romney had
dispersed a part of his fleet, and forces were
assembling at Dover. His first object was to
disperse the latter; and in his way he severely
chastised the town of Romney, and the force at
Dover fled at his approach. Bertram de Ashburnham was then governor of the castle, but
his garrison was too weak and insignificant to
contend with so daring an enemy. After a short
resistance he submitted to the mercy of William,
who barbarously beheaded him and his two sons.

This acquisition was of great importance to the Normans. The dysentery had prevailed to an alarming degree in the army; and such a commanding fortress, at that time deemed impregnable, afforded a safe receptacle for the sick and wounded. William remained here eight days, employed in surveying the works, with a view of augmenting their defensive character; and having supplied his losses, by reinforcements from Normandy, he proceeded towards London.

After his coronation, as a compliment to the superior abilities of his maternal brother, Odo, bishop of Bayeux, and to reward his eminent services, he appointed him governor of Dover castle. The bishop was also created earl of Kent, lord chief justice, and regent of England during the absence of its monarch, while on a visit to his Norman dominions; and was invested with authority to erect castles where they might be considered necessary for the defence of the kingdom.

Before the period of Odo's aggrandisement, he had been generally esteemed as a lover of justice and equity, a patron of learning, and a liberal benefactor to the cause of religion: but no sooner had the king embarked for Normandy, and left him unequalled in power, than he renounced those principles, which had formerly shed so radiant a lustre around him. In expectation of succeeding to the papal chair, at the death of Gregory, agreeable to the predictions of the astrologers of Rome, that prospect became at once the idol of his imagination. In order to obtain his object it was indispensable to amass wealth; and his rapacity for riches, increased with his means of extorting them. By constant acts of oppression, he had engrossed to himself no less than one hundred and eighty-four lordships, in Kent, and four hundred and forty-five in other counties. The kingdom was filled with exaction and rapine, and the complaints of the people only tended to increase their misery. New fines were imposed to chastise their murmurings, until their indignation burst through all restraints; and they resolved, by prompt and vigorous measures, to regain the liberty and property which had been so arbitrarily wrested from them.

A considerable body of the men of Kent, who had determined to stand or fall by each other, applied to Eustace, earl of Boulogne, Godwin's old antagonist, for assistance; and, in concert with him, devised a plan to possess themselves of Dover castle. The time, place of rendezvous, and method of attack, being previously arranged, the earl landed with his troops by night, found the Kentish confederates punctually assembled, and they all marched together, favoured by surrounding darkness, to surprise the sentinels at their posts. The bold assailants were either perceived, or betrayed; for whilst a party of them were endeavouring to scale the walls, the garrison made a sudden and furious sally; and, with the advantage of higher ground, easily repressed the aggressors, many of whom were slain, and others hurled from the precipice.

The earl having lost his best men in the encounter, retreated hastily to his ships, and left his Kentish allies to endure the vengeance of their regent, and to deplore the failure of an effort, which, although abortive, must in candour be pronounced a noble enterprise. At the time Eustace ventured this attack, the exterior walls were not erected. The sally was made at the entrance on the back of the Roman ditch, and the skirmish took place on the uneven ground between that entrenchment and the side of the perpendicular cliff.

William, at length informed of his regent's misconduct and tyranny, returned to England, and accidentally met the ambitious earl with a numerous retinue, and loaded with riches, on his way to Rome. Indignant at the conduct of the regent, who had planned all this without the knowledge or consent of his sovereign, the king commanded his guards to seize him. The earl was also a bishop, and the soldiers, fearing the displeasure of the pope, refused to obey. At the suggestion of the archbishop of Canterbury, the king seized the delinquent with his own hands, not as the *bishop of Bayeux*, but simply as *earl of Kent*, and confiscated the whole of his immense property.

Reflecting on the precarious state of affairs which then agitated England, and fearing an invasion from Denmark, William proceeded with energy in adding new works to Dover castle, in order to secure an impregnable fortress on this part of the coast. The forfeited lands of his brother Odo, and several others, were appropriated to this purpose.

He appointed a relation, John de Fienes, constable of the castle and warden of the Cinque Ports, with an entailment of those high offices upon his heirs male. He also gave him one hundred and seventy-one knights' fees, to be held of him, in capite, by castle-guard tenure; and with the revenue arising from these lands, he engaged eight knights to assist, and they were associated with him. These knights were obliged, by the condition of their tenures, to build towers, and to garrison them with their military tenants.

Their plan being matured, the constable and his colleagues commenced building, and connected their insulated towers with an exterior wall. Their masonry may be traced from the ridge of the cliff, on the south side, and by following the line of towers round the northern curve of the wall, to its termination in an opposite direction;

but the innumerable alterations that have taken place in these works, will prevent the lover of antiquity from arriving at any satisfactory conclusion, as to their primary grandeur.

The first building reared in the Norman curtain, on the side of the castle nearest the town, was a gateway, called

Canon, or Monk's Gate.[2]--This gate probably took its name from the canons, or secular priests, formerly belonging to the garrison, whose apartments, surmounted with battlements, were over the arched passage. It is uncertain at what period the gates were taken down, and the walls of the gate-way nearly levelled with the ground, on the inside of the curtain. A platform was then made, by filling up the passage with earth, and cannon placed on it.

When alterations were making at this place, in 1797, the stone frame of the old gates, and the iron hooks on which they hung, were found on the inside of the arch. It is evident there could be no necessity for a bridge in passsing to these gates, which were only a few feet above the basement of the present ditch. After the demolition of this gate, another was made a little farther from the cliff; and the arch of it remained in the curtain until 1797; but the passage had been closed many years.

---

[2] Pl. iv. fig. 30

A souterrain, excavated out of the solid rock, and several feet under the present surface, was discovered, a short time since, in sinking the ground for a new road: but the use for which it was intended, is very uncertain. A well was likewise discovered, about the same time, near Monk's gate.

Within these last fifty years, great alterations have taken place at this part of the wall A military road has been constructed, rising with an easy ascent from the town to this point. Here a new entrance was constructed, and defended with a draw-bridge, a caponniere under it, and a tete-du-pont, or an outwork, to annoy an enemy marching up the military road. Several other precautions have been taken, to defend this new entrance.

Rokesley's Tower. [3]— William de Albrincis, was the founder of this circular tower, and it was, at first, called by his name. But having deputed Thomas de Rokesley, of Lenham, his sub-governor, it thence obtained the name of Rokesley.

Fulbert de Dover's Tower. [4] — This square tower was built by Fulbert de Lucie, who came to England with the Conqueror. Being selected one of the confederate knights, by John de Fienes, for defending this castle, he changed his

---

[3] Pl. iv. fig. 31.   [4] Pl. iv. fig. 32.

name to Dover. When his personal services were not required in the castle, he retired to his baronial mansion, at Chilham. He was succeeded by his son, Hugh de Dover; and, a descendant of his, Richard de Dover, held the large possessions of his ancestors. Neither his wealth or honors could shield him from the cares of life, and, unhappy in the midst of riches, he retired to the abbey of Lesnes, which he had founded in 1179. At his death this great name became extinct, and the estates passed, by the marriage of a female, to an illegitimate son of king John.

After Fulbert de Dover, an officer named Calderscot commanded in this tower, and it was called after his name.

The Prison.—Fulbert de Dover's tower has, through a long period of years, been converted into a prison, for offenders against the revenue laws, crown debtors, and every insolvent within its jurisdiction, which extends from Margate to Seaford, in Sussex, and the towns of Feversham, and Tenterden. A house for the keeper, called the Bodar of Dover castle, is built at the back of the tower. He is also Sergeant at Arms, and holds his office under the Lord Warden.

This wretched prison had formerly only two rooms to contain its unfortunate inmates, and no food allowed to sustain life. Such a picture of misery ought to have excited pity in every human breast; and, in the year 1796, the board of ordnance granted £600, for adding three rooms and a yard. The late D. P. Watts, esq. who occasionally visited Dover, and contributed to the comfort of these prisoners, had a path paved across the yard, for them to walk on for exercise, and to preserve health; and James Neild, esq. of Chelsea, completed the work, in 1810, by causing the whole to be paved with stone, which cost upwards of £60. In the same year, by the assistance of a benevolent Quaker, he gave £800. 3 per cents. to the mayor and corporation of Dover, the interest of which is to be distributed among such of the prisoners, as are most destitute. On the side of the tower, towards the military road, is a grating, through which they solicit donations from those who enter the castle. By these precarious means they formerly obtained their only support; but their situation is now much improved.

Hirst Tower.[5]—The next tower in the wall is circular, and was also built by Fulbert de Dover. He appointed a subaltern officer, John de Hirst, to command here, from whom the tower took its name. For his services in the castle, he held the village and manor of Hirst, of the lordship of Chilham.

Arsick, or Say Tower.[6]—Part of this tower

---

5 Pl. iv. fig. 33.   6 Pl. iv. fig. 34.

E

is circular, and part square. It was built and
defended by William de Arsick, lord of Ley-
bourne, in Kent, where he had a castellated
mansion.   It was afterwards commanded by
Jeffery de Say, a descendant of William de Say,
who was a person of consequence, in the county
of Salop, during the reign of William the First.
It was called Arsick or Say tower, after the
names of its commanders.

Gatton Tower.[7]—The next tower was built
by William de Peverell, to strengthen the curtain between his own and Arsick's tower. Its
name is derived from Robert de Gatton who
held it of that nobleman, and received for its
maintenance the town of Gatton, in Surrey.

Peverell, Beauchamp, or Marshal's Tower.[8]
—William Peverell of Dover, distinguished by
that title from his illegitimate brother, William
of Nottingham, erected this stately tower; and
several lordships and manors were granted to
him, which he held by castle-guard tenure. Hugh
Beauchamp afterwards commanded here, and
was also marshal of the castle; from whence its
names.

It was built in an angle of the exterior wall, and
constructed for defensive warfare on every side,
having a noble arched gate-way, with ditch and
draw-bridge, and several apartments for the sol-

---

7 Pl. iv. fig. 35.   8 Pl. iv. fig. 36.

diers, with an embattled platform for the archers. This gave them the command of a considerable part of the Saxon vallum; and the whole of the side hill, between the castle and the town, lay open to them.

An arched passage, with a caponniere, led from the principal gate-way, between two parallel walls, to Palace gate, which has been mentioned in our account of Suffolk's tower. In 1771, the exterior curtain, from this to Porth's tower, fell into the ditch; and, in digging for a new foundation, the piers of the bridge, before the arched gate-way, were discovered.

Porth, Gostling, or Queen Mary's Tower.[9]— Hugh de Porth, whose family was of distinction in the time of the Conqueror, held of the king twelve knights' fees, to build this tower and to command in it. Porth appointed one Gostling, as his substitute, and the tower was afterwards repaired by queen Mary. Hence it obtained its names.

Fienes, Newgate, or the Constable's Tower.[10]— John de Fienes, on being placed at the head of the associated knights, and appointed constable of the castle, by his relative, the Conqueror, erected this noble gate-way The apartments over it were suitable to his own dignity, and for those who might succeed him. Several manors

---

9 Pl. iv. fig. 37.   10 Pl. iv. fig. 38.

and lordships were given him for the purpose
of erecting the building, and to maintain its garrison.

The plan of this fine edifice, raised on the site
of one more ancient, is derived from the designs
of Gundulph, who, in the construction of military
works, first introduced the high portal, and secured the passages by means of a draw-bridge,
port-cullis, and massy gates, in preference to the
low entrance, and protracted avenues of the
Saxons. The gates at this entrance were secured
by two port-cullises, and the bridge, when drawn
up in the recess, formed a complete defence.
Two embattled towers, on each side of the gates,
commanded the ascent of the hill, and the passage to the bridge. A souterrain, cut in the
solid rock, appears to have entered under this
bridge, and to have passed through the Saxon
vallum into the interior ditch.[11]

On entering the arch which leads into the
castle, a door on the left opens into the porter's
lodge. Here were formerly exhibited a sword,
an old key of the castle, and a horn. The sword,
they said, was Julius Cæsar's, the key was the
first ever used in the castle, and the horn called
the labourers to their work at its first erection.
These idle tales are worn out; and the sword
appears to resemble those, used about the time
of Edward the Second or Third.

---

11 Pl. iv. fig. 7.

On the other side of the passage is another room, in which, after the warden of the ports ceased to hold a court of appeals at Shepway, the records, the doomsday book of the ports, and other manuscripts were deposited. About the beginning of the last century, by the carelessness of those who had the command here, the door was left open, and these ancient writings were suffered to be either destroyed or taken away. Some of them, however, were copied, and have been handed down to us.

At the inner extremity of the passage, on the right hand, a flight of stone steps leads to the governor's hall, arched over with stone, and about thirty-two feet by twenty-five. The hall is over the interior of the arched gate-way, and flights of steps lead from it to the towers on each side. Another flight of steps leads to a gallery, over the exterior of the gate-way, which is about thirty-seven feet long and thirteen broad. By turning an arch on each side of the gate-way, an additional room has been made on each extremity of the gallery; and the embattled terrace over the gallery and arched roof of the hall, is now converted into three lodging rooms.

Great alterations have taken place in this tower. New fire places were constructed, both in the hall and the gallery, in 1580, and the style of the workmanship is of that age. The narrow slips in the wall, intended for the archers, have been supplanted, and sashed windows have taken their places; and the rooms, formerly dark and gloomy, are now light and comfortable. From these apartments the view is pleasing and delightful. The sea, the town, the harbour, and the Romantic hills and valleys that diversify the adjacent country, form a picture hardly to be equalled in grandeur or in beauty.

A caponniere was made at this place, during the late war, by building up the spaces left by the Norman masons, between the piers of the bridge. In this concealment, they have all the usual contrivances for annoying a besieging enemy. On the south side, near the bridge, a large mound has been raised for a platform, on which cannon is mounted in time of war. This, and other alterations, have nearly concealed the line of approach cast up by the Dauphin, when he besieged the castle.

His royal highness the duke of Clarence resided in this tower a short time since; and the present lieutenant governor, R. H. Jenkinson, esq. occasionally makes it his residence.

Clopton Tower.[12]—The next tower in the curtain is of an irregular hexagonal figure, and was also built by John de Fienes, who gave the manor of Clopton, in Norfolk, for its repairs and defence. It was held by the service of castle-

---

12 Pl. iv. fig. 39.

guard, by a person whose name was Clopton, and it took its name either from the manor which he held, or from his own name.

King Edward IV. rebuilt this tower from the foundation, and the records of the castle were deposited here in the reign of Edward VI. when one Levenste, out of mere malice, on finding his competitor, John Monyings, preferred before him to the office of lieutenant governor, burnt and destroyed the whole of these valuable books and parchments.

Godsfoy's Tower.[13]—Fulbert de Dover built the next tower in the curtain, and gave the manor of Sentling for keeping ward in it. Nicholas Veraund was appointed commander, and his successor, Godsfoy, gave his name to it.

Crevequer's Tower.[14]—This round tower, the next in the curtain, was built by Robert Crevequer, who held, in capite, five knights' fees, by castle-guard. His father, Hamo Crevequer, accompanied duke William to England, and was appointed sheriff of Kent during his life. One Cranville commanded in this tower, and was probably a substitute appointed by Crevequer.

Magminot's Tower.[15]—Gilbert de Magminot was a great favourite with William the First, and was appointed marshal of the castle, and one of the associated knights. His tower was a

---

13 Pl. vi. fig 40.   14 Pl. iv. fig. 41.   15 Pl. iv. fig. 42,43,50,51,52.

considerable building, and extended in the bend of the curtain, towards the south-east. It consisted of two circular parts, joined by a sharp angular projection; and, at a small distance, other circular parts, which had a communication with the rest of the edifice by the parapet on the wall.

Numerous alterations and improvements were made in this part of the castle by that distinguished hero, Hubert de Burgh; and we will endeavour to describe them, in a short sketch of his interesting life, which we hope may prove acceptable to the reader.

Hubert de Burgh.—This great man, no less loyal, active, prudent, and brave, than learned in the laws of his country, had distinguished himself in the time of Richard the First. In the turbulent reign of king John, when the greater part of the barons defied the power, or threatened to overturn the throne of the monarch, the few whose fidelity was unimpeached, were selected to occupy posts of honor and responsibility, and to command in the strongest garrisons. Among the fortresses in the kingdom, few were more important than Dover castle, liable, as it was, from its situation, to the first attack from an enemy, and likely to become a dangerous possession, should they take it; and among the great men of that day, no one was more eminently fitted, both by his exalted talents, and his tried fidelity and love to his sovereign, than Hubert de Burgh, to be its constable or governor. King John, therefore, appointed him to this office, at the time when the Dauphin of France was making formidable arrangements to invade the kingdom.

The constable, aware of the intentions of the Dauphin, made every preparation for the defence of the castle.

The Dauphin arriving in the year 1216 at Stonar, with a considerable force, effected his landing. The king, who was at this time at Dover, with a numerous army of more than sixty thousand men, chiefly composed of foreigners, on whom he could not place any reliance, retreated first to Guildford, in Surrey, and then to Winchester. Not meeting with any resistance, the Dauphin marched to London, where he was received with the greatest demonstrations of joy by the discontented barons. After miserably wasting Essex, Norfolk, and Suffolk, and collecting much plunder, he returned, towards the end of the year, to the capital, from whence he proceeded with a large army, to besiege the castle of Dover. For this purpose his father had sent him a military engine of the most formidable description, called the mal-voisin, or bad neighbour, with which he expected to make a breach in the walls.

This fortress happened at the time, to be very

badly defended, being deficient both in knights
and officers, who ought, by the tenure of their
lands, to have been on their station; and the
attack was made so suddenly that the constable
was obliged to arm his own servants, and place
them on the walls and towers. To prevent such
a dereliction of duty in future, he afterwards
obtained the king's consent, and the approbation
of the knights, to commute their personal services
for a sum of money. This change produced a
regular garrison on the spot, who were always
well trained and ready for action.

The Dauphin made his approaches nearly in a
straight line to the foot of the bridge, at the Constable's tower, by casting up a bank on the right
of his work, at the sharp part of the hill, where it
begins to turn to the north. The chalk cast out
of the lines raised a sufficient bank, to cover his
men from the archers in those towers that extend
from the edge of the cliff to the grand entrance,
where the sudden bending of the curtain to the
north, defended them from the towers that are
situated beyond it.

While the Dauphin was carrying on his works
on this side of the hill, Stephen de Pencester,
accompanied by four hundred horsemen, with
arms and engines of defence, had the good
fortune to enter, through the sally-port under
Godwin's tower, without being discovered; and
their arrival was hailed with joy by the scanty
garrison.

The siege was still in progress when the king died ; an event which encouraged the besiegers to hope that the constable might be prevailed on to accept honorable terms of capitulation. For that purpose the Dauphin sent William Longspee and upwards of forty barons, to treat with him. Among other arguments, they pretended that the demise of the king absolved him from his oath of allegiance, and that he might now, without any imputation of disloyalty, swear obedience to a prince whom his countrymen had already acknowledged as their sovereign; and that his compliance would, moreover, ensure to him distinguished marks of favour.

The faithful and enterprising constable, after holding a council of his officers, replied that the king his master had left a successor, (Henry the Third,) to whom he owed allegiance; and that he would continue true to his trust, and defend the castle to the last extremity. He added, that he never could believe, that the esteem of a prince could be obtained by any notorious act of baseness and treachery.

As promises could not warp his principles, they endeavoured to work on his fears. His brother was then a prisoner in France ; and they threatened to have him put to death, if he did not deliver up the castle. Their threats were as ineffectual as their promises, and the Dauphin gave up the hopeless enterprize, during the winter, and marched towards London.

The defect in the Norman curtain, which had enabled the Dauphin to make his approaches without molestation, had not escaped the notice of the constable; and he determined to apply an immediate remedy before the siege might be renewed. To effect this, he added a considerable outwork,[16] or spur, before Magminot's tower; and raised a parapet[17] of earth, after the manner of the Romans. This spur commanded the entrance into the castle, and the side of the hill, down to the place where the Dauphin first broke ground. A very wide and lofty souterrain, sunk to a considerable depth in the solid rock, led from this new work under Magminot's tower, and opened in the Saxon vallum.[18]

On the side of the souterrain, a passage led to a door nearly under the foundation of the exterior wall, where a passage, by a flight of stone steps, entered a gallery in the bank of the ditch, which formed a communication between the tower in the angle, and a new one built in the ditch before the souterrain.

In order to make a sally, and to secure a retreat, he built a caponniere across the ditch, from Saint John's tower,[19] with a gradual ascent, until it opened in the surface, about the middle of the spur, in three branches.[20] The eastern branch had a circular tower[21] (now demolished)

---

16 Pl. iv. fig. 46,   17 Pl. iv. fig. *m*.   18 Pl. iv. fig. *p*.
19 Pl. iv. fig. 44.   20 Pl. iv. fig. 45, 47, 48.   21 Pl. iv. fig. 48.

in the parapet, close by the opening, to protect the men while entering, in case of their being repulsed. Strong gates defended each of the entrances, and another secured the passage where the three branches united.[22]

The communication between the souterrain and the caponniere was through the round tower, in the ditch; and there were strong gates and a draw-bridge, to defend the entrance. There was also an arched passage in the caponniere, by the side of the tower, to keep open a communication between the different sally-ports.

Extensive as were these works, they were all completed before the Dauphin returned to make a second attempt on the castle. At this time his affairs were almost hopeless; and his last resource rested on a large army which he expected from the coast of France. This armament of eighty large ships and several transports, put to sea from Calais. Hubert had not been negligent in providing every possible means to intercept them, and had collected forty sail from the Cinque Ports to effect his purpose. The disparity of force was so alarming, that several knights refused to embark; and even the great mind of Hubert viewed with apprehension the dangerous enterprize. Before his departure he received the Sacrament; and gave the strictest

---

22 Pl. iv. fig. 49.

orders that the castle should not be surrendered on any terms, not even to save his own life, in the event of his being taken prisoner.

Hubert was soon in sight of the French, sailed past them, as if his object had been to surprise Calais, and suddenly tacking, bore down in a line upon their rear. The bowmen and archers began the engagement with a volley of arrows. As soon as the ships came in contact, they were fastened together with chains and hooks; and powder of quick lime was cast in the air, to be driven by the wind into the eyes of the enemy. The English then leaped on board with axes in their hands, and rendered the ships unmanageable by cutting the rigging. The French, unused to this manner of fighting, made but a feeble resistance; and only fifteen of their vessels out of the whole number escaped. One hundred and fifteen knights with their esquires, and more than eight hundred inferior officers, were taken.

During this grand battle the Dauphin was making his second attempt on the castle; but finding the new works cast up by Hubert, had prevented him from carrying on his approaches, and that the fleets of the Cinque Ports were continually cutting off his supplies, he soon raised the siege, and not long after, was obliged to leave the kingdom.

Few men in any age have experienced greater varieties of fortune, than this famous defender

of the castle, Hubert de Burgh. High in the
favour of his sovereign, he was honored, at the
same time, with the guardianship of the principal
castles in the kingdom, appointed sheriff of
several counties, and raised to the rank of chief
justice. All these various offices he sustained
with credit, except the last: but the loyal nobleman, the honorable sheriff, the wise counsellor,
the intrepid warrior, proved a severe and cruel
judge. In this capacity he sullied the many
honors he had before acquired; he raised up
enemies even among those who had been his
friends, and afforded a pretext for that rancour
and jealousy which his many brilliant virtues had
hitherto restrained, to burst every barrier, and
at length to overwhelm him. He on whom, not
long before, a grateful monarch had heaped
honors even to profusion, he whose wise and
prudent counsel had united and harmonized the
conflicting interests of the barons and nobles,
and whose liberal benefactions had gained him
the affections of the ministers of religion, lived
to see an angry monarch draw his sword upon him,
and strip him successively of every dignity,—to
bear the obloquy of those who were his inferiors
in every thing but in malice, and to be pursued
with unrelenting fury by an ecclesiastic whom
nothing less than his total ruin could satiate.
More than once was the wretched Hubert a
prisoner in the tower, several times was he

obliged to flee for refuge to a sanctuary, and either starved out, or dragged forth with violence.

But at length even the malice of his enemies was tired and exhausted. Nothing remained to the fallen Hubert to invite plunder, or excite envy. The storm which had so long raged, abated its fury. The black clouds that had gathered over his head, bagan to disperse; and the evening of his life, though not brilliant, was tranquil and serene. He died at Bansted in May, 1243, and was buried in the church of the Black Friars, London.

Saint John's Tower.[23]—This round tower has been described as forming a part of the great work constructed by Hubert de Burgh. The command of it was given, either by Hubert or by Henry the Third, to a person whose name was Saint John, from whom it derived its name.

Fitzwilliam's Tower.[24]—This tower was built in the curtain, on the north-east side of the castle. In the front, next the ditch, it is on the same plan as Magminot's towers, but on a more contracted scale. Several appendages to this building were added after its first erection; and besides those lands given by John de Fienes, to support the garrison, others were afterwards granted at Tunbridge, Ham, and Whitfield, for that purpose.

---

[23] Pl. iv. fig. 44.   [24] Pl. iv. fig. 55.

A souterrain[25] at this tower, had an entrance in the interior ditch, on the side of the Saxon vallum. By means of a caponniere across the exterior ditch, it was carried through the bank, and opened in the north meadow, where a large gate, hung on two large pivots, in stone sockets, and secured with bars fixed in the wall, defended the entrance. By a mechanical contrivance it was raised to nearly the top of the arch, and, when open, there fixed horizontally, and fastened in a place made to receive it. When suddenly let down against the stone abutments, the weight and velocity would have driven back any number of men that might be entering, and their utmost strength could not oppose it. Between this and the tower, was a draw-bridge to raise before the arched passage in the ditch; and higher up, a port-cullis formed a third barrier at Fitzwilliam's tower. This old sally-port was closed up for ages, but new contrivances for destroying an enemy are now added, in the modern style of military tactics.

Fitzwilliam, who commanded in this tower, held three knights' fees, by castle-guard tenure, as an associate with John de Fienes. At the battle of Hastings he was marshal of the army, where he distinguished himself in so singular a manner, that the duke, after his victory, gave him the scarf from his own arm.

---

25 Pl. iv. fig. 56.

F

This tower was afterwards commanded by William de Saint John, and it was sometimes called after his name.

Watch Towers.[26]—These towers had neither knights appointed to them, nor lands given to build, or keep them in repair, and were probably appendages to the two adjoining ones.

Albrincis, or Averanche's Tower.[27]—Of all the remaining Norman Towers, this is the most perfect and curious; and was erected, in an angle of the curtain, by William Albrincis, one of the confederated knights.

The ground being uneven, the foundation was laid below the bottom of the deep ditch, on the north-east side, and the wall, which is about ten feet thick, was carried up to a level with the Saxon vallum. A gallery was built in this wall, with platforms behind the slits for the archers, in each of the five sides of the tower. Stone steps led from one platform to another, at each of the angles, and the arch ascended in proportion to the rising of the floor. There was a room in the tower, arched over and open in front, and it appears to have been a recess for the weapons and implements of war. Over this room was a platform, and the gallery in the wall opened into it. A circular staircase led from the platform to the top of the tower, where the motions of the enemy could be observed, and signals made

---

26 Pl. iv. fig. 57, 58.   27 Pl. iv. fig. 60.

from it to the Roman fortress. In the wall, on this story, was an arched gallery, open in front, and supported with small columns and three elliptic arches; and the men on duty were perfectly secure, and sheltered from the weather. From this gallery the archers could command a considerable length of the ditch, and also the approach to Godwin's tower. Towards the castle, the two sides of the platform were quite open; and near the openings of the galleries, was a machecolation in the wall, for pouring down hot water, burning sand, or melted lead. From the platform was a covered way in the bank, on the side of the wall leading to Pencester's tower. In the additions and alterations that have been lately made, the vaulted gallery, and the room under the platform, have been enclosed by a bank of earth; but a passage to them has been left from one of the new casemates.

Veville, or Pencester Tower.[28]—This building was seated between Albriucis and earl Godwin's towers. It was probably built by that earl when he opened the entrance into the Roman fortress; and when John de Fienes commanded in the castle, Veville might be appointed to it, his name being the first on record. Stephen de Pencester was appointed to command in this tower, after he had conducted the four hundred horsemen into the castle, when besieged by the Dauphin.

---

28. Pl. iv. letter *b*.

F 2

The manors of Postling and Horton were given to support its garrison.

In the bank between this and Fitzwilliam's tower, several bomb-proof casemates have been made, which open in the Saxon vallum; and a covered way has been formed, which extends from this vallum towards the Roman fortress.

All the ancient ground plans, and the connecting parts of the Roman and Saxon works, have been destroyed between this tower and Godwin's gate-way.

Ashford Towers.[29]—These four square edifices command the eastern wall down to its extremity, at the edge of the cliff, and derived their name from Ashford, the lordship of that town being given, either to build, or repair them. They appear to have been intended for sentinels, or occasionally as advanced posts, where a small number of men might defend that quarter from attack. Their diminutive size could not admit of a garrison.

Beyond the curtain, new hills have been raised and others altered, bomb-proof batteries built, souterrains excavated, and arches of brick constructed, in order to promote a free and secure communication to all parts of the outworks. Nor has invention been remiss in providing means to destroy an enemy, who might have the temerity to enter these subterranean fastnesses, or strive

---

29 Pl. iv. fig. 63, 64, 65.

to force a more open pass into this part of the castle.

The stupendous height of the perpendicular precipice which fronts the sea, might induce the Normans to imagine that nature had here raised a secure bulwark, and that the protection of art was not necessary. We are informed by Pictaviensis, who was chaplain to the conqueror during the whole of his expedition, that the cliff, in his time, was merely cut with instruments of iron, in such a manner as to resemble, in a rude condition, walls and battlements. These chalk defences, softened by every winter's frost, soon yielded to the furious storms that beat against them, and a few centuries laid them in ruins. An earthquake, on the 6th of April, 1580, which extended along the whole range of these hills, destroyed the parts that were then remaining, and threw down a considerable quantity of the cliff, and the ends of the exterior wall that were built on the edge of it.

In sinking the ground for a road from the new entrance to the north curtain, in a line near the cliff, a well was discovered, which was partly filled with rubbish. Between this road and the precipice, and near the east angle, a new hospital is erected. The situation is much exposed to the chilling blasts of a winter's season.

From a spot near this building Doctor Jefferies and Monsieur Blanchard, on the 7th of January,

1785, took their aerial excursion from Dover to the opposite coast.   These gentlemen, having waited a considerable time for a favourable wind, and fearing a rival in Mr. Sadler who arrived in the mean time with his damaged balloon, resolved to seize the first propitious moment for their perilous enterprize.   On the 7th, the wind blew moderately from the N. N. W. and early in the morning the apparatus was prepared for the progress of inflation, and a paper kite kept flying to ascertain the direction of the wind.   Signal guns were fired from the castle, to announce the intended departure of the aeronauts to the surrounding population, who had repeatedly assembled, and had been as frequently disappointed in consequence of sudden changes in the atmosphere.

About one o'clock the balloon was nearly filled, and the adventurers prepared to take their airy flight. They accordingly affixed the car, in which were deposited nine bags of ballast, the French edition of Monsieur Blanchard's aerial voyage with Mr. Sheldon, a bladder containing several letters, a compass, a few philosophical instruments, a beautiful English and French silk flag, some refreshments, and two cork waistcoats, to guard against accidents. This cargo, with the two aeronauts so exactly balanced the machine, that after it had glided slowly and gracefully from the stupendous precipice, it remained for some time nearly in the same horizontal parallel, or about two hundred and ninety feet above the surface of the ocean.

When the aeronauts arrived within six miles of the French coast, they descended with such rapidity as obliged them to cast over the whole of their ballast; and they availed themselves of their cork waistcoats, in expectation of being plunged in the watery element. This reduction of weight so considerably lightened the vehicle, that they ascended with equal rapidity to a tremendous height, and were carried two leagues and a half inland from the coast. About three o'clock they alighted in the environs of the forest of Guines, where a numerous concourse of people congratulated them on their safe arrival, and rendered to these enterprising travellers every assistance in their power. The balloon was taken to Calais, where the car still remains deposited in the town-hall.

Queen Elizabeth's Pocket Pistol.—Near the edge of the cliff stands mounted this beautiful piece of brass ordnance, usually called Queen Elizabeth's Pocket Pistol, which was presented to the queen by the states of Holland, as a token of respect for the assistance she afforded them against Spain, in their contest to establish the independence of their country. This engine of destruction was cast, at Utrecht, by James Tolkys, in 1544. It is twenty-four feet long, and formerly had the reputation of carrying a twelve pound ball to the distance of seven miles. Its touch-hole was once decorated with an annulet of gold, but this precious metal, by the exercise of a species of Vandalism, has been long since totally invisible. During a long period this gun has not been fired; and it is moderately certain, that a charge of powder would not only blow it to atoms, but inflict serious injury on the individual who tried the rash experiment. It is adorned with a variety of rich and beautiful devices, typifying the blessings of peace, and the horrors of war, accompanied by a representation of the arms of England; and on its breech are the following lines in low Dutch:

> " Breeck scrvet al mure ende wal
>   " Bin ic geheten
> " Doer Berch en dal boert minen bal
>   " Van mi gesmeten."

TRANSLATED :

> " O'er hill and dale I throw my ball,
> " Breaker my name of mound and wall."*

General Annals ; or a Relation of Royal, and Great Personages who have visited the Castle.

Whenever affairs of state summoned our kings to the coast or continent, this castle was honored by their presence; and those of the Norman line ever esteemed it as a place of perfect

---

* It was remounted on an iron carriage, A. D. 1827.

security. On the royal precept being despatched to the constable, announcing the sovereign's intention of appearing on a day specified, it was the duty of the marshal to procure such provisions as the country afforded; and for that purpose he exacted them, not unfrequently, in an imperative tone, from the neighbouring peasants. The constable and the resident knights had usually levied heavy contributions of grain, pulse, and provender, on their military tenants, in their several districts; and such extortions were much increased, on the occasion of a royal visit. These excesses were not confined to this castle, but extended to those in every part of the kingdom, till restrained by charter in the ninth year of Henry the Third.

It has been already noticed that William the conqueror not only frequently visited the castle, but that he also greatly improved, and extended the fortifications.

In 1101, Henry the First met the earl of Flanders at Dover, where a treaty was signed between them.

During the civil wars in the reign of king Stephen, Dover castle unfurled its standard in favour of the empress Matilda; but the king, by continued importunity, at length prevailed with Wakelyn, who was then governor, to deliver it up to him. King Stephen died here in the month of October, 1154: history, however, is silent as to the precise spot where this event took place.

Henry the Second came to the castle about two years after the death of Stephen, on his way to the continent with the design of claiming the city of Nantz, as his right by succession.

Richard Cœur de Lion, son and successor of Henry the Second, visited the castle previous to his departure on a crusade to Jerusalem. His fleet lay in Dover roads, from whence he sailed with one hundred large ships and eighty gallies.

King John, having opposed the pope in matters that related to the clergy, was formally deposed by his holiness, and the kingdom laid under an interdict. Philip, of France, was also excited to invade the British dominions, and had assembled an immense army for this purpose on the opposite shores. To oppose these measures, John summoned all his military tenants to meet him at Dover, and commanded the royal navy to assemble off the port. His army was too numerous for any useful purpose, and all were remanded except 60,000 men who were able to provide themselves with a coat of mail, and complete armour; but no confidence could be placed in their fidelity.

While the king lay at Dover, he was visited by Pandulf, the pope's legate, who represented in lively colours the precarious situation of the kingdom, as well as the mighty power of Philip,

and darkly hinted at the disaffection of the English
army. John trembled as the legate spake, being
fully aware of his danger; and after a long
struggle, signed an instrument which he had
before rejected. This was on the 13th of May,
1213. The following day was spent in anxious
consultation; and, on the 15th, John, in the
church of the templars, and in the presence of
his nobles, resigned his dominions to the pope,
and consented to hold the kingdom as a vassal,
at the yearly rent of 1000 marks. The legate
contemptuously spurned at the proffered sum,
treading it under his feet, while none had courage
to revenge the daring insult.

After the king had violated the great charter
which he had granted to his barons at Runnymead,
in 1215, he resided at Dover during the following month of September, awaiting the arrival of
foreign auxiliaries, whom he had hired to repress
the liberties of his subjects.

On the 21st of May, 1216, the king again
assembled an army at Dover, to oppose the
Dauphin of France, some particulars of which
have been mentioned in our account of Hubert
de Burgh.

In the year 1255, Henry the Third, having
concluded a peace with Spain, requested permission of the king of France, to return home
through that kingdom. The request was readily
granted, and he embarked at Boulogne and

landed at Dover, accompanied by his queen, the queen's sister, the countess of Cornwall, and a suite of a thousand horsemen. On his arrival he was met by a numerous procession of the nobility and clergy, who conducted him and his splendid cavalcade, to the castle, with all the pomp and distinctions of royalty.

In 1259, Richard, king of the Romans, expressed a wish to visit his friends in England, and appeared on the coast. The barons, who had then usurped the power of the king, objected to his landing; and required, as a condition, that he should swear to assist them, in their intended reformation. On his hesitating, they fitted out a fleet, and raised an army to oppose him, should he reach the shore. These vigorous measures induced him to comply, and he was allowed to land; but not suffered to enter the castle, until he had given assurance that he would conduct himself, as required.

In 1262, the breach being healed between Henry the Third and the barons, the king came again to Dover castle, and appointed Robert Wallerand to the office of constable.

Prince Edward was appointed constable of the castle during his absence in the Holy Land, and served the office by deputy. On the death of his father, in 1272, he passed through Dover on his return home, and frequently visited the castle during his reign.

Edward the Second visited the castle in 1308, only a few months after his accession. He embarked in the Cinque Ports fleet for Boulogne, to consummate his marrriage with Isabella of France. On his return he again visited the castle, accompanied by the queen and a numerous suite, where they continued some time. After this he several times came to this fortress, assembled his council here, and transacted business of great national importance.

Edward the Third made his first visit to the castle in 1329, being the second year of his reign. The Cinque Ports fleet was assembled to receive him; and he embarked with a thousand horsemen, and a numerous train of attendants, to do homage to the French king, for his possessions in that country. On a visit here in 1331, he was accompanied by the queen, and they sailed from hence on a visit to the king of France. The king came in great haste to the castle in 1339. Chargny, the governor of St. Omer, had endeavoured to corrupt the fidelity of Amerigo di Pavia, who was then governor of Calias, which had lately been conquered by the victorious arms of Edward. To punish the perfidy of Chargny, Amerigo had consented to deliver up the town, on the last midnight of the year, and forty thousand crowns were offered, as a reward for his treachery. He informed the king of the whole design, who secretly embarked on board the Cinque Ports fleet at Dover, accompanied by three hundred men at arms, and six hundred archers. They were privately admitted into the town, and concealed in the most convenient manner. At a short distance, Chargny was posted with a body of five hundred spearmen, ready to take possession. Precisely at midnight one hundred of them were sent forward, to deliver the stipulated sum, and to sieze the fortress. They approached, the postern was opened, and they unsuspectingly entered. Edward and his noble band, like furious lions, rushed on their prey. Chargny moved forward to join the contest, and made a gallant, but unavailing resistance; and the whole were made prisoners. In this conflict Edward fought on foot, like a private knight, under the banner of sir Walter Manby. He singled out for his antagonist a valourous knight, sir Eustace de Ribeaumont. Twice he received a stroke on his helmet which brought him on his knees; twice he renewed the contest, and ultimately vanquished his adversary. The king concealed his rank until the prisoners were conducted into the fortress, where he invited them to a repast; and the prince of Wales and the English knights, waited on the guest. On rising from table, the king took from his head a chaplet of pearls, and placed it on the head of Ribeaumont, with this high encomium on his merit: "To you, sir knight," said the king, " I

" adjudge the prize of valour in the action of
" this morning, and pray you to wear my chaplet
" during the year for my sake. Wherever you
" go, tell the ladies that it was given by the king
" of England to the bravest of knights."

In 1382, the princess Anne, sister of Winceslaus, the emperor, and daughter of Charles the Fourth, arrived at Dover castle, and was splendidly received, preparatory to her marriage with Richard the Second. This monarch also came here in 1396, and embarked for Calais, with his uncles, the dukes of York and Gloucester, and a large train of nobility and gentry, to obtain an interview with the French king.

After the battle of Agincourt, in 1415, Henry the Fifth landed at Dover with the dead bodies of the duke of York and the earl of Norfolk. The crowd rushed into the water to receive him, and the victorious hero was carried in their arms from his vessel to the beach. From hence the triumphal procession continued to the metropolis, where he was welcomed with unbounded acclamations of joy.

In the following spring Henry's vanity was flattered by a visit from several distinguished personages. Among these was Sigismond, king of the Romans, and emperor elect, who was using every endeavour to extinguish a schism in the church, occasioned by two pretenders to the papacy, at the same time. For this purpose he visited France, and Henry was making splendid preparations to receive him in England. A fleet of three hundred sail was assembled at Calais to convey him and his retinue, among whom were a thousand horsemen, to Dover. Before he reached the British shore, a report had passed the channel that, while in France, he had exercised an assumption of power, in virtue of the imperial dignity. Henry was determined to preserve the rights and independence of the crown; and as soon as the emperor's ship cast anchor in the bay, the duke of Gloucester and several noblemen rode into the water, with their swords drawn, and inquired whether the imperial stranger meant to exercise or claim any authority or jurisdiction in England. He replied in the negative, and was immediately received on shore by the earl of Warwick, governor of the castle, and by several nobles and great barons, with all the honors due to the first sovereign in Europe.

In 1421, Henry assembled an army at Dover, of twenty-four thousand archers, and four thousand horsemen, and collected a fleet of five hundred sail, in which he embarked them for the continent, to revenge the death of his brother, the duke of Clarence, who was slain at the battle of Beaujé

Henry the Seventh, in 1491, came with an army to Dover, and embarked for the continent. While besieging the town of Boulogne, a treaty for peace was opened, and he returned and landed with his army at this port.

Henry the Eighth was a frequent visitor to the town and castle; and finding the rents and revenues of the fortress had much decreased, or had been applied to other purposes, he made several salutary regulations to improve them. They were formerly received at the paymaster's tower. A flag from the turret announced the day of payment; and whoever neglected to settle his account before it was taken down in the evening, was fined a double sum every time the tide flowed to the eastward. Even these severities, usually called Dover castle sursises, could not secure the prompt receipts from those manors that still remained attached to the castle; and Henry enacted that in future the rents should be paid into the king's exchequer, within fifteen days after the festival of St. Simon and St. Jude, under a penalty of their being doubled for every omission. Out of these sums the constable or his deputy received annually, by four equal quarterly payments, one hundred and sixty pounds. At this time the castle was considered as an honorable, strong, and defensible fortress. The king expended large sums in repairing the walls and towers, and the garrison was numerous and respectable.

In 1513, the king commanded the barons of the Cinque Ports to fit out their fleet to cover the passage of his army to the continent. He arrived at the castle on the 15th of June, where he remained fifteen days with his queen, Catherine of Arragon, and then took his leave of her, and embarked for Calais, fully determined to reconquer the patrimony of his ancestors.

In 1520, the emperor Charles the Fifth, nephew to queen Catherine, on passing from Spain to the Netherlands, cast anchor with his whole squadron in the harbour of Hythe. On being informed that the English court was then at Canterbury, he expressed a desire to pay his respects to his uncle and aunt. The king and queen hastened to Dover castle, where they received their nephew on the 30th of May. They continued here till the following day, being Whitsunday, when they departed, with a grand cavalcade, to join the members of the court that remained at Canterbury. Here they banqueted till the third day, when the king accompanied his nephew on board his fleet, which had sailed to Sandwich, and then returned to meet the queen at Dover castle. After making every splendid preparation they embarked, with a gorgeous train of attendants, to meet Francis the First, on the plain between Guisnes and Ardres, afterwards called le champ de drap d'or, from the costly magnificence there exhibited. After this, Henry frequently visited the castle and this part of the coast ; built the castles of Sandown, Deal,

Walmer, and Sandgate; and expended large sums of money in repairing the harbour, and in erecting bulwarks and block-houses at Dover. These military constructions were placed under the jurisdiction of the constable of the castle; but he reserved the nomination of the officers to himself.

In the summer of 1575, queen Elizabeth honored the castle of Dover with her presence, on her progress through the county; and Lambarde informs us that she spent large sums in repairing the walls and towers.

Charles the First arrived at the castle on the 13th of June, 1625. While he remained here, he was at great expense in providing apartments for the reception of his intended queen, the princess Henrietta of France, whom he came to meet on her first arrival, and he conducted her to the castle. They afterwards proceeded to Canterbury, where the marriage was solemnized in the monastery of St. Augustine.

On the 23rd of February, 1642, the same king and queen, accompanied by their daughter, the princess Mary, were again at Dover; not with a splendid train of admiring courtiers, but almost alone, solitary, and forsaken. Those shouts of joy and gladness which had welcomed their first meeting on the British shores, were now turned to sadness, and a fearful presage of impending ruin. Driven from their throne, and deprived of their revenues, their resources were barely equal to meet their present necessities. It is probable that the same room in the castle which had witnessed their joyful meeting in 1625, was now the scene of their mournful separation. The queen and her eldest daughter, then only thirteen years of age, embarked for Holland, and the king returned to Greenwich. War and desolation were the companions of his future years, and he ended the last sad period of his sufferings on the scaffold.

In the same year, on the 21st of August, the castle was surprised and taken, and wrested from its lawful sovereign, by a merchant of Dover, whose name was Blake. He, with only ten of his townsmen, all determined republicans, adventured to scale the lofty cliff fronting the sea, where no danger could be apprehended by the garrison. About midnight they began the daring enterprize, each armed with a loaded musket, and furnished with ropes and scaling ladders; while some of their companions lay in ambush at the castle gates. On reaching the summit of the cliff, they proceeded to the walls of the Saxon fortress, which they also scaled without discovery, and secured the guard. The porters refused to deliver up the keys; but a threat of instant death obtained compliance, and the gates were thrown open. These latter operations alarmed the garrison. Surrounding darkness concealed the number of their opponents; and finding the gates open, they suspected treachery, or that a considerable force had taken possession of the castle. Under these apprehensions they either surrendered, or fled with precipitance from the fortress, and the barriers were closed after them. The earl of Warwick was then at Canterbury, to whom Blake dispatched an account of his success, and an armed force was sent to his assistance. Thus secured, the parliamentarians kept possession of it during the remainder of that unhappy contest.

The loyalists of Kent, lamenting the loss of this fortress, raised forces to assemble on Barham downs, and they marched to the coast under the command of the colonels Hatton and Hammond. After reducing the castles of Sandown, Deal, and Walmer, and making themselves masters of the forts and bulwarks in the neighbourhood, they cast up works on the north-west side of Dover castle. Here they could level their cannon directly against the walls, and five hundred balls were fired without doing any material injury. Colonel Rich was sent by the parliament, with a superior force, to raise the siege, and the loyalists were obliged to retire with precipitation, and to leave their stores and artillery behind them.

On the 29th of May, 1660, at one o'clock in the afternoon, king Charles the Second landed here, on his restoration, accompanied by the dukes of York and Gloucester, and by several persons of distinction. The king embarked on board the English fleet, which waited for him at the Hague, on the 23rd, and one continued roar of cannon marked its progress till it cast anchor in Dover bay. When his majesty came on shore from the Royal Charles, he was met by general Monk, whom he cordially embraced, and was conducted by the mayor and the royal attendants to a canopy erected on the beach, where the minister of St. Mary's presented him with a large Bible with gold embossed clasps, and made a suitable harangue on the occasion. From hence he departed towards London amidst the joyful acclamations of his subjects, who pressed in infinite multitudes, from all quarters, to welcome his return. He remained one day at Canterbury and another at Rochester, and arrived on the 29th at Whitehall. As a compliment to Dover, in the same year he presented to the corporation a mace, which is still in use, inscribed, *Carolus Secundus hic posuit vestigia prima* 1660.

The princess Henrietta-Maria, duchess of Orleans, came to Dover on the 15th of May, 1670, on a visit to her brothers, king Charles the Second and the duke of York. She was received very graciously by the king, who kept his court at Dover, more than a fortnight, amidst a continued round of diversions, festivity, and mirth, until the duchess returned to France.

The princess Maria d' Este of Modena, then only fifteen years of age, landed at Dover on the 21st of June, 1672, where she was met by the duke of York, afterwards king James the Second, and married to him the same evening, by the bishop of Oxford, before they left the place. Her mother, the duchess of Modena, accompanied her, and was present at the ceremony.

From this period, the venerable pile no longer witnessed the splendour of royal residents; the courtier had deserted her battlements, and her long days of pristine beauty were drawing to a close.

The present state and appearance of the Castle.

In this ancient fortress, there have been introduced, of late years, many alterations; some of which have been necessarily mentioned to illustrate our preceding narrative, as we passed on from one tower to another.

For some time prior to the year 1727, the castle appears to have suffered much, both from neglect and violence. At that period it was visited by Doctor Stukeley, who expressed great regret, that so venerable a fortress, which had at various times, by its impregnable bulwarks, intimidated our enemies, and saved the kingdom from invasion, should become a prey to the ravages of time, and to the negligence of succeeding ages.

During the wars with France, in the time of queen Anne, fifteen hundred French prisoners were confined in the palace or keep, who, in less than twelve months, had much injured the building, and destroyed most of the timbers and floors.

The duke of Cumberland surveyed the castle, in 1745, when additional barracks were erected for 1000 men. A bastion of earth was also cast up on the north-west extremity of the fortress, and other improvements were carried on by his direction.

During the French revolution, which commenced in the year 1794, when continual threats of invasion were denounced against us, it became a subject of national importance, to secure and defend this important military station. Fifty thousand pounds were voted for this purpose, and surveyors and engineers were sent to examine the works. Miners, mechanics, and labourers, were employed to excavate the rock, for souterrains, casemates, and mines; to erect caponnieres; and to cast up additional mounds and ramparts. These immense bulwarks surround, at proper distances, the whole fortress, and consist of sod surmounted with breastworks and heavy cannon.   To ascend their steep sides, would require great exertion, even without arms or accoutrements; and to bombard them would be useless, as the balls would be merely buried in the sod.   Communications are formed with the interior works, by means of shafts and souterrains, passing under the deep ditch that encompasses the exterior wall.   The ditch is sunk in the solid rock, and the wall is built against the perpendicular sides of it.   From the height of the ground on the outer side of the ditch, and the mounts that surround it, the wall lies secure from a bombardment, except towards the summit, which forms a breastwork, from the raised surface within, both for cannon and musketry.

At the same time, extensive barracks were excavated in the solid rock.   They are several feet under ground, and light and air are admitted by apertures that perforate the surface, and by openings in the side of the perpendicular cliff that faces the ocean.   By these additions, accommodations are now provided for a garrison of three or four thousand men.

The views from the castle walls are truly romantic.   Those on the north and north-west, are bounded by the surrounding hills; between which and the battlements, a deep valley descends towards the sea.   The views from the battlements on the keep, which have been already described, extend over the hills, to the Isle of Thanet, and take in a vast extent of country.

From the western battlements the prospect is most delightful, and extends over the fertile valley, down which descend the small river Dour, and the main road from London. Other valleys branch off to the left, and are intersected by lofty hills. The populous villages of Charlton and Buckland, occupy a considerable extent in this direction.

Fronting the battlements on the south-west, and at less than half a mile distance, the extensive and lofty heights raise their fortified crest above the highest pinnacle of the castle. On this opposite hill formerly stood a pharos or watch-tower, similar to that which has been already described in the Roman works. It was called the Devil's drop, or Bredon-stone, and the site is now occupied by a redoubt. The haven formerly entered between these two light-houses, and occupied the principal part of the valley in which the present town is situated. The town now spreads across the whole extent towards the sea; and, from the utmost extremity, in conjuction with its adjoining villages, forms an almost continued range of buildings, nearly two miles up the country.

Beyond the town, and more southward than the heights, from which it is separated by a deep valley, rises the lofty and majestic head of

Shakespeare or Hay Cliff, 350 feet above the surges which beat against its base. As the steep ascent to its summit rises from a valley behind it, every fall of the cliff must considerably reduce its altitude; from which we may fairly conclude that it was much higher, when Shakespeare described it in the following lines, which are taken from his tragedy of King Lear:

" There is a cliff, whose high and bending head
Looks fearfully on the confined deep.—

How dizzy 'tis to cast one's eyes so low!
The crows and choughs, that wing the mid-way air,
Seem scarce so gross as beetles. Half way down
Hangs one that gathers samphire* ; dreadful trade!
Methinks he seems no bigger than his head.
The fishermen that walk upon the beach
Appear like mice, and yon tall anchoring bark
Diminished to her cock, her cock a buoy,
Almost too small for sight. The murm'ring surge,
That on th' unnumber'd idle pebbles chafes,
Cannot be heard so high. I'll look no more,
Lest my brain turn, and the diminish'd sight
Topple down headlong.

From the dread summit of this chalky bourn
Look up; a height—the shrill gorg'd lark so far
Cannot be seen or heard.

From the edge of the cliff, on the east side of the castle, the eye, elevated 350 feet above the

---

* The samphire is an excellent pickle, and grows in abundance on the sides of these cliffs. The persons who gather it, fasten a rope to an iron bar stuck in the ground, and then let themselves down over the frightful precipice; but who can think of it without shuddering!

ocean, wanders over a vast expanse of waters.
Directly opposite lies the coast of France, at a
distance of about twenty miles. In clear weather,
the lofty cliffs, the fields, the houses, and a wide
extent of country are distinctly seen. On the
right lies the town of Boulogne, and, on a hill
beyond it, the lofty tower, built by Bonaparte,
at the time of his intended invasion. About it,
and along the coast, were encamped his numerous armies. Twenty-three miles to the left
of Boulogne, on the low ground, is situated the
town of Calais, whose towers and battlements
are often clearly seen by the naked eye. Ships
of all nations trading with the northern ports, or
the city of London, are continually passing this
narrow neck of the channel, presenting such a
variety, as cannot be met with in any other part
of the kingdom.

Having presented the reader with such prospects as appear most interesting, when seen from
different parts of the castle, we would merely
state its appearance, when the eye beholds it at
a distance.

From the many elevated points in the neighbouring country, and particularly from the London road, it strikes the observer with all its
majestic grandeur, and he would rather consider
it as a fortified city, than a single fortress.
About thirty-five acres of ground are enclosed
within its walls, and its conspicuous appearance

in the channel, has, through a long succession of ages, guided the adventurous mariner as he passes many a dangerous mile on the briny ocean: and when fierce westerly winds drive him from his perilous moorings in the neighbouring downs, he here finds a sheltered retreat under its lofty summit.

When seen from the opposite coast of France, like another Atlas, the castle appears to lift its towering head above the clouds. Well might the inhabitants of these shores, and foreign mariners as they pass by, stand in awe of its mighty strength, and spread its ancient fame through distant climes. Should the enemies of our country assault its battlements, or those of the contiguous heights, whose strongly fortified lines would enclose a numerous army, may discomfiture and defeat chastise their insolence, and repel the bold aggression. And may the laurels of victory, the love of virtue, and the blessings of peace, for ever flourish on our happy island.

A LIST

OF THE

CONSTABLES OF DOVER CASTLE,

AND

WARDENS OF THE CINQUE PORTS.

UNDER EDWARD THE CONFESSOR, 1053.

Godwin   Harold

HAROLD, 1060.

Bertram de Ashburnham

WILLIAM I. 1066.

William Peverel   John de Fienes
Odo, Bishop of Baieaux

WILLIAM II. 1087.

John de Fienes   James de Fienes

HENRY I. 1100

James de Fienes   John de Fienes

STEPHEN. 1135.

William Maresshal   Richard, Earl of Eu
Wakelyn de Magminot   Eustace, Earl of Boulogne

HENRY II. 1154.

Henry, or Hugh de Essex   Henry de Sandwich
Simon de Sandwich   Alan de Fienes

RICHARD I. 1189.

James de Fienes
Matthew de Clere
William Devereux
William Longchamp
William de Wrotham

JOHN. 1199.

Thomas Bassett
Hubert de Burgh
William de Huntingfield
William de Sarum
Geoffry Fritz-Pier
Hubert de Burgh (2d time)

HENRY III. 1216.

Hubert de Burgh
Sir Robert de Neresford .
Hugh de Windlesore
Sir Geoffry de Shurland
William de Albrincis
Hubert de Burgh (3d time)
Stephen de Segrave
Symon Hoese
Bertram de Criol
Hubert de Husato
Hamo de Crevequer
Bertram de Criol (2d time)
Peter de Savoy
Humphry Bohun
Sir Ingelram de Fienes
Peter de Rivallis
Bertram de Criol (3d time)
Reginald de Cobham
Roger Northwood
Nicholas de Moels
Richard de Grey
John de Grey
Hugh Bigod
William de Say
Robert Waleran
Henry de Wingham
Henry de Braybrooke
Edmund & Robert Gascoyne
Henry, Bishop of London
Walter de Bersted
Richard de Grey
Nicholas de Criol
Henry de Montfort
Roger de Leyborne
Sir Simon de Sandwich
Edward, Prince of Wales

EDWARD I. 1272.

Sir Stephen de Penchester
Simon de Cray
Ralph de Sandwich
Sir Robert de Shurland
Sir Stephen de Penchester
  (2d time)
Robert de Burghersh
Sir Stephen de Penchester
  (3d time)
Sir Reginald Cobham
Henry Cobham, of Rundel

EDWARD II. 1307.

Robert de Kendale
Henry Cobham, of Cobham
Robert de Kendale (2d time)
Bartholomew de Badlesmere
Hugh Despencer, jun.
Edmund, Earl of Kent
Robert de Kendale & Ralph de Camoys
Ralph Basset
Ralph de Camoys & Robert de Kendale (2d time)
Hugh Despencer (3d time)
Bartholomew de Burghersh

EDWARD III. 1327.

Bartholomew de Burghersh
Edmund of Woodstock
Robert de Burghersh
William de Clinton
Bartholomew de Burghersh (2d time)
Sir John Peche
Ralph, Lord Basset
Bartholomew de Burghersh (3d time)
Reginald de Cobham
Otho de Grandison
Roger de Mortimer
Guy St. Clere
Sir John Beauchamp
Reginald de Cobham (2d time)
Sir Robert Herle
Sir Ralph Spigurnel
Sir Richard de Pembrugg
William de Latimer
Edmund Langley

RICHARD II. 1377.

Edmund Langley
Sir Robert Ashton
Sir Simon de Burley
Sir John Devereux
Henry de Cobham
John, Lord Beaumont
Edward, Duke of York and Albermarle
Sir John Beaufort

HENRY IV. 1399.

Sir Thomas Erpingham
Henry, Prince of Wales

HENRY V. 1413.

Thomas Fitzalan
Humphry, Duke of Glo'ster

HENRY VI. 1422.

Humphry, Duke of Glo'ster Edmund, Duke of Somerset
Humphry Stafford, Duke of Sir James Fiennes
   Buckingham Simon Montfort

EDWARD IV. 1461.

Richard, Earl of Warwick William Fitzalan
Sir John Scott

EDWARD V. 1483.

Richard, Duke of Gloucester

RICHARD III. 1483.

Henry Stafford, Duke of William Fitzalan, Earl of
   Buckingham Arundel

HENRY VII. 1485.

William Fitzalan Henry, Duke of York
Sir William Scott Sir Edward Poynings

HENRY VIII. 1509.

Sir Edward Poynings George Boleyne
Sir George Nevill Henry, Duke of Richmond
Sir Edward Poynings (2d Arthur Plantagenet
   time) Sir Thomas Cheney
Sir Edward Guldeford

EDWARD VI. 1547.

Sir Thomas Cheney

MARY. 1553.

Sir Thomas Cheney Sir William Brooke

ELIZABETH. 1558.

Sir William Brooke Henry, Lord Cobham

JAMES I. 1603.

Henry, Lord Cobham George Villiers, Duke of
Henry, Earl of Northampton Buckingham
Edward, Lord Zouch

CHARLES I. 1625.

Theophilus Howard, Earl of Suffolk

James, Duke of Richmond

Robert, Earl of Warwick

COMMONWEALTH. 1649.

Colonels John Lambert, John Deshborough, and Robert Blake

Charles Fleetwood & John Deshborough

CHARLES II. 1660.

James, Duke of York

Henry, Viscount Sidney

JAMES II. 1685.

Henry, Viscount Sidney.

WILLIAM III. 1689.

Colonel John Beaumont

ANNE. 1702.

Henry, Viscount Sidney

Prince George of Denmark

Lionel Cranfield Sackville, Earl of Dorset

James, Duke of Ormond

GEORGE I. 1714.

Lionel, Earl of Dorset

John Sidney

GEORGE II. 1727.

Lionel, Duke of Dorset

Robert D'Arcey, Earl of Holderness

GEORGE III. 1760.

Robert D'Arcey, Earl of Holderness

Frederick, Lord North

William Pitt, Rt. Hon.

Earl of Liverpool, Rt. Hon.

GEORGE IV. 1820.

Earl of Liverpool, Rt. Hon.

THE
CINQUE PORTS.

———◆◆◆———

General View of the Cinque Ports;—their Customs and Privileges.

DOVER being one of the Cinque Ports, it may be desirable, before we proceed with the history of the town and port, to give a general outline of these ancient havens, so far as a small work of this kind will admit.

Situated opposite the coast of France, and inhabited by a bold and daring population; their navies, manned by intrepid and experienced seamen, were a safeguard and defence to the nation; and the enemy generally stood in awe of their mighty prowess. To reward their services, and encourage their exertions, chartered rights and privileges were conferred on them; and their dignity in the state, was equal to their high importance. No enemy approached the shore, but the armed inhabitants of the cinque ports were ready to receive them, and to repel the bold aggression ; and their feats of heroic valour, are recorded in our ancient histories.

The modern names of the five principal ports, are Dover, Hastings, Sandwich, Hythe, and Romney. The usual number of ships provided for the king's use, was fifty-seven, each containing twenty-one mariners and one boy, making a total of 1254 persons ; to which the king added a certain number of soldiers, armed with bows and arrows, darts, spears, slings, and grapling-irons. These armaments were at the sole disposal of the king, for forty days ; the expenses of the first fifteen being defrayed by the ports. But the time of service, and the number of ships, depended on the emergency of the case, and their fleet has sometimes consisted of more than one hundred armed vessels.

Induced by the honors and privileges of the cinque ports, other towns on the coast were desirous of joining them, and were united as limbs or members of the head ports. Among these, the two ancient towns of Rye and Winchelsea stand pre-eminent, the former having the town of Tenterden, as a subordinate member. These limbs or members are first mentioned in the Red Book of the Exchequer, and in the Doomsday of the Ports.*

---

* The first of these ancient documents is supposed to have been written soon after the year 1100; the latter was an ancient manuscript, formerly kept in Dover castle, till it was destroyed in the reign of Edward VI. as has been mentioned in our history of the castle, page 63.

The following is a list of the cinque ports, with their members, extracted from these ancient records, with the proportionate number of ships each provided for the king's use. Those towns marked with an asterisk (*) are corporations.

A list of the Cinque Ports, their two ancient towns and their members, with the number of ships and mariners they provided for the king's service.

Head Ports and their Members.	Ships.	Mariners.	Boys
*HASTINGS, a head port	3 ..	63 ..	3
*Rye, an ancient town, with *Tenterden ..	5 ..	105 ..	5
*Winchelsea, an ancient town.............	10 ..	210 ..	10
*Seaford and *Pevensey	1 ..	21 ..	1
Bulverheath and Petit Hiam..............	1 ..	21 ..	1
Hidney, Grange, and Beakesbourn........	1 ..	21 ..	1
	21 ..	441 ..	21
*DOVER, a head port, with *Folkestone, *Faversham, Margate, St. John's, Goresend, St. Peter's, Woodchurch, Kingsdown, and Ringwould	21 ..	441 ..	21
*SANDWICH, a head port, with *Deal, *Fordwich, *Ramsgate, Walmer, Sarr, and Brightlingsea	5 ..	105 ..	5
*ROMNEY, a head port, with *Lidd, Promehill, Old Romney, Dangemarsh, Oswardstone	5 ..	105 ..	5
*HITHE, a head port, with West Hithe	5 ..	105 ..	5
*Total....	57 ..	1197 ..	57

The origin of the cinque ports is involved in total darkness. That four of them, viz. Dover, Sandwich, Hythe, and Romney, were Roman ports, is unquestionable; but Hastings is not mentioned in the Itinerary of Antoninus, nor does it appear that any of the Roman roads led to this place. It is probable that they were incorporated during the Saxon Heptarchy; and they appear to have conducted their business, as a collective body, soon after the Romans had left the island, by sending a bailiff to superintend their fisheries at Yarmouth. We cannot find that they had any charter of privileges, to sanction such a right; but custom, from a remote period, had given their proceedings the authority of law. Prior to the landing of Cerdick the Saxon, A. D. 485, they annually repaired to a bank of sand, on which the town of Yarmouth was afterwards built, to catch herrings; and there they dried their nets, salted their fish, and considered themselves as the legal proprietors of the soil.

From so humble an origin, this sand-bank became a general fair or mart for the finny tribe; and vessels from the opposite coast of Flanders, came to purchase of the cinque ports fishermen. Buildings were erected for their officers, a court and prison for the administration of justice, and they received annual rents for their lands and tenements.

When the town of Yarmouth began to arise on this very spot, and the resident inhabitants became numerous, continued feuds raged between them and the inhabitants of the cinque ports. In the reign of William Rufus, the bishop of Norwich built a chapel for the residents of the rising town, and sent a priest to officiate. The inhabitants of the cinque ports expelled him, and chose a priest for themselves; and the contest was carried to such extremities, that the nation became alarmed.

The town of Yarmouth was now become a place of importance, and king John espoused the cause of the burgesses, and granted them certain privileges. The cinque ports resented the grant, and employed force to establish their pretended rights; and the two parties fought and plundered each other, at intervals, with all the rancour of the bitterest enemies, through several succeeding reigns.

In the twenty-first year of the reign of Edward the First, the royal navy landed his majesty on the coast of Flanders. The mariners of Yarmouth, and those of the cinque ports, then separated their squadrons from the rest of the fleet, and engaged each other with such fury, that no threats or efforts could repress their rage, till twenty-five ships belonging to Yarmouth were burnt; several more damaged; one hundred and seventy-one of their men killed; and property lost to the amount of £15,356.

At length the cinque ports appear to have been animated with a better spirit, and to consider their claims with greater calmness and forbearance, but they continued to send their bailiff till the reign of Elizabeth.

This feud of the fishery has carried us further down the stream of time than we intended, and we must refer back to an earlier period. Camden informs us that William the Conqueror first placed a warden over the cinque ports; but whether the limbs or members were then united to the five head ports, does not appear. It is mentioned in a charter to the cinque ports, granted by Edward the First, son of Henry the Third, that he had seen the charters of Edward the Confessor; of William the First, and Second; of Henry the First; of John; and also of his father, Henry the Third; all which charters were then in existence. This is the oldest charter now extant. Most of our succeeding kings, down to the twentieth year of Charles the Second, granted new charters to the ports; all confirmatory of past privileges, and adding new ones. Even a bare mention of every one of them, would far exceed the limits of this short work.* We can merely hint at a few, as we pass on.

---

* Among these various privileges, was an exemption from all tolls and taxes, except such as were levied by themselves; a cognizance of all causes, both civil and criminal, within their own courts; to punish offenders; to hold markets and receive tolls within their own jurisdiction; to possess goods found floating on the sea; to have a guild, a court leet, and court baron; to assemble at Shepway, and keep a portmote or parliament, for the general good of the ports; an exemption from military services in the field; to assess and tax themselves, &c. &c. &c.

The freemen of the cinque ports, as a mark of high distinction, were called barons, and still retain the appellation; and their representatives in the great council of the nation, enjoyed superior dignity, and had rank among the nobility. Their courage, industry, commercial knowledge, and constant intercourse with other nations, eminently qualified them both as legistators and as advisers of their sovereign.

At this time, the great council of the nation consisted of the nobility only. The knights, citizens, and burgesses, were afterwards added, and, till after ages, deliberated in the same house with the peers. In calling over the members, they began with the lowest order, the burgesses and citizens; then the knights; and lastly, the barons of the cinque ports and the peers. Hence it appears, that the port barons ranked with the nobility, and formed a part of the great council, before the commons were annexed to that body; but when the council was divided into two houses, their importance seems to have suffered a diminution, and they now sit in the lower house. Still, however, they hold the distinguished honor of supporting the royal canopy over our kings and queens at their coronations; and to have a table on the right hand of their majesties, to feast with them in Westminster hall, after the ceremony.

Forty days before the coronation, the king's

writ is delivered to each of the ports.* A court
of brotherhood and guestlings† is then called to
appoint thirty-two barons to attend their majesties, all in one uniform, which are provided at
their own expense; but their charges, while at
court, are defrayed by their constituents.‡

---

* These writs have been discontinued many centuries.

† This court was originally held at Shepway Crosse, or
Shipway, about half a mile from Limne church or castle, on
the confines of Romney marsh. After the decay of that place,
it was held at Romney, or some other place within its jurisdiction. Formerly it consisted of seven principal persons
from each port, and the two ancient towns; but the number
has since been reduced to five; viz. the mayors or bailiffs,
two jurats, and two commoners. The chair is taken by the
chief magistrates in rotation, and he who presides has the
title of speaker. Forty days' notice is usually given for holding a court, and the summons is issued in the name of the
speaker, and of the magistrates of the town in which he resides.
Each member is sworn to defend the rights, liberties, and
charters of the ports. Here the supplies were raised for fitting
out their fleets, and the general business of the ports dicussed
and regulated; and here the bailiffs, to superintend the fisheries of Yarmouth, were appointed; and their report received
on their return.

When the services of the ports were dispensed with, the
holding of the court became less frequent. It was annually
held until the year 1601. After a lapse of many years, a court
was held in 1750; others in 1771; in 1812; and in 1821.

The entry books of the brotherhood and guestling, from the
eleventh year of Henry the Sixth, to the present time, are kept
in a chest at Romney.

‡ The canopy bearers are now chosen by each port separately. At Dover they are chosen by the mayor, jurats, and
common-council. In some of the ports the resident freemen
have a voice in the election.

The silken canopy is supported by four staves covered with silver, to each of which is affixed a small bell, the whole provided by the king's treasurer. To each staff are four barons, that is sixteen to each canopy.

After the banquet, they continue at court during the king's pleasure; and when they have leave to return, they take with them the canopies, with the bells, staves, and other appurtenances. They were formerly taken by the ports in turn, but are now equally divided among them.

The lord warden or admiral of the ports is usually constable of Dover castle; but in former times there have been some few instances, in which the two offices have not been held by the same person. His authority, as warden, is very extensive: he holds his superior court at Shipway; issues writs in his own name; and has the supreme command of the forces within the franchise. He claims a right of warren from Dover to Sandwich, two or three miles within shore; and appoints warreners to preserve the game. As constable, he holds his own court within the limits of the castle, where he takes the chief command.

General and Incidental History of the Cinque Ports.

Having given a general outline of the cinque ports, and of such other particulars, so far as our limits will admit, we will now relate a few instances, among many, in which the navy of the ports, has rendered essential services to the nation, with such other incidental circumstances, as may be entertaining to the reader.

From the reign of Edward the Confessor, which commenced in 1053, the cinque ports' fleets, says Dr. Campbell,* were particularly useful, during several succeeding reigns, in protecting the flourishing trade that was then carried on from the eastern coast of the kingdom.

If it be asked, were was the cinque ports' fleet, when William the Conqueror landed at Hastings? we answer, that a great part of it had been taken away by the rebellious sons of earl Godwin. Tostig, the fourth son, had revolted with a large squadron, and turned pirate. When his brother Harold had mounted the throne of England, this pirate, in conjunction with the king of Norway, invaded the northern counties. The cinque ports' fleet was sent against him, and defeated the Norwegian navy; and, while on this expedition, the conqueror unexpectedly landed in Sussex. As a proof that the fleet of the cinque ports was then returning triumphantly

---

* Lives of the Admirals, vol. i. p. 114.

down the channel, the Normans had no sooner
disembarked, than they burnt the greater part of
their ships, to prevent their falling into the hands
of the English.

During the reign of Henry the First, which
commenced in 1100, the fleets of the ports
rendered essential service, in his conquest of
Normandy, from his brother, duke Robert. On
his return to England, November 26, 1120, his
son, prince William, then sixteen years of age,
embarked soon after him, on board a new ship,
accompanied by a large train of young nobility
and persons of distinction. Ambitious of reaching the English coast before his father, he offered
rewards to the sailors to hasten their course; but
the father and the beloved son had embraced for
the last time in Normandy. In full sail, just as
it fell dark, the ship struck on a reef of rocks,
then known by the name of Shatteras. Soon she
begins to sink; the boat is lowered to preserve
the prince, who leaves the ship in safety. The
cries of his beloved sister, Matilda, strike his
ear, and he returns to save her. The shades of
death affright the crew; the water rushes through
the disjointed timbers; and each flies to the boat
to save his life. She sinks with the ship; and
more than two hundred unfortunate beings are
buried in the watery abyss: a butcher of Rouen
alone escapes, by clinging to the mainmast.
He only was taken from the dreadful wreck, to

carry the ~~doleful tidings~~ to the agonized king, who, it is said, was never afterwards seen to ~~smile~~.

When king John, in his 16th year, 1215, was forsaken by almost the whole of his subjects, and had retired for safety to the Isle of Wight, he was secured by the assistance of the cinque ports' ships and mariners, until he was again restored to his authority.

The famous battle fought in the channel, in the 2nd year of Henry the Third, 1217, between the mariners of the cinque ports and the French fleet, has been mentioned in our history of the castle, page 69.

In the 8th, 10th, and 11th years of this reign, the ports fitted out double their usual number of ships, completely equipped, for the king's service.

The port barons, in 1236, supported the royal canopy at the coronation of Eleanor, queen of Henry the Third. This is the first record we can find of the barons' attendance on these oc-occasions; but in a charter of the following monarch, Edward the First, it is mentioned as an ancient privilege.

The ports were defective in their usual loyalty and duty, in the 45th year of this reign, 1261. Dover, in conjunction with the other ports, took part with the discontented barons, and the cinque ports' fleet was fitted out, to prevent the king from receiving any foreign succours. They justified their conduct, by saying, That whatever was for the good of the nation, must also be for the good of the sovereign.

A sad spirit of revolt was manifested by the mariners of the cinque ports, in the 51st year of this reign, 1266. They joined in the cabal of Simon de Montfort and his son, and gave them the command of their fleet. Thus misguided, they plundered every foreign vessel they met with, and, in November of that year, burnt the town of Portsmouth, to be revenged on the king for having hung some of their barons. They persevered in their audacious practices, until prince Edward resolutely opposed them; when they agreed to submit, on condition of having a confirmation of their privileges. Winchelsea alone resisted; but after the loss of several men, the prince entered the town, took Henry Pethune, the leader of the rebellion, prisoner, and the rest submitted to an accommodation.

In no part of their history, were the cinque ports more renowned for their naval exploits, than in the reign of Edward the First, the munificent promoter of their strength and commerce. In the 10th year of his government, 1282, their navy, with a reinforcement of other vessels taken up for the service, under the command of admiral Geoffry de Say, completely excluded the continental powers from taking any interference with the affairs of Scotland; and prevented the king's enemies there, from receiving any foreign succours.

Still more convincing proofs of their prowess were manifested in the 21st year of this reign, 1293, in that furious war which originated in an affray between the crews of an English and French ship, relative to a spring of fresh water. An English ship putting into a Norman port, remained there some days. While they lay at anchor, two of the crew went to get fresh water at a place not far distant from the shore, where they were insulted by some Normans of their own profession; and coming from words to blows, one of the Englishmen was killed, and the other flying to the ship, related what had happened to his fellow sailors, informing them that the Normans were at his heels. Upon this they hoisted sail and put to sea; and though the Normans followed them, they escaped, but with some difficulty. On hearing this, the inhabitants of the English ports, sought assistance from their neighbours; and the enemy, on the other hand, retaining the same disposition, increased their strength daily, and chased all English ships. In these excursions, having had the good fortune to meet six, and to take two English vessels, they killed the sailors, hung up their bodies at the yard-arm, with as many dogs, and sailing in this manner for some time on their coasts, signified

thereby to all the world, that they made no sort
of difference between an Englishman and a dog.

This, when it came to the ears of the inhabitants of the English ports, by the relation of
those that escaped, provoked them to take the
best measures they could to revenge so signal
an affront; and having in vain cruized at sea, in
order to find out the enemy, they entered the
port of Swyn, and having killed and drowned
abundance of men, carried away six ships; many
acts of a like nature succeeding this on both
sides. At last, wearied by this piratical war,
they, by messengers who passed between them;
fixed a certain day to decide this dispute with
their whole strength. On the 14th of April,
a large empty ship was fixed in mid-channel,
between the coasts of England and Normandy,
to mark the place of engagement. The English,
before the time appointed, procured some aid
from Ireland, Holland, and other places; and
the French drew to their assistance the Flem-
ings and Genoese. On the day appointed both
parties met, full of resolution. Their minds
boiled with rage, and a like spirit seemed to
agitate the elements. Storms of snow and hail,
and boisterous gusts of wind were the preludes
of an obstinate battle, in which the French were
defeated; many thousands being slain, besides
those who were drowned; and a large number
of ships perished. The victorious English carried

off two hundred and forty sail; and with these they returned to their own ports.

Philip the Fourth, of France, was so enraged at this defeat, that he pompously threatened to invade England, and to destroy both the people and the language.

In 1296, while the cinque ports' fleet was assisting king Edward in the conquest of Scotland, the French king collected two hundred sail of ships and gallies, and embarked an army to put his threat in execution. They approached the English coast, hovering and anchoring near the shore; and spent several days in sounding and reconnoitering with their gallies. Their first attack was on the town of Hythe; and the inhabitants fled before them. Being soon joined by a reinforcement, they returned on the invaders; killed two hundred and forty of their men, and burnt one of their ships.

To revenge this loss, the French admiral immediately sailed for Dover; and landing his forces before the garrison returned from Hythe, the inhabitants retired into the country. Revenge and fury marked the progress of the invaders; women and children fell victims to their rage; and the town, the priory, and the other religious houses, were ransacked and pillaged. They were still engaged in plundering when the garrison returned on them, with a considerable reinforcement, attacked their scattered detachments, killed about eight hundred, and chased the remainder to the shore. The admiral, alarmed for his safety, retired to his ships, with as many of his men, and as much plunder as could be taken away, while several were left to perish on the beach. One Thomas, a monk, who was much reverenced for his great sanctity, was murdered in this conflict; and his brethren, to repair their losses, pretended to work miracles by his influence.

Soon after this, the French landed at Dover in the night, burnt the greater part of the town, and damaged several religious houses. This was considered the more unpardonable, as two cardinals were, at the same time, residing in the place, and negociating for a peace between the two nations.

These excesses were of short duration; and before the end of the year, the British navy not only swept the enemy from the channel, but made several descents on the coast of France.

In the latter end of August, 1297, the king sailed from the ancient town of Winchelsea, with a mighty fleet, having an army on board of nearly sixty thousand men, which were landed at Sluys in Flanders. After this, the unfortunate contest took place between the cinque ports' and Yarmouth squadrons, which we have already mentioned.

In 1326, king Edward the Second, having a

dispute with the king of France, ordered the cinque ports' fleet to guard the channel, which they did so effectually, that an hundred and twenty ships of the enemy were soon brought into English ports.

The French having assembled a large fleet in 1338, burnt the towns of Southampton and Plymouth, and insulted the town of Hastings. On the following year, the cinque ports' fleet retaliated, by burning the town of Boulogne, destroying the magazines and naval stores in the docks and arsenals, and bringing away four large ships, nineteen gallies, and twenty lesser vessels.

In 1340, the French king assembled a fleet of four hundred sail; and the British monarch, Edward the Third, drew together a navy of three hundred ships, to oppose them. Towards the end of June, the hostile fleets met on the coast of Flanders. The king of England commanded in person; and the battle raged with the utmost fury, from eight in the morning, till seven in the evening. Only thirty of the enemy's ships escaped; and their loss was estimated at thirty thousand men.

At the coronation of king Richard the Second, 1377, *six* barons of the cinque ports supported a blue canopy, on silver spears.

The king of France, in 1405, sent a fleet of one hundred and forty sail, with an army of twelve thousand men, to the assistance of Owen Glendour, prince of Wales. The cinque ports' fleet, under the command of lord Berkeley and Henry Pay, came up with them off Milford haven, where they took fifteen of their ships, burnt fourteen, and dispersed the rest. After this, the united fleets of the realm, burnt at least thirty-six towns on the coast of France, and returned to Rye, with an immense booty.

Henry Pay, the famous admiral of the cinque ports, in 1407, surprised the Rochelle fleet, consisting of one hundred and twenty sail of merchant men, richly laden, and took the whole of them.

Henry the Fifth, in 1417, united his other squadrons with the cinque ports' fleet, and assembled a navy of one thousand five hundred vessels at Dover. Here he embarked, with an army of twenty-five thousand five hundred men, for the coast of France, where his victories were so rapid, that in two years he conquered nearly the whole country. To stop his victorious arms, Charles the Sixth, confirmed, in general terms, his right to the crown of France, and gave him his daughter, the princess Catherine, in marriage, with whom he returned to Dover, on the second of February, 1421.

At the coronation of Margaret of Anjou, queen of Henry the Sixth, in 1445, the canopy bearers for Dover, were Ralph Toke, William Brewys, John Warde, and Richard Grigge, and the expense of each, while at court, was £1. 6s. 8d.

The cinque ports' fleet was called out to exercise in the Downs, on the 26th of May, 1475; and conveyed the king and his army from Sandwich to Calais, on the 26th of June.

1492, the cinque ports' fleet conveyed Henry the Seventh and his army from Sandwich to Calais. It performed the same service for Henry the Eighth in 1513, 1544, and 1545, from the port of Dover.

When the Spanish armada threatened destruction to the British isles, in 1588, the cinque ports fitted out six ships of superior magnitude, for the queen's service; and appointed for every one a pinnace of thirty tons to attend it. The whole expense amounted to forty-three thousand pounds; and among the services performed, against the enemy, the mariners of one of the ships belonging to Dover, being well acquainted with the flats and banks of the channel, decoyed the great Galleas of Spain upon them, and afterwards engaged and burnt her.

At a brotherhood holden in 1603, to decide on the dress of the canopy bearers, at the coronation of king James the First, it was ordained that they should wear "A scarlet gown made citizen fashion, to reach to the ancles, faced with crimson satin; Gascaine hose, crimson silk stockings, crimson velvet shoes, and black velvet caps."

The cinque ports, in the second year of king

Charles the First, 1626, fitted out two very large ships, which served two months, and cost the ports more than £1800.

By an inquisition taken June 12th, 1682, the jurisdiction of the ports extended from Shore Beacon, in Essex, to Red Cliff, near Seaford, in Sussex.

Thirty-two barons of the ports, in 1685, supported the canopy at the coronation of king James the Second, and his queen. They were dressed in doublets of crimson satin, scarlet hose, gown of the same colour faced with crimson satin, black velvet shoes, and caps of the same, fastened to their sleeves.

Since the royal navy has been composed of larger vessels than could, at present, be accommodated in these havens, the services of the barons have been dispensed with, in raising their usual number of ships; but their privileges, except their freedom from military service in the field, have been suffered to remain; subject to such bye laws, or other encroachments as may have taken place among themselves.

As they cannot now oppose the common enemy, on board their vessels, the government seem to have thought it reasonable, that they should unite with the military for this purpose; but the proposition has always been received with dissatisfaction.

It was enacted, in the thirteenth of Charles

the Second, 1673, that the constable of Dover castle should have the same authority, as the lieutenants of counties, to raise a militia within the liberties of the cinque ports; but this authority appears to have been exercised with much forbearance.

During the American war, which commenced in 1775, instead of a militia, a regiment was raised, to be called the Cinque Ports' Volunteers.

When the war commenced with France in 1793, it was proposed by the lord warden to raise several companies of horse and foot, to be called the Cinque Ports' Fencibles. To defray the expense, a subscription was made of £1350; in addition to which the ports raised £5171. 6s. 6d.*

In 1798, four hundred men were demanded of the ports, as an army of reserve. The men were raised by bounty, in the adjoining counties, which was restricted to £30. each.

	£.	s.	d.
*The Rt. Hon. W. Pitt, Warden of the Cinque Ports, and Constable of Dover Castle	1000	0	0
Colonel North, Governor of Dover Castle	100	0	0
John Trevanion, Esq.	100	0	0
Chas. Small Pybus, Esq.	100	0	0
John Smith, Esq.	50	0	0
	£1350	0	0
Port of Dover *(by cess.)*	885	2	6
Sandwich	887	18	6
Hastings	325	5	0
Romney......	104	17	0
Hythe	92	12	0

	£.	s.	d.
Town of Rye........	398	5	0
Winchelsea .	327	0	0
Faversham..	236	16	0
Folkestone..	144	14	0
Fordwich ..	93	0	0
Deal	218	9	0
Seaford	50	0	0
Tenterden ..	167	0	0
Margate....	538	16	6
Saint Peter's	105	0	0
Birchinton..	30	0	0
Ramsgate ..	270	0	0
Walmer....	186	0	0
Sarr	73	15	0
Beakesbourn	36	16	0
	£5171	6	6

A local militia was required of the ports in
1811, the men were ordered to Dover to complete their exercise; but the divisions from the
western ports had no sooner entered the town,
than the sparks of commotion began to blaze
among the inhabitants. When the balloted men
of Dover, who had consented to join the service,
marched down from the castle to join their comrades, from the west, in the market-place, the
indignation was so strong, particularly among
the females, that they were obliged to fly for
safety; and were marched to Deal to complete
their service. Several actually served their time
in gaol, instead of joining the ranks. The precious privilege of being exempted from serving
in the field animated many a bosom; but they
should have considered, that this privilege was
granted on condition of their raising a certain
number of ships for the royal navy; and as they
cannot now raise these ships, it is but reasonable
they should serve in some capacity; and we
cannot doubt but such would be the general impression at the present day. The opposition did
not arise from disloyalty, but from a misconcep-
tion; and if they had been invited as volunteers,
the whole population was ready to meet the
enemy.

Complaints have been made that the privileges
of the ports have been invaded, by local assessments, in the name of county rates. In fact, to

tax themselves, forms one of their privileges ;*
and if levied by the body of freemen, or by their
representatives duly elected, with open accounts
to shew how the money is expended, it still
remains an invaluable privilege. If, however,
in the lapse of ages, a number of individuals,
may have assumed this power to themselves,
and acted independently of the freemen, it certainly bears the features of a dangerous authority;
and, in the hands of wicked men, would prove
an insupportable tyranny.

If such a power really exists, it must do credit
to the moderation of those who have exercised it
with such singular lenity, during a long course
of succeeding years. It certainly would shew
great magnanimity and great patriotism, particularly among those who may hold such a
power, to place it on a fair and honorable basis;
lest at some future time, however prudently
exercised, it might become a rallying point for
disaffection or insubordination.

At the coronation of his present majesty, in

---

* One of their privileges was, "To have a guild, that is, a
fraternity or combination of men, who had all the franchise of
court-leet and court-baron annexed to them, by which they
were endowed with a power, upon emergent occasions, for the
common interest, to lay assessments and taxes upon the inhabitants of the cinque ports and their members ; the word Guild
being extracted from an old Latin word Geldo, which signifies
to tax."—*Philipott's Villare Cantianum, page* 11.

1820, the following gentlemen were selected to bear the royal canopy:

Hastings	Hon. W. H. J. Scott, M.P. James Dawkins, Esq. M.P. Edward Milward, Esq.
Sandwich	Joseph Stewart, Esq. Charles Emmerson, Esq. George Noakes, Esq.
Dover	E. B. Wilbraham, Esq. M.P. Henshaw Latham, Esq.
Romney	Cholmondeley Dering, Esq. Benjamin Cobb, Esq.
Hythe	Stewart Majoribanks, Esq. M.P. William Deedes, jun. Esq.
Rye	John Dodson, Esq. M.P. William Phillips Lamb, Esq.
Winchelsea	Henry Brougham, Esq. M.P. Lucius Concannon, Esq. M.P.*

It is curious to observe what strange mutations the hand of time, and the revolutions of centuries, have made in these once celebrated havens. The rivers which formerly passed through Hastings, Romney, and Hythe, have been either diverted from their original channels, or found

---

* In consequence of the absence from England of Mr. Concannon, and the resignation of Mr. Brougham, Sir George Warrender and Colonel Bridges, were named on the day before the coronation, to represent the town of Winchelsea; but only Colonel Bridges attended. Sir George had not sufficient time to procure his dress.

subterraneous passages to the ocean ; while the Rother and the Stour are continually diminishing in magnitude, and losing their former importance. The waters that flow down the Dour, into Dover harbour, have not been noticed to suffer any decrease; and could the head springs of the Liddon Spout, which now pass several miles under ground, till they rush into the sea between Dover and Folkstone, be turned into this valley, they would much increase the Dover stream.   These springs have evidently a communication with the Nailbourn a Drelingore, which now flows down the Dour, and probably it might not require a heavy expense, to divert the whole into this channel. With such an accession of back-water, and an ample income, the ancient port of Dubris, (now Dover,) might not only far out-live its sister havens on this coast, but remain a useful harbour through succeeding ages.

HISTORY

OF THE

TOWN AND PORT.

Topography.

THE town of Dover is situated on the eastern coast of Kent, in latitude 51° 8' and longitude 1° 5'. Being on the narrowest part of the British channel, which is not more than twenty miles in width, the opposite shores of France are distinctly visible.

The town lies in a handsome bay, bordered by a beautiful beach composed of loose and small pebbles, so moveable that the force of the waves is continually changing their position. Sometimes they rise in lofty hillocks near the entrance of the harbour, or extend in ridges along the shore, presenting an apparently fixed boundary to the ocean, and a perpetual barrier to the town. These in a few tides are demolished, and rebuilt at another point, to be again removed at the caprice of the wind and weather.

The lofty cliffs towards the ocean suddenly

break off near the centre of the bay; and the opening between them terminates a beautiful valley, which extends several miles inland, and branches into sister vallies, spreading in various directions between the lofty hills that surmount them.

About four miles up the valley, near a village called Ewell, are the two sources of the small river Dour, which, working several mills as it winds along, pursues its course towards Dover, entering the town at a small distance from the sea, into which it formerly entered by a direct course towards the eastern part of the bay. Having long since been diverted from this course, it now turns to the south-west, and, running parellel with the shore, passes through a spacious sheet of water called the Pent; and being admitted through a gate-way into another sheet of water called the basin, proceeds from thence by another gate-way, into the present harbour, and from thence into the ocean.

At high water the sea advances, in some places, close up to the base of the cliffs, dashing, in stormy weather, furiously against them, and undermining them.. The higher parts, deprived of their support, frequently fall with a tremendous crash, and are precipitated to a great distance into the sea; and in this manner were formed the rocks that are to be seen, when the tide recedes, on each extremity of the bay.

Such is the general outline of Dover in its present state, but its marine boundary, and the situation of the town, through a succession of ages, have undergone continual alterations.

————o✿o————

Ancient History of Dover before the Roman Conquest.

To repeat the fabulous tales that have been recited, and the various conjectures that have been made, as to the early history of this place, would afford but little interest. Nothing certain however can be relied on, previous to the invasion by Julius Cæsar. But it is evident, from the accounts given by that great warrior and elegant writer, that on the arrival of the Roman army on this coast, he found a rude and uncultivated people, but little removed from a state of barbarism. Their towns were enclosed in thick woods, or built on hills of difficult access, and surrounded by deep ditches. In that early period of society, when each little tribe, independent of the rest, was frequently engaged, under its respective chieftain, in predatory incursions against the territories of its neighbours, it was needful that every town should be a fortress, not only to repel an enemy, but to secure their families and property, while the warriors sallied forth to attack or pursue their enemies. The huts, enclosed in these fastnesses, were rudely built. A few stakes driven into the ground, supported a roof covered with grass or rushes.

The dress of our islanders, was as rude and simple as their architecture. The skins of beasts taken in hunting or tamed for domestic purposes, were their garments by day and their covering by night. They were armed with arrows, spears, and swords; they had shields, breastplates, and helmets. Their war chariot was remarkable, combining, as Cæsar confesses, the swiftness of cavalry with the steadiness of infantry; a refinement in the art of war, which he evidently did not expect to meet with, among a people so uncivilized. "So expert are they (says he) at this exercise, that they can stay their horses at full speed, even in the midst of a descent, stop short and turn, run upon the pole, rest on the harness, and throw themselves with great dexterity into their chariots."

The vessels or boats, they commonly made use of, were formed with branches of osiers, the sails being made of the skins of beasts, and the tackling with thongs of the same material. Cæsar informs us that the Gauls had at this time vessels of a much more formidable construction, and able to contend with the Roman fleet. "Their keels were rather flat, their forecastle very high, their poops contrived to endure the roughness of the sea, and their bodies of impenetrable

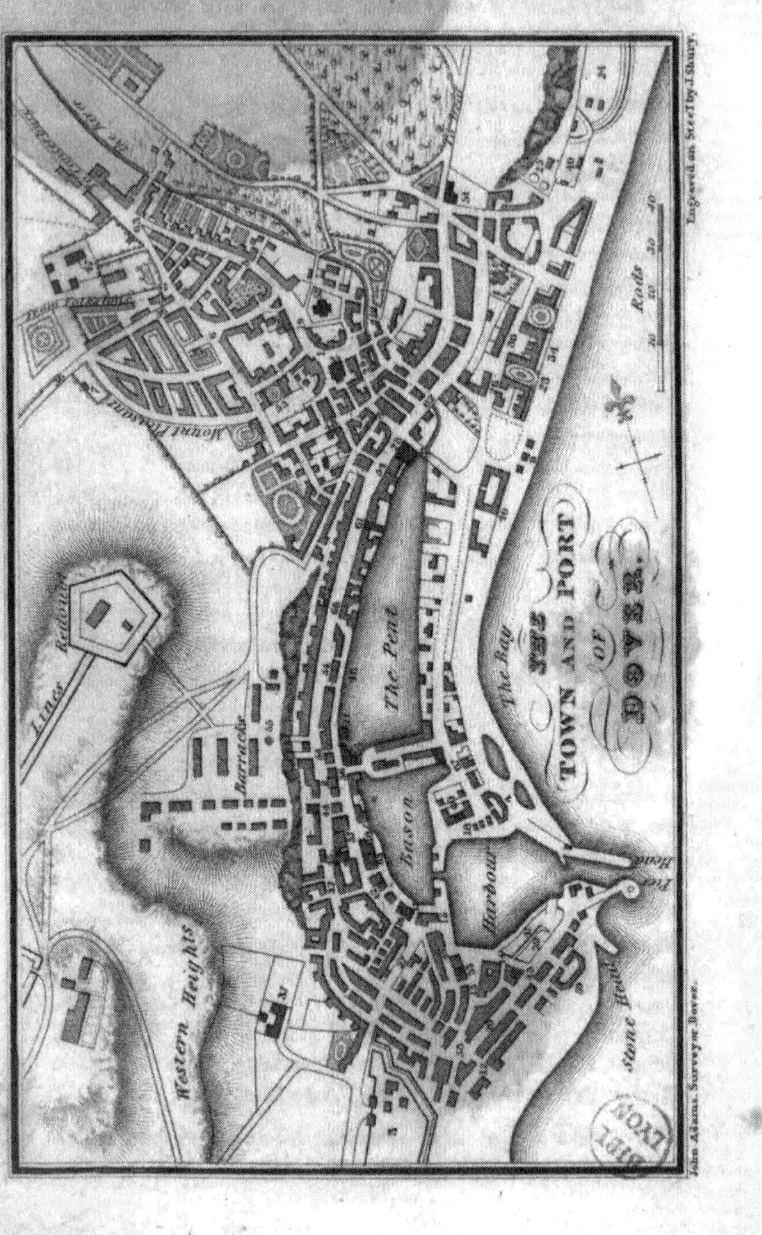
THE
TOWN AND PORT
OF
DOVER.
Western Heights
The Pent
The Bay
Bason
Harbour
Stone Heap
Light House
Barracks
Rods
John Adams, Surveyor, Dover.
Engraved on Steel by J. Shury.

References to the Plan of the Town.

←❃→

Antwerp Inn	1	Market Place	35
Albion Library	2	Military Road	36
Archcliff Fort	3	Military Hospital	37
Amherst Battery	4	New Bridge	38
Biggin-street	5	New Dry Dock	39
Black-ditch	6	Ordnance Yard	40
Bowling-green	7	Outer Basin	41
Bench-street	8	Post Office	42
Bathing Rooms	9	Providence Hotel	43
Bank, J. M. Fector & Co.	10	Paris Hotel	44
Bank, Latham & Co.	11	Packet Boat Inn	45
Beach-street	12	Pent-side	46
Council-house-street	13	Priory Buildings	47
Crane-street	14	Queen-street	48
Cross-wall	15	Round Tower-street	49
Custom-house	16	Royal Oak Inn	50
Custom-house Quay	17	St. James's Church	51
Castle Inn	18	St. Mary's Church	52
Canon-street	19	St. Martin's Church-yard	53
Fisherman's-row	20	Snargate-street	54
Fish-market	21	Shaft (Grand)	55
Folkstone Road	22	Snargate-st. Over Sluice	56
Guilford Lawn	23	Strond-street	57
Guilford Battery	24	The Plain	58
Gas Works	25	Townsend Battery	59
Hammond Place	26	The Buildings	60
Hawkesbury-street	27	Theatre	61
King's Arms Library	28	Townwall-street	62
King's-street	29	Victualling Office	63
Liverpool Terrace	30	Union Hotel	64
Lauriston Cottage	31	Wright's Hotel and Ship	
Limekiln-street	32	Inn	65
London Hotel	33	William's Library	66
Marine Parade & Library	34	York Hotel	67

*** *The figures on the scale should have been* **20, 40, 60, 80,** *the whole being eighty rods.*

oak." From which we may conclude that our islanders had also vessels of a similar description.

The Britons, like the Celtic nations, were much addicted to sloth; and, like the Gauls, fond of intoxicating liquors. They either wasted their days in listless indolence, or in rioting to excess: or if roused for a time by the excitements of war, or the chase, in both of which they displayed courage, intrepidity, and perseverence; yet no sooner did they lay down their weapons, than they sunk again into their habitual supineness.

General and Incidental History of the Town during the Roman Government in Britain.

FROM what has been stated, the reader will be enabled to form a general idea of the people with whom Cæsar had to contend, in attempting the conquest of this island. Pretending that the Britons had assisted his enemies, the Gauls, he sailed from Boulogne on the 26th of August, fifty-five years before the Christian era, with two legions of infantry, and commanded the cavalry to follow him. His fleet, consisting of eighty ships and two gallies, arrived before Dover about ten o'clock in the morning, and cast anchor in the bay. Observing multitudes of the natives, marshalled on the declivities of the surrounding hills, and ready to receive him with their missive weapons, he hesitated to land.

About three o'clock in the afternoon, after calling a council of war, he changed his course, and sailing eight miles to the eastward, cast anchor near the low lands in the vicinity of Deal. The natives following the motion of the fleet, urged their horses into the waves, and, by their gestures and shouts, defied the invaders. The appearance of the naked barbarians, and a superstitious fear of offending the gods of this unknown world, spread a temporary alarm among the Romans. After a short pause, it was dispelled by the intrepidity of the standard bearer of the tenth legion. Calling on his comrades to follow him, he leaped with his eagle into the sea: detachments instantly rushed on from the nearest boats, to defend their standard: the beach, after a short, but sanguinary conflict, was gained; and the untaught valour of the natives yielded to the arms and discipline of their enemies.

On the fourth night after their landing, many of the ships, were injured by the violence of the tide. The British chiefs who had come to the camp to solicit peace, observing the consternation occasioned by these events, retired separately, and concealed themselves, with their forces, in the neighbouring woods. They sprang on the seventh legion, which had been sent out to forage, and nearly overwhelmed them; and,

assembling the other tribes, an assault was made
on the Roman camp. Though this failed, it
taught Cæsar to reflect on the dangers that would
attend his remaining here during the winter.
To save his reputation, he gladly accepted an
illusory promise of submission from a few of the
native chiefs, and hastened back to Gaul with
his army, after an absence of three weeks.

Each party was engaged in active preparations
until the next spring, when Cæsar again sailed
from Boulogne, in May, with an army of five
legions and two thousand cavalry, on board a
fleet of nearly seven hundred ships. On seeing
them approach the shore, the astonished Britons
fled to the woods, while the invaders proceeded
to their former camp. Cæsar immediately pursued; but a storm having destroyed forty of his
vessels, during the night, he was recalled the
next day. After ten days' labour, the fleet was
drawn on shore, and surrounded by a fortification.
Many and furious were the conflicts that followed.
At length three of the legions, with all the horsemen, were sent out to forage, and their apparent
disorder invited the Britons to attack them with
their whole force. Descending from the hills,
they poured through every opening, and pene-
trated as far as the eagles; but the veterans
received them with coolness. The conflict was
fierce and dreadful; the avenues of retreat were
closed up; and but few were able to regain the

woods and mountains. Dispirited by this defeat, many of the confederate tribes returned to their homes. Some again sought the clemency of the conqueror, gave hostages, and engaged to pay a yearly tribute to the Romans. As the equinox was now approaching, Cæsar was willing to accept of their submission, and returned to Gaul with the whole of his forces, in the month of September.

After long and severe contentions, the Roman government was firmly established in Britain, in the reign of Titus, by Agricola, about the year A. D. 90. The south had submitted, but the northern nations were still in arms; and the flames of war and desolation were continually bursting forth in every part of the island.

In the time of Dioclesian, who became emperor of Rome in 284, the hardy and adventurous pirates of the north, infested the narrow seas, and plundered, without mercy, the inhabitants of the coast. In order to remedy this evil, the emperor deputed into Britain an officer of the degree called *comites*, having ships and men under his command. He established garrisons on the coast, and repressed the depredations of the barbarians. Dubris, now Dover, was a principal station, and had for its defence a commander and a detachment of Tungrians.

Between the years 364 and 367, in the reign of Theodosious, the father of Theodosious the

Great, a numerous cohort of Roman soldiers
being posted at Dover, they built on the banks
of the river Dour an extensive bath. It was
situated in what is now St. Mary's church yard,
and extended under the steeple, and part of the
church. After a lapse of fourteen hundred
years, the remaining parts are firm and compact,
and require great exertion to separate them.
The greater part has been destroyed within these
last sixty years, for the purpose of interring the
dead.

Dover, during the time it was occupied by the
Romans, was called by various names. Ptolomy
the geographer calls it Darvenum, and Darver-
num. By other writers, it was called Doris, and
Durus. Antoninus, in his Itinerary, calls it
Dubris.

The precise spot where this ancient town and
port were situated, it is difficult to determine.
When the Roman eagles were first unfolded on
the coast of Britain, it is obvious, from the Commentaries of Cæsar, that the sea flowed a considerable distance up the valley. The haven
was pent in between the hills, and the armed
natives were marshalled on each side of it; from
whence it appears obvious that the site of the
present town, was at that time occupied by the
sea. Somner, Doctor Plot, and others, have
supposed that the ancient port was in the neighbourhood of Charlton, about a mile and a half

within the present shore; and Camden, from the number of anchors and planks of ships that have been dug up in this part of the valley, is of the same opinion.

We learn from Darell, that the port long after this, occupied the site of the present market-place. He informs us that St. Martin's church, built in the year A. D. 696, was erected on the spot, where, before the reign of Arviragus, ships used to ride at anchor. This Arviragus appears to have been a tributary king, and contemporary with the emperor Claudius, who began his reign A.D. 46. That this space of ground was formerly occupied by the sea can hardly be doubted from the nature of the soil, which is a continuation of either sand or beach down to the present shore.

It is however certain, from the Roman bath under a part of St. Mary's church, that the waters had receded from this side of the valley a considerable time before that warlike people left the island in the year A. D. 447.

From these premises, and from the names of two of the gates of the city wall, we conclude that the city Dubris occupied the present site of the Market-place, Church-street, Canon-street, Market-street, King-street, Bench-street, Queen-street, Above Wall-street, the upper part of Snargate-street, and probably Town Wall-street, with their intermediate lanes and passages.

By some authors we are informed, that the

Roman road or Watling-street, entered at Biggin-gate, formerly situated at the lower end of Biggin-street. Harris says it passed down by what is now called the Park-wall, at the lower part of the Maison Dieu field, entered the town on the west of St. James's church, and thence proceeded to its end, at Ford's corner, which was the landing-place from foreign parts, and of course the true Portus Dubris. We should hence conclude that a branch of this road descended on each side of the haven; and, as Ford's corner is supposed to have been in the lane that now leads to the river from King-street, on the south-east of the Flying Horse inn, we should rather conceive that the branch which entered at Biggin-gate proceeded to this place.

Some have doubted whether the Romans ever fortified Dover with a wall. That two of the gates, that of Adrian and Severus, which afterwards formed a part of the Norman wall, should bear the name of two of the Roman emperors, is however a strong presumptive proof, that they were built by this people before they left the island. The former of these emperors, Adrian, built a famous wall eighty miles long, from the river Eden, in Cumberland, to the Tine in Northumberland, to prevent the incursions of the Picts and Scots; and the latter, Severus, after many victories over these barbarians, died at York, A.D. 211; and Kilburne assures us that the gate in the old wall, called Severus's gate, was built by Severus, a Roman, in 209. As the emperor Severus was at that time in this island, we have no doubt of its being built by his direction, which we shall further notice in our description of it.

As a further proof that the Romans fortified the town with a wall, we may add that they had a burying-place on a spot of ground just without Adrian's gate, which will be also noticed as we proceed.

About the year 410, the fabric of the Roman empire began to give way, its very foundation being threatened by the barbarous nations that surrounded it. Instead of carrying their victorious arms to attack distant countries, they were obliged to concentrate their forces to defend their own. They recalled their troops from Britain, and the sun of Roman glory, which, during four centuries and a half, had shone with meridian lustre, set to rise no more, leaving the natives a prey to intestine broils, and to the ravages of the Picts and Scots.

———o❀o———

General and Incidental History of the Town during the Saxon Government in Britain.

THE Saxons, who were called in to the assistance of the natives, in the year 449, instead of affording support, turned their swords against them, and usurped the Government. Hengist,

the adventurous leader of this people, not less
ambitious, but more ferocious than the polished
writer of the Commentaries, inflamed like him
with the love of glory, and no less bent on death
or conquest, spread the ravages of devastation
from shore to shore. It was a war of extermi-
nation. Blood and fire, buildings rased to their
foundations, and hillocks of human bones, marked
their fiend-like steps in every path; and this
scene of carnage and desolation continued till
the thrones of the Heptarchy were set up.

During these commotions, most of the edifices
raised by the Romans in this valley, were consumed in the general devastation, and they
probably remained in ruinated heaps, until the
time of Alfred the Great. Some of the walls of
the town, however, and the towers that secured
the gates, seemed to have braved the hand of
violence and the storms of ages, and have been
seen in our days.*

Alfred, ever anxious to promote the welfare
of his people, encouraged them to rebuild the
desolated towns and cities, and to assemble in
communities, for their general security. From
this period, the town of Dover gradually arose
to its former importance. A guild, or social
confederation, was obtained, which enabled the

---

* Darell informs us that Withred, king of Kent, fortified the
town with a wall towards the sea, about the year 690. It is
probable he repaired the Roman works, or extended them
farther towards the east.

inhabitants to provide a certain number of ships for the king's service, and for which they were rewarded by a charter of privileges, in the reign of king Edward the Confessor. At this period they were able to arm twenty vessels, each to carry twenty-one experienced mariners, and to maintain them at sea fifteen days.

Earl Godwin was their patron and warden. The proud and haughty conduct of this potent earl, and the unbounded authority which he assumed within his jurisdiction, had so incensed his sovereign, that the king waited for a favourable opportunity to chastise his insolence. This was soon afforded him by the following occurrence which took place at Dover.

In the year 1051, Eustace, earl of Boulogne, who had married Goda, sister of king Edward, came on a visit to his royal brother, and was passing through Dover, on his return home. One of his train, being refused admission to a lodging which had been assigned him, attempted to force his way, and, in the contest, wounded the master of the house. The inhabitants revenged this insult by the death of the stranger; the earl and his retinue had recourse to arms, and murdered the wounded townsman; a tumult ensued, and about twenty persons were killed on each side; and Eustace, being overpowered by numbers, was obliged to save his life by flight from the fury of the populace. Hastening back to court, he complained of the insult to the king, who entered very warmly into the quarrel, and commanded earl Godwin to punish the townsmen. Godwin refused; and perhaps very justly. Disparing of a reconciliation, he armed against his sovereign; but doubting the constancy of his adherents, and finding the king's army to be more numerous than his own, he fell from his lofty pre-eminence, and fled into exile.

The annual rental of the town, in the reign of Edward the Confessor, was valued at eighteen pounds.

General and Incidental History of the Town, during the Norman Government, and to the Present Time.

At the period of the Norman conquest, this town was so miserably burnt, that, with the exception of twenty-nine houses, the whole of it was reduced to ashes. Neither the origin of this fire, nor the precise time when it took place, have been transmitted down to us; but as forces were assembled here to oppose the conqueror, who dispersed them; and as William himself afterwards besieged and took the castle, beheaded the governor, and was guilty of other acts of cruelty towards the inhabitants, it is probable that it occurred during these disputes. Hence the rental of the town could not be ascertained at that time.

When seated on the English throne, not only the castle, but also the town of Dover became an object of the conqueror's solicitude and favour; and in his eighteenth year, the rental was computed at forty pounds, and by the return of the king's bailiff, it amounted to fifty-four.

Mr. Lyon informs us that the conqueror, towards the end of his reign, enclosed the town with a wall, gates, and towers, and that some of the foundations were laid with stone, brought from Caen in Normandy; and further adds, that these were the first enclosures. That the town was not fortified prior to this period, must, according to ancient authors, be evidently a mistake. We should rather conceive that the Roman walls and towers, at least some of them, were still standing; and that the conqueror repaired, and probably extended them more towards the east, the sea having, at this time, left a larger portion of its former bed in the valley.

From an old plan of the town, taken in the reign of queen Elizabeth, and from several of their foundations, we will endeavour to trace the wall, and the situation of ten gates,[1] and the towers, from Eastbrook-gate to Biggin-gate.[2]

---

[1] We confess that the *precise* situation of three gates, is rather doubtful; but the situation of the other seven, is clearly pointed out.

[2] We intended to have given a plan of the wall, and the situation of the gates, as far as could be ascertained; but found the expense would be too great for this small work.

Eastbrook-gate.[3]—This gate was situated at the foot of the castle hill, near St. James's church, at a place called Mansfield's corner; probably at a short distance below the church.

Saint Helen's-gate.—The wall was continued from Eastbrook-gate, in a south-west direction, to a tower in the curtain, between Eastbrook, and the next gate, named St. Helen's, which stood near a mansion called Copthall, and afterwards Moor's hall, probably on, or near the site of the present mansion belonging to Mrs. Rice.

The Postern, or Fishers' gate.—This gate was so called from its being used by the mariners, in bringing their fish into the town. It led to the old harbour, and stood near the back of the present Fox public house.

Butchery- gate.—The tower of this gate, and the remaining parts of the wall on each side of it, were taken down in 1819. The foundations could now be found under the pavement, the paling, and the northern wall of Mr. Shipdem's mansion. The tower was used for a night prison till the time of its demolition, when the materials were perfectly firm, and almost as compact as a solid rock. The river flowed directly under the western part of the tower, and still continues to empty itself at the same place.

Severus's-gate.—This gate, says Kilburne,

---

[3] There was formerly an Eastbrook-street. A house in this street, valued at five shillings, belonged to the Maison Dieu.

was built by Severus, A. D, 209, four years after this emperor had built a castle at Reculver.[4] It led from the present Bench-street. The tower stood considerably in advance from the line of the town wall, and flanked it, both to the east and westward. On the western foundation of the tower stands the eastern front of the King's Arms Library, and the northern front of the library and house, on the straight and continued foundation of the town wall, from Butchery-gate. These foundations were so firm and compact, as almost to bid defiance to the pick-axe or chisel.

The customer of the port formerly received the king's dues in apartments over this gate. Here was also a place or exchange paved with stone, where merchants used to meet at eleven o'clock in the forenoon, to transact business; and, in the course of time, it was called Penny-less Bench.

The corporation claimed a right to the town wall, gates, and towers ; and when the customer removed his situation, his apartments were converted into a prison.

After the gate was taken down, a platform was constructed for three cannons, and it was called the Three Gun Battery. It continued in this state until the year 1800 ; when several of the

---

4 In an old manuscript, still preserved in the Dering family, it is said that the emperor Severus fortified the town with a wall.—*Harris.*

inhabitants obtained a grant from the corporation
of the ground and materials, on condition that
they built a bridge over the pent, to open a
communication, for carriages, between the town
and the rope-walk, and it was done by subscription.

As there was a considerable distance between
this and Snare-gate, the curtain was defended by
a square tower which stood in the intermediate
space, the foundations of which are now covered
with houses.

Snare, or Pier-gate.—This gate stood near
the foot of the cliff, and crossed the street, now
leading to the pier. On a stone placed in the
wall, where the gate stood, is an inscription, by
which we are informed that the gate was taken
down in the year 1588. This stone is also the
boundary between the freehold and leasehold
estates, in the town.

Adrian's, or Upwall-gate.—This gate (supposed to have been built by the emperor Adrian)
was situated a short distance from the cliff, just
above Snare-gate, and led to the common, now
called the heighs. Just without the gate was a
Roman burying ground,[5] which has been already
noticed;[6] and, on the hill, at a short distance,

---

[5] In clearing the ground for a building, in 1797, several urns
were found, in which were pieces of Roman coins, but their
inscriptions were not legible. Several more were found in 1804.

[6] See page 144.

stood the Roman pharos, the walls of which were remaining in the reign of Henry the Eighth.

Common, or Cow-gate.—This gate also led to the common, and stood at the upper extremity of Queen-street. By an order of the corporation it was taken down in 1776. The foundations, and some remains of the wall, may be traced at several places, from this, to Adrian's-gate.

Saint Martin's, or Monks-gate.—This was a private gate for the use of the monks, and was situated in the wall that bounded the collegiate church; and the present wall, at the upper part of the old church-yard, is built on the foundation of the old town-wall.

Biggin, or North-gate.—This gate was situated at the lower extremity of Biggin-street, at the north-western corner of Saint Mary's church-yard; and was taken down in the year 1752. Apartments were built over this gate for a watchman, to sound an alarm, or make signals, in time of danger. Part of the wall, adjoining the gate, was taken down in 1827, to make room for the present Rose public house, when the materials were perfectly sound. Bricks, of an extraordinary size, were found intermixed with the stone; and traces of fragments or foundations, may be found, from this place, to Cow-gate.

Leland says, that the wall, in his time, could not be traced beyond the church-yard, and that it took a direct course from thence to the river.

Mr. Leland might have gone a little farther ; and we are credibly informed that the foundations were clearly discernable, within the last fifty years, to the extent of the wool factory, belonging to Mr. Jennings. From hence, we should suppose, they passsed on under the present footpath, to the bridge ; and from thence across the meadows, to Eastbrook-gate, which has been already mentioned.

Some have supposed that, instead of passing down to the river, the wall branched off at the lower part of the church yard, or at the lower extremity of Mr. Jennings' factory, to Stembrook; and from thence, skirting the backs of the houses, proceeded on to Eastbrook-gate. To reconcile this hypothesis with Leland's account, either the river must have passed much nearer to the church-yard than it does at present; or a brook, of which, perhaps, the ditch in front of Elsham's cottages is the bed, which Leland calls the river, may have emptied itself near what is now called Stembrook.

There still remain, to the eastward of the bridge at Eaststone, some traces of the East-brook, which branches off, at a few rods from the present stream. We may reasonably conclude that it anciently crossed St. James's-street, near Eastbrook-gate, which appears to have taken its name from it; and from thence flowed into the old haven, situated at the lower part of

Woolcomber-street, which will be mentioned in our account of the harbour.

In the reign of William the Second, the inhabitants of Dover witnessed a most flagrant insult offered to Anselm, archbishop of Canterbury, in 1095. The king had imbibed an inveterate enmity against this prelate; and, on his asking permission to visit Rome, commanded him immediately to quit the kingdom. To conceal his disgrace, and to hide himself from observation, he laid aside his archiepiscopal habit, and proceeded on his journey alone, in the garb of a pilgrim.

While waiting for a passage at Dover, he was overtaken by a king's messenger, who not only exposed him to the scoffs and derision of the multitude, but stripped him of what little property he had, and sent him off to the continent, destitute and forsaken, with only a scrip and a staff.

From the year 1132 till 1227, during which period the Priory and the Maison Dieu were built, Dover seems to have enjoyed her brightest days of opulence and splendour. Her walls and battlements were then entire, and the watchman's nightly voice was heard from tower to tower. The majestic pile of St. Martin le Grand, and the five parochial churches, were then standing in their beauty. The joyful hymn of praise and thanksgiving, resounded from one sacred edifice to another; and we may reasonably conclude that the streets and private buildings, in some degree, corresponded with the public edifices, in taste and elegance.

At the same time, looking towards the north-west, imagination beholds the stately towers and lofty pinnacles of the Priory and Maison Dieu, rising in progressive grandeur. Troops of ar-tizans occupy every quarter; and prosperity, the fruitful companion of industry, gladdens every bosom.

Towards the east stood the magnificent and elevated castle, still rejoicing in her pristine beauty, strength, and excellency. Numerous armies assemble in the neighbourhood; [7] kings and princes visit the castle and the religious houses; and all prove the rising prosperity and importance of the place.

During this bright period, an act of retributive justice took place here, which ought to be mentioned. Longchamp, bishop of Ely, being a favorite of king Richard the First, was raised from a low condition, and made regent of the kingdom, when this monarch departed on his expedition to the Holy Land, in 1191.

Proud and imperious, he governed with a heavy hand. Geoffrey, the king's illegitimate brother, was elected archbishop of York, and had obtained his investiture from the pope; but

---

7 See Pages 82 and 83.

omitted to consult the regent. This was an affront, not to be forgiven. Landing at Dover, on his way home to take possession of his see, he perceived that orders had been given to arrest him ; and he fled, for sanctuary, to the church of St. Martin le Grand. The sanctuary was violated, the archbishop torn from the altar, dragged through the streets in his archiepiscopal vestments, and conducted a prisoner to Dover castle.

This act of tyranny, united with others, roused the resentment of the nation. The regent was accused, condemned, and imprisoned. He makes his escape ; flees to the port of Dover in women's apparel ; and passes as a pedlar, with a measure in his hand, and a roll of cloth on his arm. Seated on a rock, awaiting the first opportunity to pass the channel, the sailors suspect him, and the cheat is discovered. He is arrested, and conducted to the castle. The infuriated mob deride, insult, and follow him to that dungeon, lately occupied by Geoffrey, who had fallen a victim to his pride and ambition. Pride! thou parent of tyranny and oppression, contemplate this picture, and view the fate that must meet thee, either in this busy scene, or in that which rises just before thee, where repentance nor reformation can afford one gleam of hope, to cheer thy doleful prison-house.

Dover was the first of the cinque ports incorporated by charter. The town had long enjoyed special privileges; but Edward the First, who began his reign in 1272, not only confirmed their privileges, but granted them a charter, by which he acknowledged the corporation, by the name of mayor and commonalty.

To encourage the inhabitants after the loss they had sustained, by the landing of the French in 1296, which we mentioned in our account of the cinque ports,[8] the king (Edward the First) established a mint here for the coinage of money; and, by patent, A. D. 1299, appointed "The table of the exchanger of money," to be held here and at Yarmouth.

In the seventeenth year of Edward the Second, 1323, as appears by the patent rolls of that year, the town was divided into twenty-one wards,[9] each of which was charged with one ship for the king's use; and, on that account, each had the privilege of a licenced packet boat, called a *Passenger*, to convey goods and passengers from this port to Whitsand, which was then the usual

[8] See Page 123.

[9] Names of the Wards:

1 Charlton	8 Rolvenden	15 Bumaris
2 Biggin	9 Bell	16 Ox
3 St. Mary	10 St. George	17 Ballast
4 Canon	11 St. Nicholas	18 Parks
5 Morian	12 Ore	19 Seagate
6 Shingle	13 Wolves	20 Snaregate
7 Nankin	14 Horsepool	21 Adrian's

place of embarkation, on the opposite coast of France.

In the tenth year of Edward the Third, 1336, it was enacted, that all merchants, travellers, and pilgrims, going to the continent, should not embark at any other place than Dover.

The price of passage was regulated in the reign of king Richard the Second, which commenced in the year 1377.[10]

This king, in 1396, demanded in marriage, Isabella, a princess of France, then only seven years of age. The kings and courts of each nation met on the plains, between Ardes and Calais, where the espousals were solemnized, amidst a profusion of magnificence. The object of the English monarch was to obtain peace, and a large marriage portion; but, in passing from Calais to Dover, a violent storm destroyed a part of his fleet, buried much of the golden treasure under the furious surges, and the king was so poor in 1398, that the mayor and good people of Dover lent him forty pounds, to alleviate his pressing necessities. Forty pounds was a considerable sum in those days, and proves that the town had recovered from the fatal disaster, that had nearly consumed it towards the close of the preceding century.

---

[10] The price was 6d. for a single person, and 1s. 6d. for a horse, in summer; and 1s. for a single person, and 2s. for a horse, in winter.

To remedy the violations of former statutes respecting the passage, another was passed in the fourth year of Edward the Fourth, 1464, which also ordained that all persons passing to Calais, should sail from the port of Dover.[11]

During the reign of Henry the Eighth, which began in 1509, Dover appears to have suffered very considerably, both in splendour and opulence, by the dissolution of her religious houses. Their stately towers and lofty spires no longer grace her avenues: monks and friars no longer parade her streets: the aged, the orphan, and infirm, no longer share their ample bounty, or crowd their hospitable gates; while mouldering walls and scattered ruins proclaim their utter extinction. Their princely incomes fell into other hands; and the poors' rate and the poor-house are substituted in their place. The heated imagination still recoils at the name of monk or friar, and their characters are painted in odious colors by the pens of those who seized their property; but whether the poor and needy have profited by the change, may long remain a question hard to be decided.

If we accuse Henry for destroying these ancient establishments, we must not forget to thank him for defending our port, by building Archcliff fort, and Moat's battery under the

---

11 This Statute was repealed in the 21st year of James the First, 1623

castle; and by erecting platforms for cannon. Some of the materials of those sacred edifices, probably found a place in these warlike constructions; and the king appears to have been a better friend to the mariner, by improving the harbour, than to those who officiated at the altar.

Leland, in his Itinerary, informs us that the town wall, at this time, was in a ruinous state, and that part of it could not be traced in several places.

In the eighth year of queen Elizabeth, 1565, commissioners were appointed to survey the towns on the coast. Dover, according to their report, contained only 358 houses, 19 of which were not inhabited. There were, belonging to the port, twenty trading vessels,[12] which employed three hundred mariners.

A curious circumstance occurred at this place on the 1st of July, 1605. Several Spaniards of distinction were waiting here, and a Dutch fleet lay at anchor in the bay. This republic had refused to pay the usual compliment to the English navy, by striking their flag in proper form. Sir William Monson entered the bay, at the same time, with an English fleet, on board

12 Ships.		Tons.	Ships.		Tons.	Ships.		Tons.
1	of	4	1	of	20	4	of	41
1	of	10	1	of	25	1	of	43
2	of	15	1	of	26	1	of	101
2	of	17	1	of	33	1	of	120
2	of	18	4	of	40			

of which was an ambassador from the emperor Rodolphus the Second ; and the Dutch admiral struck his flag thrice, and then advanced it again.

After landing the ambassador, Sir William sent a gentleman to the Dutch admiral, entreating his company the next day to dine with him ; to which he readily assented. The gentleman then requested him to take in his flag. This was sternly refused ; but on being told that the English fleet was ready to decide the point of honor, or sink in the contest, the flag was taken in ; and the Dutch admiral immediately stood out to sea, firing a gun for the rest of his fleet to follow him.

The strand was covered with spectators, anxious to see the event of this dispute ; and when Sir William came on shore, the Spanish general, Sciriago, told him, that he should have thought, had the Dutch been allowed to wear their flag, that times had been strangely altered in England since the days of his old master, king Philip the Second, whose flag was shot at by an English admiral, when he came to marry queen Mary ; and the king was not allowed to display it in the narrow seas.

In the fourth year of James the First, 1606, the waste ground below Snare-gate, from which the sea had receded, being granted by charter

---

13 Twenty-eight years afterwards the tythe of these buildings was claimed by the vicar of Hougham, as a part of his

to the commissioners of Dover harbour, was soon covered with buildings and warehouses.[13] To include these additional buildings, it was necessary to make a new division of the wards, as inserted in the following note.[14]

A sharp conflict taking place between a Dutch

---

parish, which extends to the edge of the cliff, but, by a decision of the court of exchequer, it was confirmed to the parish of St. Mary in the year 1638.

[14] A list of the present wards in the town of Dover, with their limits :

Charlton.—All Charlton, to the victualling office.

Biggin.—From the end of the town to Gardiner's lane.

St. Mary's.—From Gardiner's lane, to Biggin Gate.

Canon.—From Biggin Gate, including the Market.

Morian.—The street from the Market to Bench Street, and the buildings on the left hand side of Bench Street.

Shingle and Nankins.—St. James's side of the river, to Bean's Corner.

Holvenden and Bulls.—St. James's parish, above Bean's Corner.

St. Nicholas, including St. George.—Cowgate.

Snargate.—All the right hand side of Bench Street to Snargate.

Hither part of North Pier.—From Snargate to Robinson's Lane.

Lower part of North Pier.—From Robinson's Lane to the Dock, including Over the wall.

Hither part of South Pier.—From the Dock to Vinegar Sluice ; and from thence straight across Paradise Pent, through the little alley next Hudson's garden, to Thomas Pascall's.

Lower Part of South Pier.—The remainder of the Pier not mentioned.

and Spanish fleet, near the shore, on the seventh
of September, 1639, the latter were obliged to
take shelter under the Dover batteries, and
to claim the rights of hospitality from a neutral
power.

The plague, which destroyed upwards of
98,000 people in London, was brought to Dover,
in 1665, by a young person, who had been
employed in that metropolis, as a servant. It
raged with great violence, and destroyed upwards
of 900 persons in this town. The dread of the
infection was so great, that the dead bodies,
some in coffins but more without, were carried
to a place of burial, in carts.

A piece of ground on the side hill, above
Archcliff-fort, and close to the new military
hospital, was consecrated for this purpose. It
is called *The Graves*; and many respectable
families have continued to bury here, till within
these few years. In the general consternation,
no account of the funerals appears to have been
kept; as no traces of such a number can be found
in the register book, either of the church of
Hougham, in which parish the ground is situated,
or in those of the churches in Dover.

On the 3rd of November, 1688, the inhabitants
of this town were gratified with a sight truly
grand and magnificent. The prince of Orange
had sailed from Holland with an army, and
a fleet of more than five hundred ships and

transports, to deliver our native country from oppressive tyranny, and despotic power. When off this port, he cast anchor till the whole of his fleet came up; on board of which were numbers of our nobility and gentry, and among them the two famous historians, Rapin and Burnet. Here the prince called a council of war, and remained till the following morning. How delightful a prospect to the noble and the free: but how different must have been the feelings of those who had lately fawned on the tyrant; and, but a short time before, to obtain the favour of his dissolute and capricious predecessor, had delivered up their charter, and bartered the liberties of their fellow townsmen.

On the first of August, 1714, being the day on which queen Anne died, the great duke of Marlborough landed here, under a discharge of cannon, and amidst the acclamations of the people. The queen's death was not known either by the duke, or by the mayor and corporation, by whom he was received in their formalities.

King George the First, on a voyage from Holland to England, was overtaken by a violent storm. On the third of January, 1726, his fleet lay in great jeopardy before the port of Dover, and one of his yachts entered the harbour; but his majesty was driven on to the port of Rye, where he landed.

A horrid act of cruelty and vengeance was

perpetrated here, in 1737, by a young woman, whose name we forbear to mention, as some very respectable branches of her family are still resident in the neighbourhood. She resided, as servant, with a Mr. Fagg and his wife, in St. James's-street, who had an only daughter, about four years of age. One sunday morning Mrs. Fagg, previous to her going to church, gave directions to this domestic, how to cook a pig for the family dinner, saying, "Do the two ends well, and the middle will roast of itself." Either through ignorance, knavery, or, we should hope, from a disordered mind, she literally fulfilled the injunction, by cutting the pig in three parts; roasting the two extremities, and leaving the middle in a pan by the fire. A reproof for such anaccountable conduct, excited the rancourous spirit of the enraged female, and she determined on a speedy revenge.

Rising early the next morning, she dressed the child, who always slept with her, and of whom she appeared to be particularly fond; and, under pretence of having a walk before breakfast, took it abroad muffled up under her cloak. The morning was yet dark, and she was met by a custom house officer, who suspected she had contraband goods; but was so remiss, as neither to stop, nor question her.

With her unsuspecting victim she proceeded to a jetty under the castle; and, without hesitation, threw the devoted innocent into the sea. The raging billows, more merciful than her late pretended friend, washed back upon the shore the little trembler, who, in her innocence accosted her ruthless tormenter, with, "Oh! Margaret, the sea is very cold; why did you throw me in? Don't throw me in again." The malicious wretch made no reply, but repeated her infernal aim, and again the waves brought the dear infant to the shore. What heart could refuse to relent at such a warning voice a second time! but the rancour of this murderess was not to be mollified. Collecting all her strength, she again siezed the exhaushed infant, and threw her in a third time, as far as she was able. The effect was fatal; and the hapless victim sunk, and rose no more.

Her malignant purpose being accomplished, re-awakened conscience took the alarm; and, as she afterwards confessed, she would have given her own life to retrieve the child. Replete with horror, and not knowing where to flee, she wandered on till she came to a hole in the cliff, near St. Margaret's bay; and, groping into it, hoped their to lie concealed from every human eye. Providence, however, had determined otherwise. After she had remained here some days, a company of hunters passed by, and their dogs set up such an incessant din, at the mouth of the cavern, that no efforts could call them off. Wondering at so strange an incident, they

alighted; and the miserable refugee was discovered. Exhausted with want, and haunted
with terror, she made a full confession of her
guilt, and stated the circumstances we have
related.

The place of her apprehension being beyond
the limits of the town, she was assigned over
to the cognizance of the county court. After
sustaining a trial, during which, it is said, she
manifested great contrition for her heinous crime,
she suffered the sentence of the law, and was
hung at Canterbury. For the credit of humanity,
we cannot forbear hoping that this unhappy
woman acted under the influence of temporary
derangement; and we can hardly conceive it
possible that any one, possessing a sound intellect,
could be guilty of so flagrant an act of cruelty.
Still it should prove a warning to ungoverned
passion, lest, deviating from the path of virtue,
it be hurried on from one excess to another;
and corrupted nature, left to her own enfeebled
powers, will soon fall a prey to temptation, sin,
and hopeless misery.

We now turn to another scene, where dangerous adventure is made a subject of amusement.
In the same year, 1737, a person whose name was
Cadman, a sort of fool-hardy mountebank, and
who made a trade of rash enterprise, amused the
people of Dover, by flying across the harbour,
from the highest point of the cliff, towards the

lower extremity of Snargate-street. A rope was extended from the summit of the cliff, to high water mark, and he descended, with expanded wings, without sustaining any injury. Thousands were assembled from all parts to view this novel sight; but poor Cadman afterwards lost his life, at Shrewsbury, in practising a similar prank, in that city.   This high point of cliff was formerly called Sharpness, and was the tarpeian of ancient Dubris, from whence, it is said, they hurled down their malefactors, in the same manner, as from the tarpeian rock at Rome.

An act was obtained in 1763 for a turnpike road from Dover to Folkstone. It entered the town at Archcliff fort; but, about twenty years afterwards, a new cut was made through the valley, by Maxton, which joins the old road about three miles from Dover.

An extraordinary circumstance took place at Dover on June the 20th, 1768. A highwayman, who had robbed a Mr. Harriotson, at Waldershare, was secured in this town, armed with two pistols and a poniard, with the stolen property in his possession. After entering the castle gates, where they intended to confine him during the night, he fled from his guard; and availing himself of a rope that had been suspended from the top of the cliff, by a person who had been gathering samphire, he let himself down, and nothing more could ever be heard of him.

His majesty the king of Denmark, with his retinue, landed here on the tenth of August, 1768, and was welcomed on shore by salutes from the cannon of the castle, forts, and vessels in the bay; and by every possible mark of distinction and respect. After visiting the royal family of England, and several parts of the kingdom, his majesty came again to Dover, on the 14th of October, on his return to his native country. Mr. Fector, the grandfather of the present heir who is still in his minority, had the honor, on both occasions, to entertain the royal visitant, in his hospitable mansion, at the old bank. On his departure, the king presented to his courteous host, a gold box, curiously set in mosaic, as a testimony of respect, for the attention that had been paid to him.

On the 24th of February, 1772, a large section of Shakspeare's cliff fell down with a tremendous crash, the noise of which was heard at several miles distance; and the road along the sea beach to Folkstone, was completely blocked up. A few days before this, nearly 100 feet of the castle wall, opposite the town, fell into the ditch; and a building, that had been lately erected near the cliff, also fell; the chalk under it having given way. Several falls of the cliff also took place in Snargate-street about the same time; and the alarm was so great, that many left their houses.

About the year 1777, Guildford battery was

built near the south pier head; Townsend battery, near the north head; and North's battery, where the present ordnance yard is situated; but the latter was soon destroyed by the sea.

In 1778, an act was obtained for paving, cleansing, lighting, and watching the town, which imposed six-pence on every house, one shilling on every chaldron of coals imported, and a toll, equal to what the turnpike act allowed, payable at the gate on the London road. These imposts being inadequate for the purpose intended, another act was obtained thirty-two years afterwards, by which the duty on the houses and coals was doubled

In 1784, an act was obtained for the recovery of small debts, above two and under forty shillings; and a court of requests is held for this purpose, on the first Tuesday of every month.[15]

In a severe thunder storm, on the 14th of August, 1795, a man and four horses were struck dead by the lightning, on the heights, near the present citadel. The man was in the employment of the late Mr. Coleman, and was returning home with an empty waggon and four horses, when the violence of the storm induced him to take

---

15 The cognizance of this court extends not only over the liberties of the town and castle, but to the parishes of Charlton, Buckland, River, Ewell, Lydden, Coldred, East and West Langdon, Ringwould, Saint Margarets at Cliff, Whitfield, Guston, Hougham, Capel le Ferne, and Alkham.

shelter under a solitary hawthorn, where they were all found dead, about two hours after the storm had passed over. The lightning seemed first to have struck the head of the fore horse, and close to the pastern of the shaft horse, to have entered the ground; a hole being found there of one inch in diameter, at the surface, and more than three feet deep in a perpendicular direction.

The eyes of the horses were opaque; and a few hairs upon the breast of one, were slightly singed; but there was no external appearance denoting a mortal wound. On opening them, the carotid artery, on the right side of the neck of the second horse, was found to be ruptured; and the hearts of the other three, were all ruptured across the right ventricle, in an oblique direction. The poor man was sitting under the bush, having the neck of the fore horse lying across his thighs. His body was much distended, but his features were neither discomposed, nor discolored. The bush was not injured.

In 1796, an act was obtained for a turnpike road from Dover to Sandwich, which passes through Deal.

Soon after, an act was obtained for a turnpike road from Dover, through Waldershare and Eastry, to Sandwich; and which branches off from the London road about three miles from Dover.

The gloomy prospects that ushered in the year 1798, were truly alarming. England had seen the continental nations, one after another, fall a prey to the overwhelming power of France; her overtures of peace had been rejected, and the whole continent was in arms against her. Threats of invasion assailed her ears; and the inhabitants of Dover saw the gathering storm approach the channel. Camp after camp covered the coast of France, and the lengthened train of war spread along her cliffs. The sons of Britain flew to arms. Volunteers and military associations were immediately formed; and England became a nation of soldiers. From Caithness to Kent, from Kent to Cornwall, the flame of military ardour animated every bosom. The foe stood appalled at these mighty preparations. They had forced the defiles of the Alps and the Apennines, guarded by myriads in arms, fighting for their *masters;* but the plains of Kent and Sussex contained noble bands of free-born Englishmen, ready to fight for *themselves,* and burning for the contest. Abashed and confounded, the enemy ventured not to tread this sacred soil of freedom; but turned their haughty front, and pointed their devouring swords towards Africa and our possessions in the east, being more assailable than the envied isle of Britain.

Even here our noble warriors were ready to receive them. And when Nelson's prowess, on the first of August, shone triumphantly on the coast of Egypt, and proclaimed to ancient Nile the heroic deeds of Britain, the joyful news was celebrated at Dover, with all the fervour of military parade. Not a cannon that could bear a ball, but joined the deafening roar; while the voice of victory swept the channel, and echoed on the Gallic shores. All our splendid deeds of arms, all our joyful acclamations, have resounded from these lofty cliffs of Albion, and proved to our opposite neighbours, that the loyalty of this land of heroes, is equal to her high renown among the nations. But we must now descend to minor subjects.

Three men were killed on board the Osprey sloop, on the 29th of September, 1798, by a cannon ball accidentally fired from Archcliff fort.

Turnbull, a soldier, who stood charged with having stolen from the mint, in the tower, two bags, each containing 1000 guineas, was apprehanded, at Dover, on the 6th of June, 1799. He had offered thirty guineas for a boat, to take him to France, and 1010 guineas were found on his person.

In 1801, threats of invasion were again denounced by the government of France. Again their armies advanced towards the channel; the forces of Britain were ordered to the coast; and the camps of the two nations were in sight of each other, on the opposite hills. The channel

was covered with ships of war; the hero of the
Nile attacked the port of Boulogne; and the
frequent conflicts and bombardments were seen
by the inhabitants of Dover, assembled by thousands on the surrounding cliffs, till the deadly
sound of cannon became almost familiar to
the ear.

During the year 1804, several attacks were
made on the coast of France, by Sir Sidney
Smith, and other naval heroes, particularly on
the ports of Calais and Boulogne. These conflicts usually took place during the night, when
the continued hollow peal was more solemn and
terrific. To sleep was almost impossible; and
many passed the hours of midnight, walking on
the cliffs.

We must now turn again from these scenes of
warfare, to notice, in chronological order, circumstances less striking and important.

A private in the Northampton militia, fell from
the high cliff in the castle, towards the sea, on
the 13th of July, 1805. Though the cliff is more
than 300 feet high, he escaped without breaking
a bone, and survived the fall.

After the battle of Trafalgar, which was fought
on the 21st of October, 1805, great rejoicings
took place at Dover. Soon, however, our joy
was clouded, and the Victory anchored in the
bay, where she remained several days, with the
body of our renowned hero on board.

On the 8th of October, 1806, more than 300 Congreve rockets were thrown into the port of Boulogne, which destroyed a part of the flotilla, and set the town on fire in several places. The flames were distinctly seen at Dover.

A corporal of the Lincolnshire militia, on the 9th of May, 1807, in attempting to take a raven's nest, built in Shakspeare's cliff, fell from an elevation of more than 100 feet, and died almost immediately. It was affirmed by some ancient people, that a raven's nest had been annually built in this place more than seventy years.

An alarming fire broke out, on the 10th of May, 1808, in the warehouses of Mess. Fector and Co. near the York Hotel, which raged with alarming fury during the afternoon. It was occasioned by a person coopering some casks of turpentine; and the damages were estimated at upwards of £30,000.

The jubilee was celebrated here on the 25th of October, 1809, with every mark of dutiful affection to our late revered sovereign. The morning was ushered in by a discharge of fifty cannon, at sun-rising. This was repeated at one o'clock, and at sun-set, with a feue de joie from the infantry, drawn up on the beach; and the whole concluded with a general illumination.

Soon after midnight, on the 14th of December, 1810, an immense mass of cliff precipitated on the house of Mr. Poole, situated in the ordnance yard, near the gasometer. The unfortunate man, his wife, and six children, were all wrapped in sleep, unconscious of danger, when the hand of destruction fell upon them. All were destroyed except Mr. Poole himself, who was dug out of the ruins, much mutilated, and is now living. A stone in St. James's church yard, points out the place, where the wife and six children were buried.

On the 23rd of May following, a pig, supposed to have perished under this mass of earth, was, on removing the rubbish, actually dug out alive, after remaining in this gloomy situation, *one hundred and sixty days without food.* The sty was excavated in the chalk rock; and the animal, when found, was lively, and as white as snow; but reduced from about eight score to two. It was exhibited for some time, as a curiosity.

About the same time, several other masses of the cliff fell down in various places, particularly in Snargate-street; but no material injury was sustained by it.

During the year 1811, the flames of war still raged in the channel, and on the opposite coast of France. On the 13th of January, the ship Cumberland, from Quebec, was attacked by four French privateers, between Dover and Folkstone. During a sharp contest, the Frenchmen boarded three times, and were three times repulsed, and either killed or thrown overboard. The Cumberland then poured in a discharge of round and canister, which so far disabled the enemy, that they made off. The mate of the Cumberland was wounded, and one man killed: and three Frenchmen taken prisoners. The enemy's loss was supposed to be about sixty.

The American ship, Mary, was taken in the channel, by a large privateer, on the 12th of March, 1811. Part of the privateer's crew were conducting her towards Calais; but before they reached the port, the Americans rose upon the French, killed some, and threw the rest overboard. The privateer observing this, made after the Mary, and the Americans seeing no chance of escape, took to their boats, and arrived safely in Dover harbour.

Our limits will not allow us to enter into particulars respecting the privateers. They were very active and troublesome about this time, and frequently obliged our vessels to take shelter under the fortresses. Even here the enemy engaged them, and the shots have sometimes come on shore. The batteries generally gave them a warm reception; but though the balls appeared to dash in the water close by their sides, they seldom sustained much injury. Late in the evening was the more usual time for these encounters, when the garrison has sometimes beat to arms, and assembled on the beach. It was curious, on these occasions, to see men, women, and children, running in multitudes, and as eager to witness these conflicts, as they would have been to view some harmless amusement. None seemed conscious of fear; but the field pieces, firing unexpectedly before the crowd, would sometimes cause them to scamper behind the buildings.

While Buonaparte was reviewing his flotilla, at Boulogne, in the month of September, 1811, he sent out seven praams, each carrying twelve long twenty-four pounders and 120 men, and ten gun brigs, to attack the Naiad frigate. She engaged them two hours, and beat them off in grand style. The day after, the Naiad being joined by the Rinaldo, Redpole, and Castilian brigs, and the Viper cutter, they dashed in boldly under the batteries, drove the whole flotilla before them, and took one of the praams. This must have been highly mortifying to the emperor, and ought to have taught him that the invasion of England would prove no easy task.

When the scourge of war, after many years of desolation, blood, and carnage, had ceased to rage on the continent, and the allied sovereigns had entered Paris, the exiled monarch, Louis the Eighteenth, then residing in England, was invited, by the voice of his people, to ascend the throne of his ancestors. On the 23rd of April, 1814, great preparations were made at

Dover, to honor his majesty, on returning to his
native country, after a banishment of more than
twenty-one years. The military lined the streets
from the entrance of the town to the harbour;
a fleet was in the bay to receive him; and all
was expectation till towards evening, when the
prince Regent, (now our beloved Sovereign,)
the duke of Clarence, and several of the nobility,
entered the town; and soon after them, the king
of France, with a train of French princes and
royal dukes, and the duchess of Angouleme. The
batteries, and the shouts of the multitude, gave
them a hearty welcome as they passed. During
the night, the prince Regent slept at Mr. Fector's,
and the king of France, on board the royal
sovereign yacht, which moored close to the quay.

Dover had never before witnessed such an
influx of strangers. Carriages were not to be
hired; numbers had travelled more than forty
miles on foot; refreshments were obtained with
difficulty; and beds were almost out of the
question. The next day every thing was ready
for the king's departure; the prince Regent took
his station on the north pier head; the military
lined the harbour; the yachts and ships of war,
were sumptuously decorated with the flags of
both nations; and ten minutes before one o'clock
his majesty sailed out of the harbour, under a
grand salute from the batteries, and amidst the
joyful huzzas of an immense multitude; and in

less than three hours, was safely landed in Calais harbour.

On the 6th of June, 1814, Dover again displayed a splendid scene of magnificence. The emperor of Russia and the king of Prussia, with a splendid train of heroes, princes, and nobility, who had signalized themselves in the various conflicts that terminated in the defeat and abdication of the famous Napoleon Buonaparte, landed here, after a pleasant voyage from Boulogne.[16] As the fleet was crossing the channel, a large squadron from the Downs advanced and saluted them. Multitudes, who had assembled from all parts of the country to view this imposing spectable, covered the cliffs and beach. At six in the evening, the Impregnable, commanded by the duke of Clarence, and on board of which were the emperor and king, entered the bay, followed by the royal yachts, and the whole fleet. The garrison, consisting of a strong brigade of artillery, the Scotch greys, the 43rd, 51st, 52nd, and 95th regiments of the line, and the Galway militia, were under arms to receive them.

16 The chief of those who landed with the two monarchs, were the prince royal of Prussia; prince William, the king's brother; prince Frederick, the king's nephew; prince Augustus, the king's cousin; marshal Blucher; count Platoff, general of the Cossacks; baron Humbolt; count Hardenburgh; count Nesselrode; baron Anstet; prince Adam Garldriske; general Czernicheff; doctor Wylie; sir Charles Stewart; colonel Cook; captain Wood, &c. &c. &c.

It being low water, the royal visitants, contrary to expectation, landed on a platform at Archcliff fort. The rush to this point was dreadful; but no accident occurred. Now the cannon began to roar. The sailors fired their broadsides; manned the yards; and were answered by a thundering peal from the batteries on shore; while the acclamations of the multitude rent the air. The emperor slept at the late Mr. Fector's; the king of Prussia, at the York Hotel; and the two heroes, Blucher and Platoff, at the Ship Inn. Early the next morning, this constellation of magnificence took its departure towards the metropolis.

After visiting several parts of the kingdom, on the 26th of June, the royal strangers, accompanied by the emperor's sister, the duchess of Oldenburg, again honored Dover with their presence. The multitude assembled to witness their return, were nearly equal to those who welcomed their arrival. The enthusiasm was equally great, and the military parade no less splendid.

They arrived from Brighton late in the evening; and the emperor proceeded to Mr. Fector's, and the king to the York Hotel. On the 27th, his Prussian majesty, about twelve at noon, embarked on board the Nymphen frigate; and at six in the evening the emperor and his sister took their passage, the former on board the

Queen Charlotte yacht, and the latter on board the Jason frigate, for the continent. Each was saluted with a grand farewell from the numerous batteries, and by the loud acclamations of the people.

The next day, the 28th, the Rosario arrived in the roads, and fired a salute. Shortly afterwards the yards of the several vessels of war were manned; a salute took place through the whole squadron; and the launch of the Nymphen frigate advanced towards the harbour, with the duke of Wellington. The batteries poured forth a hearty welcome, and the hero was no sooner on shore, than the townsmen mounted him on their shoulders, and carried him in triumph to the Ship Inn. Nothing could exceed the anxiety to get a glance of the noble victor, and the house was surrounded the whole day.

The renowned heroes, Blucher and Platoff, still lingered on our happy island. The former arrived at Dover on the 11th of July, at five in the afternoon; dined at the Ship Inn, and sailed for Calais, in the Jason frigate, at eight in the evening. The latter entered the town at one o'clock on the 24th; dined also at the Ship Inn; and took his departure in the Jason frigate, for Calais, at six in the evening. Salutes from the batteries, heart-felt peals of applause, and joyful acclamations, followed them from the British shores.

The royal yacht arrived here on the 25th of May, 1818, with their royal Highnesses the duke of Cumberland and his bride, the late duchess of Hesse, who were received under a royal salute. The duke and duchess of Kent were also saluted here, on the 6th of September following, when they embarked, with their suite, in the royal sovereign yacht, for the continent.

April 23rd, 1819, the duke and duchess of Kent landed here, under a royal salute; and, on the 25th, the Persian ambassador came on shore, under a thundering peal from the batteries. His attendants, habited in silks and turbans, with long beards, and daggers by their sides, excited no small degree of attention.

An outrage of a most daring description, was committed in this town, on the 26th of May, 1820. A smuggling galley had been taken, and her crew, consisting of eleven men, were confined in Dover gaol. They were to have been removed on that day to the receiving ships in the Downs. Numbers of strangers had been noticed parading the streets, in all directions, during the morning; and an attempt at rescue was apprehended. Constables and a military force were drawn to the market place; and some of them marched into the gaol. The mayor and one of the magistrates attended, about twelve o'clock.

When the prisoners appeared at the gaol door, a general shout of "Liberty" resounded from every quarter; and the rush to rescue bore down all before it. The prisoners were taken back; and the furious work of destruction now began. Pick-axes, crow-bars, saws, and hammers, were all in readiness. Some mounted the roof of the prison, while others attacked the wall. The riot act was read, and the soldiers advanced with fixed bayonets, while the smugglers stood as firm as a rock, blocked up every avenue, and treated the pointed instruments of death, with perfect indifference. Prime and load, make ready, present,—now struck the ear; and the fatal word, *fire,* was every instant expected. Had it been uttered, the effusion of human blood would have been excessive; but mercy seemed to hold the scale of justice. The prisoners were soon released from their cells, and taken away in triumph by the mob. It is very remarkable that this large body of smugglers, who appeared to be in disguise, were totally unknown to the constables, or to the townsmen; and must have come from a considerable distance.

The unfortunate queen Caroline, accompanied by lady Ann Hamilton and alderman Wood, landed here, on the 5th of June, 1820, after an absence of six years. She was received with a royal salute from the commandant of the garrison, who appointed her a guard of honor; and the multitude assembled on the beach, near the York Hotel, paid her that respect which was due to her

exalted rank.   The mayor and corporation were
not prepared to wait on her majesty; but some
of the inhabitants presented an address to her at
the Ship Inn.   On her departure for London,
at six in the evening, the road was crowded with
people who cheered her as she passed along, to
a considerable distance beyond the town.   Her
majesty bowed respectfully to the multitude,
and seemed to thank them with a sorrowful
smile.

Twelve witnesses against the queen, (eleven
men and one woman,) all miserable looking
beings, and of the lowest order in society,
landed here on the 7th of July, 1820.   Their
object being ascertained, a mob collected, who
vented their indignation by beating and violently
insulting the wretched foreigners.   The military
were called out to their assistance; and instead
of going through Canterbury, they turned aside
towards Folkstone, and took the lower road to
London.   This unfortunate affray has been
charged to the disloyalty of the town of Dover.
That the thing itself was illegal, unjustifiable,
and perverse, cannot be doubted; but when the
whole nation was in a state of irritation and
almost of commotion, it cannot be surprising that
a few individuals should be found here ready for
such a frolick, or that numbers should join them
out of mere curiosity.   We are quite of opinion
that the charge of disloyalty is totally unfounded,

and that a more loyal and patriotic town cannot exist in the whole kingdom.

For some time previous to the 19th of July, 1820, placards had been posted in several parts of Dover, calling upon the inhabitants to assemble on the parade, on that day, to form themselves into volunteer corps, for the protection of the queen. Early in the morning, on the 19th, troops marched in from Canterbury, and the garrison was under arms all the day; but not a rebel dared show his face. We cannot suppose it possible that a single individual, in Dover, could be either wicked or mad enough, to have contemplated such an egregious act of folly; but the government showed a promptitude in being ready to resist any thing of the kind. Some wag, or some one whose object was to disgrace the town, must have been at the bottom of it.

Among the numerous arrivals that had graced this port, during the last few years, none were more grateful to the inhabitants of the town, than the return of the worthy family of John Minet Fector, esquire, after an absence of two years. He had passed the channel to accompany them home, and they arrived in the harbour on the 14th of October, 1820. The pier heads were crowded by multitudes of people, who testified their grateful feelings, by reiterated shouts of joy. Mr. Fector had been previously solicited by his fellow townsmen to represent them in parliament, an honor which he declined, intimating that his son, however, might probably at some future time, accept of such an offer. He was sensibly affected by this new and spontaneous effusion of their attachment, and on the day after his landing he published a circular, to express his gratitude for such kind attentions.

His eldest daughter, now Mrs. Bruyeres, attained the age of twenty-one, on the 14th of October, 1820; and a splendid ball and supper were given, at his mansion, on the preceding evening, to all the beauty and fashion of the town and neighbourhood.

On the 27th of October, 1820, nearly the whole male population of Dover, above the age of twenty-one, consisting of about 2300 persons, were entertained at the assembly rooms, in celebration of the return of Mrs. Fector and her family to England. The whole were divided into five classes, to be admitted at eleven, one, four, six, and eight o'clock, as specified in their cards of admission.

The bells of St. Mary's and St. James's churches ushered in the joyful morning. Barons, and several other joints of beef, were placed on a car, drawn by six fine horses, with riders in scarlet liveries. The car then moved on from Mr. Fector's mansion towards the assembly room, preceded by a band of music, and followed by a long procession. Flags, ensigns, and banners, tastefully decorated with laurel, adorned the room. The president's elevated seat was surmounted with an arch, round which was inscribed, in large letters, "BRITISH HOSPITALITY," with three transparencies, surmounted by a large union jack, on which were the following mottos: "*The HOUSE of FECTOR, so honorable to the town of Dover: may it flourish for ages, and perpetuate its high character for probity, liberality, and benevolence.*" "*Health and long life to John Minet Fector, esquire, the munificent entertainer of crowned heads, and the liberal benefactor and kind friend of his townsmen.*"

Eleven small cannon announced the admission of the first class, when 435 persons sat down to an excellent repast, the band playing, "*O the Roast Beef of Old England.*" Soon Mr. Fector made his appearance, attended by his only son, then eight years of age, and took his seat on the right hand of the president. At the same time, Mrs. Fector, attended by her three accomplished daughters, and a train of female friends, entered the gallery, amidst the hearty cheerings of the company.

The repast being ended, the president proposed the first toast, "*John Minet Fector, esquire, our hospitable host; health and long life to him;*" which was drank by acclamation. Mr. Fector shortly addressed the company, expressing his gladness at seeing them all assembled, and the hope of meeting them again at the termination of thirteen years.[17]   On taking leave he presented a letter to the president, expressive of his kind feelings towards the town, and of his intention, shortly to propose the formation of an institution for the benefit of the aged and infirm.

The president then proposed the second toast. *"Mrs. Fector and her daughters: a hearty welcome to Old England; and may happiness attend them."*   This was drank with enthusiastic cheers; and the last toast was then proposed. *"John Fector, the son of our host, and heir apparent to the Fector House: may he inherit the excellent qualities of his father; and, like him, possess the friendship and esteem of his townsmen."*   This toast was drank with equal enthusiasm; when the company retired, and the other classes succeeded in rotation.

In the evening, a numerous assemblage, with bands of music and lighted torches, paraded the streets; while the voice of harmony, benevolence, and social friendship, resounded in every quarter. After a hearty cheer, at the mansion of Mr. Fector, they separated with the same order and decorum that had marked the whole proceedings of this festive day.[18]

---

17 His son would then be of age.

18 In this truly Old English entertainment, were consumed 2514 lb. of beef, 362 loaves, and 4752 pints of ale. And 684 plates, 104 salts, 74 mustards, 200 tumblers, and 350 mugs, were provided for the purpose.

How short, how transient are all human joys, and human devices! and how soon are these festivities to be followed by a very different scene! How soon were sorrow and mourning to surround this seat of hospitality; and, instead of music, flags, and torches, dancing in the train of cheerfulness and mirth, scarfs, and palls, and plumes of black, are seen gliding through the same streets, and followed by the same people, with countenances downcast and sorrowful. Before he had time to put his benevolent design in execution, of providing for the aged and infirm, and of cheering the declining years of poverty, he was suddenly taken hence on the 12th of June, 1821.

His funeral was attended by the whole town and neighbourhood; and the mournful procession extended from his venerable mansion to Saint James's church yard, where he lies buried in a mausoleum, built for that purpose.[19] May his son, in the course of a few years, succeed to his ample fortune, and to the many virtues that have long adorned this worthy family.

Among other improvements lately introduced, an act was obtained in 1822, to light the town with gas, which is now in pretty general use, not only in the streets, but in most of the principal shops and inns, and in some private houses.

---

19 He was sheriff of this county in the year 1805.

Another flying exhibition took place at Dover on the 5th of September, 1825. A rope was extended across the pent, from the highest point of the cliff, under the Redoubt, to the Ropewalk, and a person, whose name was Courtney, descended amidst the cheerings of the people. In the course of a few days he repeated the dangerous enterprise, and fortunately escaped a second time without breaking his neck.

An act was obtained in 1826, to build a new Fishmarket, which was completed in 1827; and to make great improvements in the Market-place, which are expected to be accomplished in the course of a short time.

The streets of Dover, like those of all ancient towns, are very irregular; and, in many places, narrow and inconvenient. We may fairly conclude that the first buildings were erected where fancy or inclination prompted, and that no settled plan of system or design was ever adopted. Succeeding generations followed the same course; and though great changes and alterations must necessarily have taken place, the same want of system has continued. Such a defect of regularity may, perhaps, be more excusable in this place, than in many others. As the sea receded, new rows of houses were built on the firm ground, which was irregular, in the first instance, and left by the water, at different intervals, far remote from each other. From these circumstances, the position of new erections, must have depended more on chance, than on any premeditated plan.

At all events, the evil is now past a complete remedy, unless the greater part of the houses could be taken down and rebuilt. Great improvements may certainly be made; and, we are happy to say, are in rapid progress. The old houses are giving place to new ones; the streets are well paved and lighted; and made wider in many places; and a few years will give a more pleasing aspect to the whole town.

The lodging houses are built on a regular plan, on a new spot of ground; but as we hope, should our limits permit, to give a general description of Dover, as a Watering-place, we now proceed to our history of the Churches and Religious Houses.

CHURCHES

AND

RELIGIOUS HOUSES,

In and near the Town.

SAINT MARTIN LE GRAND.

Having, in our history of the castle,[1] described the ancient church in the Roman fortress, no farther notice need be taken of it here. This church excepted, among the ancient structures, either of those that now exist, or of such as have long since been swept from their foundations or laid in ruins, that of St. Martin le Grand claims the first place in point of antiquity. It occupied a considerable portion of the present Market-place, on the western side of which, some of its massy ruins still overtop the adjoining houses.

We have already noticed that the haven formerly occupied the site of this ancient structure; and that it was erected by Withred, king of Kent, in 696, for twenty-four secular canons.[2]

---

1 See Page 17.　　　　2 See Pages 22 and 142.

Under their royal patron they were exempt from all jurisdiction, except to the sovereign and the pope ; and had large endowments and grants of land, several of their members being prebends, and chaplains to the king, who had a royal chapel in this church.

In the reign of Harold the First, 1036, many of their immense possessions were taken from them. At the time of the conquest, 1066, it should appear that celebacy was not enjoined to the priests, several of their sons being mentioned, in the annals of this church, who had succeeded their fathers, about this period, in the sacred offices of religion.

We hear no complaint of their morals before the year 1124, when William Corboil, archbishop of Canterbury, made grievous and heavy complaints to king Henry the First, of the dissolute and abominable lives of his canons at Dover; and plainly told his majesty, that he, as their patron, would have to answer for all their crying sins and iniquities. During six years these complaints, with increased aggravations, were continually repeated ; and the prelate being joined by his brethren, the prior and monks of Christ church, in Canterbury, the king resigned his canons of St. Martin le Grand, into the hands of the archbishop and his monks, who were to send a superior to govern the house at Dover.

It does not appear how far their morals were

improved under the new patron; but he seems to have appropriated the greater part of their income to his own use.

With these revenues, in 1132, he laid the foundation of Dover priory, then called the New Work, or Saint Martin the Less. Contentions now arose between the archbisop and his monks, respecting the appointment of a prior to the new house at Dover; during which, the canons of St. Martin le Grand, appealed to the bishop of Winchester, the king's brother, and obtained a confirmation of their ancient rents, which they continued to receive till 1139. At this period, after they had remained in the town more than four hundred years, the strong arm of power again deprived them of their whole revenues; and the church then became parochial.

Suffragan bishops[2] were afterwards appointed to this church, and divine service was performed

---

2 Their office was to assist the archbishop, or bishop. The first we can find on record was Eadsin, bishop of St. Martin's, in 1052. We can find no regular succession of them prior to the year 1508. There is extant a continued list of those who officiated at Dover, from this time till 1597, in which year died Richard Rogers, the last suffragan bishop of Dover, the title having continued fifty years after St. Martin's church was desecrated. Among these suffragan bishops, Richard Thornton, whose vacillating principles in religion were easily accommodated to any change, made a very conspicuous figure. He was consecrated bishop of Dover in 1539, and became a protestant during the latter part of Henry the Eighth's reign, and thatof

in it till the thirty-sixth year of Henry the eighth, 1546. Here the grateful hymn of praise and thanksgiving resounded eight hundred and fifty years; and here the ancient inhabitants of Dover crowded round the altar, and worshipped at the footstool of Jehovah. They are all gone, and the generations after them, are following in speedy succession.

Two or three years after it was desecrated, it was taken down, except the steeple and some of the walls, by Thomas Wingefield, Ralph Bufkin, (then mayor,) and Robert Nethersole. Wingefield and Nethersole had the old materials, and Bufkin the bells and ornaments of the church, which he said were given, by the king, to the chamber of Dover.[4]

This was the mother church in the town; and none of the priests were allowed to sing mass in the other churches, until St. Martin's priest had

---

Edward the Sixth. When Mary came to the crown he was again a zealous catholic. Several accused of heresy were brought before his horrid tribunal at Canterbury, and were there found guilty of denying the tenets of the church of Rome, and cruelly condemned to the flames. Twenty-four of these good and pious persons were burnt in that city, two at Ashford, and seven at Maidstone; besides those that suffered the like punishment in other parts of the county. How deplorable that any sect of Christians should be guilty of such enormities; and we much wish the protestants had, in no cases, imitated the sad example.

[4] The pews were given to St. Mary's church in 1546; but the altars were not removed till 1549.

begun, which was announced by tolling the great bell.

The remains of massy columns still bear witness to its ancient grandeur. The place of burial, now called the Old Church Yard, is still used for that purpose by the inhabitants of St. Mary's parish. By what means it became private property, is not known; but it was sold, in 1583, by John Toke to John Lovedale; and the present proprietor claims a right of herbage, and demands a fee of five guineas for permission to erect an altar tomb, on the premises, and ten shillings and six-pence for a head stone The General Baptists have a piece railed off for a burying place, and a part is used for a carpenter's yard.

Tradition informs us that one John Hewson, a merchant of Dover, gave the inhabitants of St. Mary's parish, the privilege of burying in this ground.

Among these venerable dead, the mortal remains of the celebrated poet, Charles Churchill, were laid, in 1764. A small stone, with the following inscription, points out the spot:

" Life to the last enjoyed
" Here Churchill lies."

CANDIDATE.

Another inscription to his memory, is also affixed in St. Mary's church.

The ecclesiastical fair of St. Martin, is still kept in the Market-place, on the 23rd of November, and continues three market days. It was originally granted to the priory, and from thence was transferred into the town.

Saint John's Church.

This church was situated at the entrance of the town from Canterbury; and, from the number of wax lights provided to burn before several saints, not only in the church, but also in the undercroft and sepulchre, it appears to have been a magnificent structure.

The church was taken down about the year 1537, by Thomas Wingefield, Robert Nethersole, and Ralph Bufkin ; and the materials and ornaments, consisting of silver censers, cruets, crosses, and chalices, appear to have been divided among them. The premises were then given or sold to John Bowle, who constructed a stable in some remains of the church, and a pig sty in the church yard. Not a wreck can now be found to point out its situation; but, in the year 1827, a large quantity of human bones were dug up, on rebuilding the second right hand house, on entering the town.

Saint Peter's Church.

This church was situated on the north-east of the present Market-place, and a row of houses is now built on the site of it. It was a rectory in the patronage of the crown, valued, in the king's books, at £3. 16s. 10d. and had a cemetery adjoining it. Formerly it paid tenths to the crown; but being certified not to exceed the yearly value of £24, it was discharged from the payment of first fruits and tenths.

From the wills in the prerogative office, in Canterbury, we find that Thomas Toke of Dover and Westbere, was buried in the chancel of the Blessed Virgin, in 1474; Richard Palmer, in the church, in the same year, and mention is made of the image of St. Nicholas; William Warren, in our Lady's chapel, in 1506; Richard Fineux, before the image of St. Mary Magdalen, in 1520, and he gave a legacy to St. Roque's light in this church; Peter Mace, before the chapel of St. Michael the Archangel, in 1540; William Paynter, before the chapel of our Lady, in 1540; Robert Vyncente, in the chapel of St. John the Baptist, in 1540; Hugh Braket, late mayor, before the high altar, in 1549; John Williams and Thomas Fynett, jurats, in the church, both in 1558; and Jane, widow of John Warren, in our Lady's chapel, in 1572.

Henry Fravel, of this parish, who was buried at the priory, by his will, proved in 1514, gave to the reparation of the north roof, over St. Stephen, and to mending the windows against St. Tronyon, five marks; and to St. Tronyon's light, a cow; and another cow, to the light of St. Trofymus.

In passing down the above list, we surely find the sire of that unfortunate son, the worshipful Robert Fynett, who, twenty years after the funeral of his father, tainted his name, and brought odium on his character, by placing his name at the head of those, who deprived their fellow townsmen of their chartered right, to nominate and elect their chief magistrate. Where does his troubled spirit wander? It looks back; it weeps for mercy, and says, " Had I contemplated the lasting disgrace of such base injustice, the repentant tear should have fallen on the accursed signature, and blotted it out for ever.

How deplorable, that any rational being should be so blinded with the insiduous glare of a few day's honor, and so act, as to transmit his sullied name with ignominy to succeeding ages. May this example prove a salutary warning; and may better principles inspire the future patriot's bosom, and point his vision to that near tribunal, where impartial justice holds the scale.

The preceding notices of funerals, and the places of burial, have been introduced that the reader may take a retrospect of past ages. Our forefathers seem to have filled the earth with churches, chapels, images, and altars, which plainly denote a due sense of their dependence on that Being to whose service they were dedicated; and ~~while we pity~~ their superstition, let us forbear to defame their misguided piety. They lived in an age of mental darkness; while we, who still admit the honor due to holy places, enjoy a brighter day; and, with more expanded faculties, admire the magnificent temple that fills the universe. With such advantages, how can we pollute the sacred edifice, or insult the Majesty that shines in every part of it!

This church seems to have been in use in 1611, at which period John Gray was rector. The parish was afterwards united to that of St. Mary, the churchwardens of which still pay a yearly fee farm rent of 10s. 10d. for a tenement, called St. Peter's church or chantry.

The mayor and members of parliament were formerly chosen in this church. In 1585, these elections were removed to St. Mary's church; and, in 1826, an act of parliament was obtained to remove them to the court hall.

We have already mentioned, in page thirty-six, the head which was found in sinking a cellar near the Antwerp Inn, in 1810, and which was supposed to have been that of the unfortunate duke of Suffolk. We have since discovered that this ground belonged to St. Peter's church, instead of St. Martin's. The duke was beheaded, by Nicholas Towers, in the year 1450. When found, this scull was nearly perfect, the jaws and teeth being entire; but after it had been exposed a short time to the air, it crumbled to dust. The chalk receptacle was afterwards deposited in the wall.

SAINT NICHOLAS'S CHURCH.

This church was situated in the centre of Bench-street; and several persons are recorded to have been buried in it, and in the adjoining cemetery.

Among these, are Robert Colwell, in 1488; Robert Randolph, before the altar of St. John of Brydlyndton, in 1489; Thomas Haxtal,[1] in the chancel, in 1486; Edward Haxtal, his son, in our Lady's chapel, in 1518; and John Brown, jurat, before the Great Rood, in the body of the church, in 1522.

John Joiner was minister of this church, in 1518; and it seems to have been in use till 1526.

The famous Robert Nethersole had the lead; Bowle, the church yard; and John Plane, of London, two tenements, which appear to have belonged to the church, with the land adjoining them. We cannot find who ran away with the materials, images, and sacred utensils, as

---

[1] He served in parliament for Dover, in 1471. By will, proved in 1486, he gave his estates to his son Edward, on condition that he assigned to the churchwardens of St. Nicholas, a croft of arable and pasture land at Maxton. One moiety of the rent was to be given to the minister, and the other to the repairs of the church.

neither Bufkin nor Wingefield are recorded to have had any concern in this sacrilegious transaction.

It does not appear how Bowle and Plane disposed of the premises: but the corporation had possession of the tower and a part of the ground, in 1729, when they sold it to Thomas Pyall, carpenter, for £124. 15s. Part of it had been converted to a stable. The porch was taken down in 1796; at which time Mr. Ashdown,[2] the Baptist minister, had part of the church yard for his garden, and the tower for his parlour, with other apartments adjoining.

The tower of the church is still standing, and was formerly called Marshes, or Prison tower, having been used for the purpose of confining French prisoners. Mr. Hasted says that the body of the church stood on the east side of the tower; and that the crypt is now used as cellars for the adjoining houses. If so, the church must have had three bodies, as these cellars are on the north and south sides of the tower.

From the quantities of human bones that have been dug up, the church and cemetery seem to have occupied the entire space between

---

[2] This old gentleman appears to have been a good moral character, but strangely excentric. He wrote a book to prove there was no devil, which obtained but little notice; and does not appear to have made a single convert. He died in 1810, aged 87 years, and was buried at Guston.

the whole length of Bench-street, and the next lane, at a few rods to the eastward of it; all which is now covered with houses, yards, or gardens.

SAINT MARY THE VIRGIN'S CHURCH.

This structure, situated in Canon-street, near the Market place, is still in use; and probably is one of the three religious houses, built by the canons of St. Martin's, during the latter period of the Saxon government. The tower,[1] bases, columns, capitals, and arches, are all indications of Saxon architecture.

Two rows of massive pillars, some round and others of a parallelogramic form, with demi-columns at each side, support the roof. The bases, capitals, and columns, as well as the width of the arches, have a considerable variation. Some of the arches are circular, some elliptical, and some pointed. The distance between the pillars varies from seven to thirteen feet.[2]

---

[1] The tower stands at the west end, surmounted by a spire covered with lead. A faculty was obtained in 1634, to take down a large leaden cross at the top of it, and to replace it with a lighter one of wood and iron. A faculty was obtained at the same time, to make a gallery at the lower end of the middle aisle. In 1497, there were only two bells in this tower; but they were afterwards, at different times, increased to six; and these six, in 1724, were re-cast into the present peal of eight.

[2] A pillar in each row was taken down in 1804, and two arches thrown into one.

The nave consists of three aisles, and three transepts, with a recess towards the east, in which are placed the communion table and the magistrates' seats. The recess has the appearance of a small chancel; but the parishioners claim and repair it, as a part of the nave. All the remaining space is filled with pews; and commodious galleries[3] extend on each side: the length being about one hundred and twenty feet, and the breadth fifty-five.

The advowson was in the gift of the crown, in the reign of king John, who gave it to Hubert de Burgh; and, in 1384, we find it appropriated by the abbot of Pontiniac, and it was then valued at £5. 6s. 8d. After this it belonged to the master and brethren of the Maison Dieu, who provided a priest daily to officiate in it; and churchwardens were appointed to keep it in repair. When the hospital of the Maison Dieu was suppressed, in 1534, it again reverted to the crown, and John Thompson, who was then master of that hospital, estimated the value of the parsonage, at £6 per annum.

King Henry the Eighth being at Dover in 1547, the inhabitants entreated that he would give them the church for a place of worship.

---

[3] The north gallery was built by subscription, in 1611; that on the west, by the pilots, in 1699; that on the south, by Henry Furness, esq. member of parliament for Dover, in 1721; and that on the east, by the parish, in 1749.

As there were no tythes, nor any provision for the maintenance of a minister, he readily consented; and, on his departure, the parishioners put a seal on the doors, in token of possession.[4] It then became a perpetual curacy, the advowson of which was vested in the inhabitants.

By taking down the images and altars, and selling the vestments of the priests, the chalices, and other sacred utensils, the parishioners did but imitate the example of those who despoiled the other religious houses at this period; and, by these means, they raised a sum of £63. 9s. 5d. With this fund, which was considerable in those days, they were enabled, in 1550, to remove the chapels, shrines, and stalls in the choir; and to beautify the church.

When queen Mary came to the crown, in 1553, the inhabitants were required to conform to the popish religion; and it cost them nearly three pounds to provide a mass book, candlesticks, tapers, a pix, a cross, a holy loaf, and hallowed fire; and to watch the sepulchre at Easter. The famous suffragan bishop Thornton, before mentioned, was the first to say mass.

On the accession of queen Elizabeth, the protestant worship was again introduced; and, in 1585, the elections for mayor and members of

---

4 The inhabitants were, however, fined by the king's footmen for not ringing the bells on his arrival, though the church was not then in their possession.

parliament, were transferred from St. Peter's, to this church. Since that period, instead of mass and matins, and the joyful hymn of pious adoration, horrid imprecations and the voice of violence have, on these occasions, resounded through the sacred edifice; and barriers have sometimes been placed between the contending parties, to prevent the effusion of human blood. The communion table has been covered with poll books, and made a desk for the recording clerks; while perjury, black perjury sat on the quivering lip, and moved the faultering tongue of those, who still could feel remorse at the stings of a guilty conscience.

Where are the guilty shades of those who, in this hallowed place of worship, challenged the Majesty of heaven, to witness their free unbiased suffrages, while they knew that compulsion, or a hope of gain, had superseded their deliberate choice? And where the still more guilty shades of those who spurned at poverty, and compelled a needy brother to perjure his own soul, through fear of want, or of losing the means to provide sustenance for himself and family? Do they haunt this polluted place; and, when the solemn hour of midnight speaks peace to the tranquil mind, do they sit trembling here, awaiting that judgment, when the doleful prison doors shall close upon them, and seal their ever-lasting doom! We have before observed that these elections are removed to the court hall; and may such scenes of enormity never more be practised under the awful canopy of heaven.

Duty obliges us, in presenting to our readers a faithful description of Dover, to revert to another subject, highly offensive to many friends of decency and propriety; but which, we humbly hope, is a mere trifle, when compared with the former.

No records remain earlier than the reign of Charles the Second, which began in 1660, of any particular seats in the church being appropriated for the mayor and jurats. The propriety of such a distinction, can hardly be doubted; and the respect which every good man must necessarily feel towards the magistracy, seems to justify it. In the present instance, the only objection seems to arise from the peculiarity of the place.

Soon after the period above mentioned, seats were erected for the mayor, the jurats, and the governor of Dover castle, in the centre of the north gallery; and colonel Stroude (who was then governor) and Walter Braems, esq. were at the whole expense. The corporation did not approve of the situation; and took away the altar, and seated the mayor in the place of it, above the communion table.

When king Charles visited Dover in 1670, he was conducted, with great pomp, into the magisterial chair. His majesty, struck with the impropriety of such an arrangement, with great humility declined the use of a seat, placed, as he emphatically observed,

————————." above
" The Majesty of Heaven."

This severe rebuke, or a respect for their sovereign, induced the magistrates to leave these seats during a short period; but the impression soon wore off, and the places were occupied as usual.

The greater part of the corporation were at this period attached to the presbyterian form of worship; while the true members of the establishment were offended at what they termed, the indecent situation of these seats; and cited the mayor and his brethren, to appear at the consistory court, at Canterbury. Here a faculty was granted to the churchwardens, to remove these seats to the north gallery again, or to any other convenient part of the church; and to put the communion table in its proper place

This was accordingly done; but a vestry was called in 1688, which was attended by six jurats, and two or three other persons, and an order was obtained to replace the seats again at the east end, where they had formerly been, above the communion table, which was done at the expense of the parish; and they remain there at the present day.

The body of the church was ceiled in 1706. Before this period, the rafters and timbers were open to the sight; but, the whole roof being covered with lead, the appearance was less unpleasant, and the inconvenience from the weather was prevented.

One of the chandeliers was purchased, by subscription, in 1738; and the other, by the pilots, in 1742: in which year the organ was built.

In 1804, the magistrates caused locks to be put on their seats, and on those of the common council men. The parishioners objected to it; and, when the pews in the middle aisle, during the same year, were new fronted, the church-wardens presumed to remove these locks. A law suit ensued; and, after expending about £1000, the cause was dropped, and the seats continue to remain unlocked, as usual.

An evening lecture was established in 1825, which has been well attended, and is a great accommodation to the town. It was at first ordered in vestry, that should a subscription to pay the minister, prove inadequate for that purpose, the deficiency should be advanced from the church cess. This order has since been cancelled; and the whole now depends on a subscription.

The lead was taken from the north roof of the church in 1827, and replaced with slates and tiles. The galleries were new fronted at the same time, and the church beautified, which has now a very handsome appearance; but is much too small to contain the parishioners.

The parish is very populous; and, according to the last census, in 1821, contained 1645 houses, and 8653 inhabitants.

Three sermons are preached on each Sunday, and the morning service is read every Wednesday and Friday, and on each fast and festival.

Charities.—The charities and donations[5] to this church are very numerous; but some of

---

[5] Thomas Fuller, by will, 1482, gave to the master of the Maison Dieu, certain messuages in the town, to provide a priest to say mass in St. Mary's church, and 6s. 8d. to repair the church, for ever.

Thomas Toke, buried in St. Katharine's chapel, 1484, gave seven acres of land, at Dungate, under Windlass Down, to repair the church, for ever.

Thomas Toke, buried in the same chapel, 1509, gave two acres of land, under Stepping Down, to maintain a light for ever, before the rood in this church.

John Templeman was buried in St. Michael's chapel, and John Claryngbould before the altar of St. Erasmus, both in 1513. No charities are mentioned.

William Smith, buried in Trinity chapel, near St. Anthony's altar, gave 2s. in 1522, towards building a new chapel in this church.

Thomas Lybens was buried in St. Lay's chapel, in this church, before the image of St. Thomas of Canterbury, in 1527, and gave, by will, 3s. 4d. to the cover of the font; and 6s. 8d. to glaze the windows in the chapel of our Lady.

Thomas Coorye was buried in our Saviour's chapel, in 1545.

them are lost, and it is doubted whether others were ever appropriated to the purposes intended. From those that remain, which are still very

---

Mention is also made of St. Nicholas's chapel; but they were all removed at the Reformation.

Thomas Pepper, in 1573, left to the poor, yearly, 20*s.* from lands in Hougham.

Thomas Elwood, in 1604, left to the poor, in bread, at Christmas-eve, 20*s.* yearly, payable from a house near the church, now in the possession of captain Dell.

Thomas Chellice, in 1613, left to the poor, in bread, 10*s.* yearly, from a house called the Saracen's Head.

Joice Evering, in 1635, gave 50*s.* to purchase plate for the communion.

Ann Booth and Mark Wills, in 1664, left an annuity of £7. 10*s.* to six poor widows, from lands at Whitfield.

Jacob Windsor, in 1669, left to the poor, in bread, 24*s.* yearly, from a house in Bench-street, occupied by Mr. Grant.

Thomas White, in 1669, left 40*s.* yearly, to four poor widows, from the Shakespeare inn.

Anthony Percival gave two large silver flagons, and George West, two silver plates, for the communion, in 1684.

John Hewson, in 1692, left an annuity of 20*s.* to poor widows of this parish.

Nicholas Cullen, in 1699, left the rent of a small tenement near the fish-market, to be given to the poor, in bread.

Nicholas Cullen also left to twenty poor widows, who do not receive alms from the parish, £6. yearly, from a house in Strond-street, and £7. yearly, from certain lands in Romney Marsh; making, in the whole, £13. each widow to receive 13*s.* every New-year's day. This charity is much improved, in consequence of the fee of the lands falling to the parish, and each widow now receives nearly £5. yearly.

William Richards, in 1701, left £5. annually, payable out of certain lands, occupied by Mrs. Horn, of Buckland.

Anthony Church, in 1709, left 20*s.* yearly, to the poor, in bread.

numerous, and from the alms at the sacrament, large quantities of bread are distributed to the poor every Sunday.

Ann Jell, in 1719, left 40*s.* yearly, to eight poor widows who do not receive parish relief, payable from a house in the possession of Mrs. Farbrace.

John Deckewer, in 1760, left the interest of £500. stock, to be distributed every Sunday, in bread, and coals on Christmas-eve, on condition that the minister and churchwardens do keep in repair the tomb of Benjamin Devinck.

Susannah Hammond, in 1767, left 48*s.* yearly, to be given in bread.

Elizabeth Roalf, in 1777, left £12. yearly, to ten of the poorest families, who do not receive constant alms from the parish.

Thomas Knott, in 1777, left 20*s.* yearly, to forty poor widows, payable from the houses, many years in the possession of the late Mr. Thomas Pattenden.

Thomas Gibbon Boykett left, by will, in 1799, £5. a year, to be given to the poor, in bread.

Rebecca Saure left, by will, in 1808, the interest of £400. for keeping in repair the tomb and vault of her late husband; the overplus to be laid out in coals, for the benefit of ten poor widows of the parish, who do not receive alms from the same.

Peter Fector, by will, in 1806, left the interest of £200. 3 per cent. cons. bank annuities, to be distributed, yearly, on Christmas day, among twelve aged persons of this parish. The widows of seamen are recommended in this bequest.

Thomas Pattenden, gentleman, of Dover, left, by will, in 1817, in trust to the minister and churchwardens of the parish of St. Mary, for the time being, the sum of £800. 3 per cent. reduced bank annuities, the dividends arising from which, to be partly appropriated towards repairing, from time to time, the fencing round his grave; and the remainder, to be yearly applied to the relief of six poor widows, who have most recently been so unfortunate as to lose their husbands by the dangers of the sea.

Ministers.—Before the suppression of religious houses, this church had a rector, a curate, a deacon, and a sub-deacon; but how they were paid does not appear.

Soon after the inhabitants had obtained possession of the church, their poverty or indifference has been such, that they have, in some instances, pawned and sold the rich vestments, left by the catholic priests, to pay their minister; and the church has sometimes been without one.

The following is a list of the ministers, during the last three hundred years, with the dates of their appointments.

Sir Robert Yonge or Long, 1522, appointed by the master of the Maison Dieu.

Sir Anthony Rogers, 1547, assistant to Sir Robert, at a salary of £6. 12*s.* per annum.

Sir Monge Thornton, 1549, at £8. per annum, and 13*s.* 4*d.* for his lodgings.

Sir Harrie Caine, 1550, at a salary of twenty marks, and the Easter offerings. His stipend not being paid, he left the church, till two rich copes were pawned to pay his arrears.

Sir Christopher James, 1553, who took the occasional duty for the Easter offerings only. The Roman catholic religion being again introduced by queen Mary, he was dismissed because he was a married man.

Sir Geoffry, 1553, at £10 salary, and his lodgings.

Sir John Lambert, 1555, at the same salary. He was buried in this church.

Sir William, 1558. He was the last who retained the title of Sir; and resigned in 1562.

The Rev. Thomas Turpyn, 1562. He was buried in this church.

The Rev. George Joye, 1574. The vestry book was lost at this time, and no particulars are known of him.

The Rev. Robert Joye, 1582.

The Rev. Richard Pickering, 1589. He was buried in this church.

The Rev. Walter Richards, 1601. His salary was £30 a year.

The Rev. John Graye, 1608. He resigned in the year 1616.

The Rev. John Reading, 1616. He was chaplain to lord Zouch, constable of Dover castle, and accompanied his noble patron on a visit to that fortress. St. Mary's parish had no minister at the time he was here, and he obliged the parishioners by taking the duty several weeks. They very much approved of him; and he was induced to accept the curacy, at £100 a year. He appears to have been a pious, worthy, good man; and was appointed chaplain to king Charles the First.

During the civil commotions, the taint of new doctrine had infected his flock; and he was no longer considered to be an orthodox divine.

The respect that had formerly been paid to him, was now changed to malice and rancour; and his path was continually strewed with hardships and sufferings. His library was plundered by a military force, in 1642; and, on the following year, while engaged in writing his Paraphrase of St. John's Gospel, a company of armed men hurried him away to prison.

The king was moved with compassion at the cruel treatment, so unjustly inflicted on his worthy chaplain; and endeavoured to alleviate his losses, by procuring for him the rectory of Chartham, and a prebend's stall, in Canterbury cathedral. Sir William Brockman also gave him the living of Cheriton, where he afterwards resided; and he was appointed, by the assembly of divines, one of the nine persons, to write annotations on the New Testament. But neither this sacred employment, nor his sequestered retreat at Cheriton, could secure him from the frantic rage of his enemies. He was seized and conducted to Dover castle, and from thence to Leeds castle, in this county, where he wrote his Guide to the Holy City.

After obtaining his enlargement, in 1650, he publicly disputed with Samuel Fisher, of the Baptist persuasion, in Folkstone church; and he also opposed the doctrine of John Godwin, a lay teacher, who, during his imprisonment, had occasionally taken the duty at St. Mary's church.

It is not certain whether Mr. Reading returned

to his church, at Dover, after the restoration; but he was here, and appointed speaker by the corporation, when his majesty landed, and presented to him a gold embossed Bible. He died at Chartham in 1667, and was buried in the chancel of that church.

During Mr. Reading's imprisonment, the service of St. Mary's church appears to have been much neglected; but several persons were, in the mean time, appointed to the cure.

The Rev. Michael Porter, 1643. His salary was £60, and afterwards increased to £100.

The Rev. John Dykes, 1647. He came from Tenterden, and his salary was £100.

The Rev. John Robotham, 1650. He was the first who engaged to preach two sermons on each Sunday; and his salary was £100.

The Rev. Nathaniel Norcross, 1653. He consented to take a part of the duty, and to be paid by voluntary subscription; but resigned at the end of six months.

The Rev. Nathaniel Barry, 1654, at £100 salary.

The Rev. Samuel Hinde, D. D. 1662. He agreed for a salary of £100, which was very indifferently paid; and, after a long scene of contention, he resigned in 1671.

The Rev. John Lodwich, 1671, at a salary of £80, and the church fees. He was at the head of the opposition, to restrain the extensive power of the magistrates, who, at this period, had great influence in the vestry. The parish clerk died in 1698, when the minister chose a person to succeed him, and the parish, or magistrates, chose another. An appeal was made to the ordinary, who determined in favour of the parish. A series of continued discord having imbittered the life of this minister, he died in the course of of a few months after the termination of this dispute.

The Rev. John Macqueane, 1698, at the same salary that had been given to his predecessor. In the course of two years, it was proposed to deprive him of the church fees, and some other trifling emoluments, in order to lessen the parochial cess.

This minister appears to have been of an easy and pliable disposition; and his whole deportment was better calculated for private life, than for the sacred offices of religion. Though sobriety did not rank among his chief virtues, yet his mildness covered a multitude of imperfections; and thirty years glided on without much contention. Strange stories, however, are still told of his nightly rambles, with his jocose and facetious clerk; and his eccentricities are no less remarkable, than his kindness and good nature. When the great duke of Marlborough, on his landing here in 1714, attended divine service in St. Mary's church, Macqueane depicted his brilliant victories and splendid feats of arms in such glowing colors, that the duke's modesty was overpowered, and he was obliged to withdraw. Observing this, the minister raised his voice, and said, " My brethren, you see I have been able to do more than all our potent enemies could ever achieve.——I have made the noble hero turn his back."

Worn out with age, in 1728, he requested an assistant, which was acceded to; but a dispute arose whether he should be chosen by the minister, or by the parishioners. The good natured man waved his claim, and the Rev. W. Nairne was chosen, at a salary of £80 a year. Less flexible than usual, the old gentleman then objected to the choice; and after five month's contention, a vestry was called. It was here declared that the parishioners had a right to dismiss their ministers; and that Macqueane should preach no more.

Not to be intimidated by these threats, he mounted the desk on the following Sunday; but the parishioners were determined that he should not preach. They began to sing the 119th Psalm, and twice they finished this long hymn of 176 verses. The minister sat very patiently till they began it a third time, when he rose up, and requested to be heard. When silence was obtained, he jocosely said, " My friends, I think we are now even. I have, in this place, often told you a very pretty story; and, to day, you have entertained me with a very pretty song: so now farewell." He then left the church; but the affair did not end here.

Application was made to the archbishop, who considered the church to be canonically filled, during the life of the minister; and he issued a prohibition to restrain Mr. Nairne from officiating. The parishioners replied, and said that only a small number would attend the church when Macqueane took the duty; that the parishioners would not receive the sacrament from him, nor suffer him to baptize their children, sixty of whom were then unbaptized; and that while many idled away the sabbath, others went to the meeting houses, who might never return. If there really was just cause for such serious complaints, good nature must hide her face, and can no longer palliate such a character.

It was finally settled, and probably by the advice of the archbishop, that Macqueane should be paid £15 a quarter, which he accepted, on condition that he should remain minister, and be allowed to officiate as often as he chose.

The Rev. W. Nairne, 1729. He was assistant to Mr. Macqueane.

The Rev. W. Byrch, 1731. His salary was £80 a year, and the surplice fees; and he was also rector of Great Mongeham. In his time, the inhabitants, assisted by their representatives in parliament, purchased a house for the use of the minister, who, before this period, had been obliged to hire lodgings.

The Rev. Thomas Edwards, 1756. He had the same salary, and was chaplain of Dover castle; and died of a consumption in 1772.

The Rev. John Lyon, 1772. He had the same salary, as had been given to his predecessor. His researches into the antiquities of this place, do him great credit: and we feel much obliged for the information we have derived from his works, in forming this small treatise. He was author of a history of Dover, and of Dover castle, published by subscription, in two volumes quarto, in 1814. He also wrote an account of a Roman bath,[6] which is partly under St. Mary's church; and other ingenious treatises, inserted in the Archæologia of the Antiquarian Society.

A more honest or upright man could hardly be found. Influenced by neither power nor flattery, his words expressed the undisguised dictates of his mind; and, conscious of his own rectitude, he little regarded those bending civilities which a more polished society now deems necessary. This cast a shade of moroseness on his character; but his honest frankness was more than a counterbalance to such a defect. He died at Dover, in 1817, at a very advanced age, and was buried at St. Nicholas's church, in the Isle of Thanet, near the place of his nativity.

---

[6] See Page 141.

The Rev. William Wise, 1806.   He was assistant to Mr. Lyon, at a salary of £100 a year; and resigned in 1812.

The Rev. John Maule, 1812.   He was also assisting minister, at a salary of £100 a year, till the demise of Mr. Lyon, in 1817.   Many were of opinion that he ought to have succeeded without a new election; but a vestry determined against it.   Though several candidates offered themselves, he obtained a majority in his favour, and is now vicar of this parish; and also of St. Margarets, at Cliffe.   The parsonage house was rebuilt for him, in 1818.

At the demise or resignation of a minister, the pulpit is opened to as many candidates, in holy orders, as may choose to offer themselves. They are invited by a general advertisement, and each officiates during one Sunday.   When they have all taken a regular course of probation, the parishioners, who pay church cess, proceed to an election; and the candidate who obtains a majority, is licenced by the archbishop, and succeeds to the living.

SAINT JAMES'S CHURCH.[1]

This is an ancient structure; but whether of

---

[1] Kilburne calls it St. James the Apostle, or St. James of Warden Doune; and Leland, St. James of Radby, or, more likely, Rodeby, a statione navium.

Saxon or Norman origin, cannot be determined. It is a rectory, in the gift of the archbishop, and stood in the king's books, at £4. 17s. 6d. but being valued at only £24 a year, it was discharged from the tenths and first fruits.

Archbishop Tenison augmented this rectory with a gift of £200; and the governors of queen Anne's bounty, added a like sum.

Archbishop Secker left £2000 for the purpose of repairing or rebuilding the parsonage houses, in poor livings. The Reverend Thomas Tournay obtained £200 of this bounty, to which he added £50, and liberal subscriptions were raised by the inhabitants. With these sums the present parsonage house was built, by this worthy rector, in 1786. This new structure was erected on the site of the old parsonage house, which, from the masonry, appeared to have survived three or four centuries.

At the eastern extremity of the south aisle in this church, the lord warden usually held his courts of chancery and admiralty; and the court of loadmanage was also held at this place. The courts are still opened here, and the business is then adjourned to the Antwerp Inn.

Mention is made in the prerogative office, in Canterbury, of several persons who were buried in this church. Among them was John Claryngbould, buried in the choir, in 1485, before the image of St. James, and near to that of St. Nicholas.

Elizabeth, widow of John a Wodde, buried in the choir, in 1523. She gave half a sheet to the high altar, and a kercher to cover the chalice: also, her best coverlet, to be laid before the high altar, for poor child-wives; and a table cloth of drap, to make two towels; one for St. James, and the other for the cross.

John Broke was buried in our Lady's chapel, in this church, in 1529. He ordered certain lands to be sold, and forty pounds of money to be given for a complete suit of vestments, to obtain the prayers of the priests for ever.

William Warde, jurat, was buried in the east corner of Saylor's chancel, in 1623.

Simon York was buried here, in 1682; and Philip York, his son, who was town clerk, and father of the chancellor, in 1721.

Henry Matson, merchant, who gave Solton farm to Dover harbour, was buried in the chancel, in 1722.

This church consists of a nave and chancel; the nave being divided by two aisles and a transept. The square embattled tower, in which are six bells, is erected, on massy pillars, over the centre of the north aisle, having the pulpit, desk, and several pews under it. These pillars and their arches, give a heavy appearance to the inside; which was still more exceptionable on this account, till most of those that incommoded the other parts of the church, were taken down in 1825. At the same time, the gallery, which was formerly confined to the western extremity of the north aisle, was extended across the other. The church was also new roofed, slated, ceiled, and beautified; and the whole, being well pewed and spacious, has now a neat and handsome appearance.

There was only one service, on a Sunday, in this church, prior to the year 1827. Since that period, a sermon is preached in the morning, and the evening service read in the afternoon.

According to the census of 1821, this parish contained 289 houses, and 1821 inhabitants: but the number of houses, and the population, are much increased since that period; numerous lodging houses having been built in that part of the town.

Charities.—The charities of this church, are very few, when compared with those of Saint Mary's parish; and are contained in the following note.[2]

---

2 Thomas Beane, August 15, 1704, left the interest of £200. towards repairing the tomb and vault of Jane Boyd and Clement Buck; the overplus to be given in bread, to the poor, who do not receive alms from the parish.

Thomas Dawkes, April 17, 1705, left the interest of £50. to be distributed to the poor, in bread, on the feast of St. Thomas.

Peter Fector, esq. by will, March 3, 1806, left the interest of £100. 3 per cent. reduced annuities, to be distributed yearly, on Christmas day, among six aged persons of this parish. The widows of seamen are recommended in this bequest.

Rectors.—The Rev. William Ryall, 1484.

The Rev. William Noole, 1542.

The Rev. John Thompson, 1553. He was master of the Maison Dieu, at the time of its suppression, in 1536; and was a great benefactor to Dover harbour, by devising means for its improvement.

The Rev. William Watts, 1579. He resigned in 1606.

The Rev. John Gray, 1606. He resigned in 1608.

The Rev. Walter Richards, 1608.

The Rev. John Vaughan, 1643.

——Vincent, 1644. Supposed to have been put in by the parliament

——Davis, 1656. He was ejected in 1662.

The Rev. Thomas Swadlin, 1662. He was also vicar of Hougham, and resigned in 1664, on being presented to the rectory of Allhallows, in Stamford.

The Rev. Thomas Bostock, 1665. He resigned in 1675.

The Rev. William Brewer, 1676. He was also rector of Charlton, and vicar of Hougham.

The Rev. Michael Bull, 1700.

The Rev. Edward Hobbes, 1703.

The Rev. Thomas Tournay, 1762. He was also vicar of Hougham; and was much esteemed by his parishioners. A grave stone points out the place of his burial, in this church.

The Rev. William Tournay, D. D. who succeeded his father, in 1795. He was also vicar of Hougham, and was elected warden of Wadham college, Oxford, in 1809. On his being appointed a prebend of Westminster, and also of the cathedral church of Peterborough, he resigned his rectory at Dover, in 1818.

The Rev. Thomas Morris, 1818. He is the present rector, and also vicar of Hougham.

Dover Priory; or, Saint Martin the Less.

The foundations of this priory, as we have already noticed,[1] were laid by archbishop Corboil, in 1132. Having, in conjunction with the prior and monks of Christ Church, in Canterbury, obtained a grant, from Henry the First, of the revenues of the collegiate church of St. Martin le Grand, the archbishop erected, in the fields near Dover, this new edifice, called the New Work, St. Martin the Less, or Dover Priory.

According to the original grant, this house was to be filled with canons regular, of the order of St. Augustine only; and the prior was to be chosen from the house at Canterbury. But the archbishop was partial to the canons of Merton, with whom he secretly intended to fill the new house at Dover; and obtained a new grant from

---

[1] See Page 195.

the king, for this purpose, which allowed them to elect a prior from among themselves.

Dreading the resentment of his monks, at Canterbury, whom he intended completely to dupe, he privately sent the bishop of Norwich, the bishop of St. David's, together with his own archdeacon, and a company of Merton canons, with their goods and chattels, to Dover, to consecrate, and take possession of the new mansion.

The monks of Canterbury posted after them, vowed vengeance, and threatened to justify their right, by an appeal to the pope. The bishops, the archdeacon, and the poor canons of Merton, were all alarmed; and returned, laden with their household utensils, to lay their complaints before the archbishop, who was then in London. He flies to Canterbury; expostulates and threatens; but all to no purpose: the prize was too great to be given up. Vexation and disappointment agitate his spirits; and, in less than twelve days, he pays that debt of nature, which silences for ever the voice of discord, and places the cold seal of mortality on the furious tongue. Here might contention read an impressive lesson, and avarice shudder at the poisonous cup that stands before her; while duplicity might turn aside the polluted veil, intended to hide her distorted countenance, which will soon appear in all its ghastly deformity.

The monks of Canterbury, embracing this

opportunity, sent twelve of their brethren to take posession of Dover priory, before it was consecrated. Soon, however, the king's brother, who was bishop of Winchester, and the pope's nuncio, chastised their insolence, and obliged them to retrace their sullen steps back to Canterbury.

Theobald succeeded Corboil in the metropolitan see; and having learned prudence by the misfortunes of his predecessor, sent twelve of his monks to Dover, again to take possession of the new house, Ascelin, their sacrist, being appointed prior. Theobald having been a Benedictine, the new settlers agreed to adopt the rules of that society, in compliment to their patron; but soon after they became established here, their pride was mortified, in being obliged to receive their future priors, from their old house, at Canterbury.

This choice of a prior was a source of continual feuds between the two houses; and the revenues of Dover priory being spent in useless litigations, the society was reduced to extreme poverty.

Archbishop Baldwin regretted these disgraceful contentions; and, hoping to establish peace at the expense of justice, appointed Osborn, a member of the Dover house, to be their prior, in 1189. This was resented by the monks of Canterbury, who obtained of pope Adrian, in 1258, a confirmation of the original grant; and they resolved to oblige the poor monks of Dover, to live according to the strict rules of Saint Benedict, which their predecessors had adopted out of pure complaisance to archbishop Theobald, and which enjoined poverty, and obedience to superiors.

Anselm de Estria was elected at Canterbury, and sent to be prior, at Dover, in 1275. This rigid disciplinarian would scarcely allow them the necessaries of life; and their brethren of Canterbury had drawn so heavily on their funds, that their house was eleven hundred marks in debt. They had often petitioned the crown to relieve them; and, by command of the king, Robert de Whitacre was appointed prior, in 1289; and being one of their own members, it was hoped he would correct abuses. Still, however, their sufferings continued; and the French, as we have before noticed,[2] ravaged their house, in 1296.

Some faint rays of royal favour occasionally cheered their hopes with brighter prospects; and king Edward the Second lodged in their house, in 1307. The archbishop, who at this period seems to have acted more independently of his monks than formerly, obtained the exclusive jurisdiction of this priory, in 1320, which was confirmed to him by Edward the Third, in

---

2 See Page 123.

1330; and this king gave the profits of the port, and the tolls of the market, to Dover priory, in 1337.

The monks of Canterbury were all this time watching every opportunity, to regain their former influence; and obtained a grant of Edward the third, in 1356, to unite the priory of Dover to that of Christ Church, in Canterbury. The revenues and expenditures of each house were to remain separate; but the brethren of Canterbury, as patrons and visitors, were to supply the house at Dover, with a prior, and to furnish it with monks.

This, however, did not produce peace. The house at Dover, after this union, claimed a voice in electing an archbishop; but the house at Canterbury would not, by any means, consent to it. The house at Canterbury insisted on a right to send novices, at their pleasure, to the priory at Dover; which was resisted by the Dover monks.

After many processes, much money spent, and a final appeal to the pope, the priory of Dover was obliged to submit; and remained an appendage to that of Canterbury, till the time of its suppression in the twenty-fifth year of Henry the Eighth, 1535, when its annual income was £232. 1s. 5½d.

The commissioners were to sell effects sufficient to pay the debts of the monks; and the remainder, and all the rich valuables, were sent to the tower.

The king gave the lands, tithes, and buildings, to the famous Richard Thornton, suffragan bishop of Dover, to hold for life, or till promoted to a benefice, worth £120 a year. This promotion appears soon to have taken place, as the premises and estates were given to the archbishop, in 1537; and they still belong to the see of Canterbury.

Here again we find the famous trio who destroyed Saint Martin le Grand, and other churches; and these stately buildings became a prey to their devouring grasp. The ruins are very extensive, and are surrounded by a stone wall. The exterior walls of the refectory, which is now converted to a barn, are more than 100 feet long, and are still remaining. The gateway is nearly entire, and part of the church is yet standing. A farm house, lately rebuilt, is erected among the ruins; and the premises have many years been occupied by a respectable family of the name of Coleman.

THE MAISON DIEU.

The hospital of the Maison Dieu, or House of God, was erected by Hubert de Burgh, in the reign of king John, for the accommodation of pilgrims, passing to, or from the continent. A master, and several brethren and sisters, were placed in it, and were enjoined to use hospitality to strangers.

The house being intended to afford temporary relief, no church was erected, in the first instance, for the accommodation of the society. But two sisters, it is said, Agnes and Beatrice, gave lands and tenements, to provide a priest, who officiated for them, in a chapel within the church of St. Mary the Virgin, in the town.

The inconvenience of not having a church, adjoining the house, was supplied by king Henry the Third, on condition that the whole should be resigned to him; and he was present at the dedication of it, to St. Mary, in 1227. When Hubert resigned the patronage to the king, he reserved to the brethren the right of electing their own master.

Several lands and rents were given to this hospital by Simon de Wardune; all of which were confirmed to it by king Henry the Third, who also granted to the society, the tithes of the passage and ten pounds a year out of the profits of the port.

This hospital had large revenues arising from numerous manors, houses, mills, and other property; and was visited by several royal and noble personages.

Edward Prescot of Guston, 1482, gave, by will, to every member of this society, being a priest, three shillings and four pence; and to every novice, one shilling, to sing dirge and masses, on his obit day, month day, and twelve month day, and for all departing souls.

William Warren of St. Peter's, Dover, 1506, gave houses and lands to his son John, on condition that he paid yearly to the master and brethren of the Maison Dieu, for ever, £4 for a yearly obit.

At the time of its suppression, in the twenty-sixth year of Henry the Eighth, 1534, the clear revenue was £159. 18s. 6d. and the annual income £231. 16s. 7d.

Mr. Lyon seems to confound the church of this hospital, with that of St. John; and has copied the bequests to St. John's church, the utensils, and even the value of the living, in his account of the Maison Dieu.

The tower and body of the church, a small building at the east end, and the park wall, are still remaining. The ravages of time, and the desolating hands of Bufkin, Nethersole, and Wingefield, says Mr. Lyon, have destroyed all the rest. The windows are large and lofty, and the roof appears to have been supported without pillars. This sacred edifice was converted into a brewhouse and bakehouse; and into store rooms for wheat, flour, and biscuit: and the premises have been used, by the victualling department of the royal navy, from the time of its suppression till the peace of 1814.

On the opposite side of the road, and a little farther from the town, was a Saxon burying ground, where several swords, spears, and beads have been discovered in digging the chalk.

Saint Bartholomew's Hospital.

This hospital, intended for poor leprous persons, was built, about the year 1150, either by Osborne and Godwin, two monks of Dover, or by Theobald, archbishop of Canterbury; and was subject to the prior of Dover.

It was situated at Buckland, on a piece of land called Thega, on the western side of the present London road, and directly opposite the Wesleyan chapel. The house was dedicated to St. Bartholomew, and was intended for ten brethren and ten sisters; but the first donations being insufficient for this number, they were reduced to eight of each.

The warden was to keep an inventory of the goods in the house, and the images in the church; and to have the lamps lighted at the entrance of the chapel. A light was kept continually burning before the crucifix; and the gates of the dormitory were to be kept shut during the night.

This hospital was suppressed in 1535; and the church and buildings, says Mr. Lyon, were demolished by one John Bowle, a leading man in Dover, without any commission for this purpose; and he did his work so effectually, that he did not leave one stone upon another : the graves were plundered, and the grave stones taken up.

We are happy in being able, in some measure, to defend the conduct of this Bowle, so far as relates to his *commission*. It appears by a patent of Edward the Sixth, dated 1542, that his father, Henry the Eighth, in 1587, gave this hospital, by patent, together with all its lands and immunities, to his well-beloved John Bowle, during his natural life. After this, it reverted to the crown : and king Edward gave it, by patent, in 1542, to Sir Henry Palmer, knight, and to his heirs for ever. This patent is in the possession of William Kingsford, esq. of Buckland, who purchased the estate a short time since.

Hence it appears that this John Bowle did not act without authority ; but we cannot say that he had any greater reverence for religion, than his royal friend and sovereign. Though he could not bear the sight of an image or a crucifix, he possibly did not scruple to pay his daily devotions to that more popular idol, *Self Interest,* and bow down before her, with all the fervour of devout adoration. Do not her ten thousand temples yet remain ? do not her myriads of worshippers fall prostrate before her ? and is not the world parading in her bewitching train ? These are the idolaters who think lightly of holy things and of holy places. Their potent goddess set her destroying foot on our sacred edifices,

and they crumbled into ruins; while *her* temples
are found at the corner of every street; at
the portals of every house; and this facinating
idolatry covers the earth.

How narrow is the boundary between superstition and rational devotion; and how difficult
to discern the idol of our adoration. The images
of our forefathers, if worshipped, were certainly
abominations; and their rites and ceremonies
were gross and corrupt: but whatever we place
in competition with the great Creator, and pursue
as our chief good, becomes the idol of our choice.
Some fondly worship the riches, the pleasures,
or the vanities of life: some, the passions or
affections of the heart; and some, the golden
image in the likeness of man or beast. The
man who bows down to his wooden idol laughs at
the senseless phrensy of worshipping perishable
riches, or transient pleasures; and the devotee
of vanity, mocks at the stupidity of adoration to
lifeless idols. But neither can see his own folly;
and both, perhaps, are shocked at the ridiculous
mummeries formerly practised in these venerable
structures. So strange is the infatuation of
the human heart, that even the riches of these
religious establishments, were plundered to supply coffers, wasted by offerings daily devoted to
the goddess of licentious pleasures: and, in the
present instance, a few poor lepers were sacrificed
at the shrine of avarice and rapacity.

The society had a grant of holding, within the limits of their hospital, a fair, which has been continued to the present time, and is kept on St. Bartholomew's day.   Most of the ground on which the hospital was situated, is now sold for building on, and is nearly covered with houses.

LANGDON ABBEY.

This abbey is about four miles from Dover, on the north-west side of the Deal road; and originally belonged to the convent of St. Augustine, in Canterbury.   The abbey was founded about the year 1087, by Sir William Auberville; and was filled with canons of the Præmonstratensian order.

One Harebert, a brother of the society, about the year 1097, recovered five mansions, which William Peverel had unjustly extorted from them; and Hugo, the abbot, in 1110, recovered the lands, at Langdon, from Manasses Arsic, and others.

They obtained the king's licence, in 1288, to purchase lands; and defended their liberties, before the justices itinerent, in 1313.   King Edward the Second was residing at the abbey, in 1325; and their manors were confirmed to them, in 1336, by Edward the Third.   A further confirmation was also obtained from Henry the Sixth, subsequent to the year 1422.

But little delicacy was shown by the commissioners of Henry the Eighth, when sent to examine this abbey. They entered the house, at midnight, by violence, broke into the abbot's chamber, and accused him of keeping a mistress.

When this monastery was suppressed, in 1538, the gross annual revenue was £56. 6s. 9d. The manor was given to the archbishop, who soon returned it to the crown; and the king then gave the fee of it to John Master, who died at Langdon court, in 1588. James Master, who died at Langdon in 1631, aged eighty-four years, rebuilt the mansion; and his son, Sir Edward Master, kept his shrievalty here, in 1639.

The site of the ancient abbey, some of the ruins whereof still remain, is occupied by a farm house, called the abbey farm. The cellar of the monks, which is nearly entire at the present day, is curiously arched over.

SAINT RADIGUND'S ABBEY.

About three miles south-westward of Dover, on the high ground, are the remains of Saint Radigund's, or Bradsole abbey, which, about the year 1190, was founded for Præmonstratensian canons; but by whom is rather uncertain, though that honor has generally been given to Jeffery, earl of Perch, and Maud his wife. Its first endowments appear to have been splendid; and its revenues having been increased by several benefactors, it was of sufficient importance, in the latter part of the reign of Edward the First, for its abbots to have summons to parliament.

King Edward the Second visited this abbey, and transacted business here, in the thirteenth year of his reign, 1319.

In a manuscript visitation of this order, it is recorded that the abbey was in a very ruinous condition, in 1500, and deficient in the number of its inmates, the abbot having wasted the income of his house on licentious pleasures. When Leland visited this monastery, a short time before its dissolution, the dilapidations had been repaired. The choir of the church, he says, was large and fair; but the whole had declined from its ancient magnificence. At the time of its suppression by Henry the Eighth, in 1535, the annual income was £142. 8s. 9d. and the clear yearly receipts £98. 9s. 2½d.

Among many others who were buried in this sequestered spot, were several of the Criols, lords of Westhanger; William Malmayns, in 1223; Henry Malmayns, in 1274, both lords of Waldershare; Thomas, lord Poynings, in the midst of the choir, before the high altar, in 1375; and John Kyryel of Lympe, in the high chancel, in 1504. He gave £6. 13s. 4d. for licence of sepulture, and to eight priests 20d. each, to bring his body from Bellavowe to St. Radigund's.

John Byngham, of the parish of St. John the Baptist, in Dover, in 1513, gave, by will, 3s. 4d.

to the chapel of our Lady of St. Radigund's; and Elizabeth Wood, in 1523, gave half a sheet, to cover the altar of our Lady.

After the suppression of this abbey, it was given to the archbishop, who, in the course of a short time, returned it to the king. In 1537, his majesty let the premises and estate, which contained about 444 acres, to Richard Keys of Folkstone, at the yearly rent of £13. 10s. 4d. The fee was then given to Thomas Cromwell, afterwards earl of Essex; and, on his attainder in 1530, it again reverted to the crown. In the reign of Philip and Mary, it was given to Edward, lord Clinton and Saye, who, in the reign of Elizabeth, sold it to Simon Edolph, esq. who repaired the mansion, and resided here. He died in 1597, and was succeeded by his son, Sir Thomas Edolph, knt. who died at St. Radigund's in 1645. After passing through the families of the Chandlers and Cavendishes, it descended, by entailment to the Sayers of Charing, in whose possession it still remains.

The whole precinct of this abbey appears to have been surrounded by a broad ditch and rampart, enclosing an extensive area; and the walls of the out-buildings, gardens, &c. occupy a considerable extent of ground. The walls of the entrance gateway, which are of great strength and thickness, are nearly entire, and are finely mantled with ivy, as well as most other parts of

the ruins. This entrance opens by a large arch
in the centre, now underset with brick, and has
also a small arch adjoining for foot passengers;
and five lozenges, with a rose in chief, are
sculptured on the key stone.

The north and west sides of the chapel, and the
walls of the canons' dwellings, formerly part of
the mansion occupied by the Edolphs, and now
patched up as a farm house, are still standing.
The chapel had a projecting porch in the centre:
but this now forms the end of the building. That
portion of the front which adjoins to it, is
curiously chequered with flints and stones; but
the chief part of the ruins are of flint, coined
with free stone. The barn and offices in the
farm yard, have some of the arched door-ways,
still remaining in their original state.

Beneath the parlour of the farm house, are
said to be subterranean passages extending to a
considerable distance. In the farm yard is a
large broad pond, which is said to have been
anciently of much greater extent, and to have
given the name of *Broad-sole*, (corrupted into
Bradsole,) to this manor and abbey; the word
sole, or *soale*, being a Kentish provincialism for
a pond.

KNIGHTS TEMPLARS.

This society had a house, or grange, at Ewell,
about three miles from Dover, on the north side

of the London road. The house was built about the year 1185; and was given to the Knights Hospitallers, when the order of Templars was dissolved, in 1312. This structure was situated about eighty rods from what is now called the temple farm, but the last ruins were destroyed in 1760.

At Swingfield, about six miles from Dover, this society had a famous preceptory, which was founded before the year 1190; but by whom is not known. At the suppression of the Templars, it was given to the Knights Hospitallers, whose arms, and other insignia, still remain carved on the front of the present farm house, which is a remnant of the ancient building.

The eastern and oldest part was the chapel; and the east wall still exhibits three very early lance windows, with the same number of circular ones above them. In the western part, which has been altered into a different style, are two apartments, with fire places, similarly ornamented on the stone work, with sculptures of shields, charged with an anchor, and with the cross of the Knights of Malta. The same arms appear on a brick chimney, on the south side, together with the cross of St. George. Remains of foundations, to a considerable extent, may be traced in different parts of the farm yard. At the

dissolution of the house, in 1540, the clear annual
value was £87. 3s. 3½d. and the total annual
income £111. 12s. 8d.

Our more ancient historians of this county,
such as Lambarde, Kilburn, and Harris, affirm
possitively that the Knights Templars had a
house at Dover; and our more general historians
inform us that king John resigned his crown to
Pandulf, the pope's legate, in a house of the
Templars, at this place, the disgraceful deed
itself being dated, "*Apud domum militum Templi juxta Doveram.*

Honest Lambarde says that the house of the
Templars was not far from the Roman pharos,
or Bredenstone, the site of which is now occupied
by a grand redoubt, situated on the heights, just
above the town.   Kilburn and Harris have supposed that this structure was either in, or near
Archcliff fort.

In the face of these authorities, and not being
able to find the ruins, some later writers have
doubted, and others positively denied, the existence of such a building, at Dover, and have
persuaded themselves that no edifice of the kind
was ever erected here. To reconcile their assertions with the disgraceful farce of king John's
humiliation, some, following the error of Rapin,
suppose it might have taken place in St. Mary's

church, or in the Maison Dieu; while others go as far as Temple Ewell, or even to Swingfield, to find the polluted spot. The Templars had certainly nothing to do with St. Mary's church or the Maison Dieu, and their houses at Ewell and Swingfield, were at a considerable distance from Dover.

A discovery made on Dover heights, in the year 1806, seems calculated to reconcile this long train of doubt and contradiction. The engineer labourers, in constructing a new road, laid open the foundations of a very ancient stone edifice, which had been covered for ages under an accumulation of soil.[1] These foundations consist of a circular part whose extreme diameter is thirty-two feet, and a square vestibule, on the east side of it, which measures twenty-four feet by twenty. The walls of the circular part, which were four or five feet high when cleared from the earth that had covered them, were thirty inches thick, and were ornamented with pilasters and niches, and the whole interior was coated with a white cement.

These ruins are situated opposite Archcliff fort, above the military hospital, on the highest ridge of the hill, as it declines towards the east, and not far, as Lambarde says, from the Roman

---

[1] Our attention was particularly directed to these ruins by Mr. John Mummery of Dover, whose researches respecting them, have greatly assisted us.

pharos. Though the ruins are by no means striking, as to their magnitude, the erection appears to have been a small elegant structure; and, from concurring testimonies and the locality of the place, we are induced to consider this to be the fatal spot, where, more than six hundred years since, our degraded and unfortunate monarch signed the disgraceful deed, that tarnished the brighter pages of British history.[2]

It is impossible to say how long these ruins might have lain concealed under the surface; and others, still more extensive, may yet lay buried not far from them. In fact, another foundation, eighty feet long and thirty-six broad, and discovered at the same time, does exist about thirty feet to the east of them; but, as the materials are mostly brick, we conceive they are of a much later date.

It is a curious fact that the church of the Templars, in London, called the Temple Church, is a round building, similar to this on Dover heights. There are three other churches of this description, in England, all of which, it is supposed, belonged to the Knights Templars, a part of whose duty obliged them to defend the holy sepulchre, at Jerusalem, which is a circular structure, and these churches appear to have been built in imitation of it.

---

[2] We have mentioned this transaction in pages 82 and 83.

Our Lady of Pity's Chapel.

This small chapel was situated on the sea shore, to the eastward of Archcliff fort, and was built by a northern nobleman, on the spot, as tradition reports, where he had been shipwrecked. It was dedicated to St. Mary: but when erected is not known.

At the time of its suppression, about the year 1536, the sacred vessels, and gold-embroidered vestments were valued at two hundred marks, and were taken for the king's use. On a stone over the door, were the arms of England empaling those of France; and, on another stone, near the stairs, the date of MDXXX, with a rose and crown.

After the chapel had lost its furniture, it was taken for an habitation by a poor fisherman; but, in time, the sea laid claim to its shattered remains. It was totally washed down, during a tempestuous gale, in 1576; but the place is still called The Chapel, or Chapel Plain.

The General Baptists' Chapel.

In the midst of the fatal contests between king Charles the First and his parliament; and at a time when the blood of thousands, shed by the sword of civil discord, stained the glory of our beloved country, the Baptists were first introduced into this county. A century before this period, the ancient structures that adorned our island, had been thrown down and destroyed by the hand of violence; and during the century that followed, the established church had worn the garments of prosperity and gladness. But she was now fallen, and sitting in the shade of adversity. Her ministers were driven from her places of public worship, and her revenues had passed into other hands. Had she forgotten to adorn herself with the robe of humility? or had she forborn to extend that forbearance and compassion towards others which now, in her evil day, she would have implored on her own behalf? We lament her fall; and may the salutary lesson it should inculcate, remain fresh in her own memory, and prove a lasting warning to others.

In the year 1643, the Baptist missionaries, who had previously settled in London, came into the county of Kent; and Anne Stevens of Canterbury received them into her house. She became a convert, and was the first, in these parts, who, at their hands, received the rite of water baptism by immersion. Several were baptized about the same time;[1] among whom were Nicholas Woodman of Canterbury, and Luke Howard and Mark Elfreth, both of Dover; and these three were teachers from among their new converts. Woodman married a respectable widow of Dover, whose name was Katharine Brown; and Howard, who afterwards left the

---

[1] Some of these early converts went to London, to be baptized by William Kiffin, who resided at Redriffe.

Baptists to join the Friends, married Anne Stevens of Canterbury, whom we have just before mentioned.

At first, they held the doctrine of particular election and reprobation; but the whole of the converts in this county, Daniel Coxe of Canterbury excepted, soon changed their opinion, and adopted the faith of a general redemption: and some of them were re-baptized into this faith.

Mr. Richard Hobbs[1] was their pastor in 1643; and it is certain that they had a meeting house at Dover in 1655, at which time Mr. John Feetness was a co-pastor. Mr. Edward Prescot, of Guston, was also a co-pastor with Mr. Hobbs about the same time; but it does not appear how

---

1 Mr. Hobbs suffered much on account of his religious sentiments. During his imprisonment, his rectitude procured him the liberty of occasionally leaving the place of his confinement, except on the Lord's day. But, on his writing to Doctor Hinde, the minister of St. Mary's church, the Doctor, instead of answering his letter, seems to have made, in the true spirit of the times, such representations to the magistrates, that they sent for the gaoler in a rage, and commanded him to fetch Mr. Hobbs from his house, to which he had been allowed to retire, and gave positive orders that no farther indulgence should be given. This drew from the unfortunate prisoner the following remarkable appeal. " Now consider, says he, how like are these proceedings to those practiced at the court of Rome, where, if a person do but question the truth of their religion, he will soon feel the tortures of the inquisition; and doubtless, added he, these proceedings savour more the spirit of the pope's anathemas, than the mild and gentle spirit of Christianity."

R

long their place of worship had been established here prior to that period.

The congregation were driven from their meeting house in 1661, and a lock placed on the door, by order of the mayor; but it was taken off during the night, and thrown into a porch before the mayor's house. After this, they assembled secretly in their private houses; and some of their members were imprisoned in Dover castle, on account of their nonconformity.

Mr. Prescot was instrumental in converting Captain Samuel Tavenor. Prescot was preaching in a field; and Tavenor, at that time governor of Deal castle, was led by curiosity, to conceal himself behind a hedge. In this singular situation, the truth of Mr. Prescot's doctrine so powerfully convinced his understanding, that he became a convert to the Baptists' faith, into which he was baptized, by immersion, in1663 .[2]

It does not appear how long these three ministers held the pastoral office, in conjunction with each other; but Hobbs had a controversy with Luke Howard, in 1672, which will be mentioned

---

2 Mr. Tavenor was born at Rumford, in Essex, in 1621, and was made a captain of a troop of horse, in 1643. He received a commission from Oliver Cromwell, in 1653, and was appointed governor of Deal castle. His duty frequently required his attendance at Dover castle, where he was occasionally stationed. He was baptized, as before related, in 1663, and resigned his commission, in 1665.

in our account of the Friends : and Mr. Tavenor was ordained pastor, in 1681.

At this period the congregation was become numerous, and many resided in the neighbouring towns and villages. To meet their convenience, it was agreed to separate into three divisions, and elders were to be chosen by each of these churches. Samuel Tavenor and Richard Cannon were chosen by the church, at Dover ; Henry Brown and Isaac Slaughter, by the church, at Sandwich and Deal; and Messrs. Author and Hadlow, by the church, at Folkstone and Hythe. Unnited meetings of these separate congregations, were annually held, at Dover, on the first Sunday in May, during a period of fifty-three years.

Mr. Tavenor suffered much on account of his nonconformity; and was not only frequently taken from the meeting house, while preaching, and had before the magistrates ; but, in several instances, was harassed by warrants to take away his goods. He was once imprisoned ; but, having interest at court, he soon obtained his release. After this he departed to London, where he continued to preach, as often and as publicly as the times would admit, till he could again return to his flock, at Dover.

The Baptists were so cruelly persecuted, at this place, in 1686, that they could not assemble for public worship, without danger of imprisonment or prosecution; and they mutually agreed, that if any person should suffer loss, on account of their meetings, which appear at that time to have been held in their private houses, the other members would bear their equal proportion, to retrieve such damages.[3]

Mr. Tavenor licenced the south end of his dwelling house, for a place of public worship, in 1692; the licence being signed in that year, by Thomas Beddingfield, town clerk of Dover. It cannot be discovered what places of worship they might have had before this period, when free from the lash of persecution. When that cruel scourge was held over them, they were obliged secretly to hold their meetings in sequestered places, or in their private houses.

At the same time that Mr. Tavenor licenced a part of his dwelling house, he let to the congregation, on a renewable lease, the piece of ground adjoining St. Martin's church yard, for a place of burial; and his own remains were deposited here in 1696.[4] In our account of St. Martin's church, we have supposed that this piece of ground might have formed a part of the

---

3 This agreement is signed by the following persons, viz. Samuel Tavenor, Richard Cannon, William Mellon, John Simpson, Richard Marsh, Cornelius Garrison, Henry Hobbs, Thomas Neales, Thomas Stokes, and Henry Spillett.

4 He died on the 4th of August, 1696, aged 75 years, as inscribed on his tomb stone.

church yard; but it appears to have been a
garden prior to the time when Mr. Tavenor let
it to the congregation, and it probably might
never belong to St. Martin's premises.[5]

After the death of Mr. Tavenor, and of his
co-pastors, Richard Cannon and Thomas Partridge, Messrs. John and David Simpson were
ordained co-pastors about the year 1712. Mr.
David Simpson, at his death, gave £100, in
trust, to Edward Prescott of Guston, and to his
son, John Prescott, for the use of the minister,
or the poor, at the discretion of the trustees;
and, in 1723, (supposed to have been the following year,) several members of the society
subscribed £100 for the same purpose, and put
it into the hands of the trustees.

The Simpsons were succeeded by Mr. Robert
Pyall, who was ordained November 20th, 1732,
having previously been a minister in the society
six years. During Mr. Pyall's ministry, Mr.
Prescott, a relative of the former pastor of that
name, by will, bequeathed £70 for the use of
the congregation; and this sum was appropriated,
in 1745, to purchase premises for a chapel, which
was erected on, or near the site of the meeting
house, which Mr. Tavenor had licenced for a
place of worship, forty-seven years before this
period.

Mr. Pyall died in 1759; and no other pastor

---

appears to have been appointed till Mr. William Ashdown and Mr. Stephen Philpott were ordained co-pastors, October the 30th, 1781. Mr. Philpott left this society, in 1789, to take charge of another, in connexion with it, at Saffron Walden, in Essex, and Mr. James Porter was ordained pastor, June 12th, 1792. He was expelled March 14th, 1794, and Mr. Ashdown resigned July 5th, 1795; but continued in communion with the society till the time of his decease, in 1810.[6]

Though Mr. Benjamin Marten had officiated as minister, both before and after Mr. Ashdown's resignation, he did not accept of the pastoral charge till August 21st, 1800.

A Sunday school, the first of the kind in Dover, was instituted in 1803, by a female member of this congregation, who is the lineal heiress of Mr. Tavenor. She took the sole management of the school on herself, during several years; but has lately been assisted by the juvenile members of the society.

The foundation stone of a new and elegant chapel, designed by Mr. Thomas Read, was laid, on the 15th of February, 1819, by Mr. Sampson Kingsford, elder of the Baptists' church at Canterbury, who delivered an appropriate discourse

---

[6] We have mentioned Mr. Ashdown in page 203. In addition to his Treatise on the Scriptural Meaning of the word *Satan*, he wrote a Key to the Evangelists and the Epistles of the New Testament.

on the occasion.   This chapel, which is situated above the Fivepost-lane, leading from Snargate-street, was opened for public worship on the 2nd of May, 1820.   Several vaults, with entrances from the adjoining cemetery, were constructed in the basement ; and some remains were removed from the old burying ground, and interred in this new place of sepulture.

Mr. Marten's long and zealous ministry was drawing to a close ; and only three years were allowed him to officiate in this new structure. Afflicted by one of the most painful maladies to which our fragile frames are subject, he sought relief in London ; but exhausted nature sunk under the weight of a severe, but necessary operation ; and he died in that metropolis on the 14th of November, 1823, aged fifty-four years. He was generally esteemed, not only by the society, but by all who knew him ; and his remains were deposited in the new chapel, at Dover, where an appropriate monument has been. erected to his memory.

Mr. George C. Pound, after officiating as a minister of this society fourteen years, was chosen pastor on the demise of Mr. Marten ; and is assisted in his charge, by Mr. John Marten, son of the late pastor.   The present deacons are Messrs. John Igglesden, John Marsh, John Tilly, and William Kingsford, esq.

Of late years, most of the members appear to

have embraced the Unitarian doctrine; but we are informed that this does not affect the denomination, as General Baptists. Their Sunday school consists, at present, of about 120 children.

THE FRIENDS' CHAPEL.

These people made their first appearance, at Dover, during the time that Oliver Cromwell held the reins of government. At this period, the hierarchy was prostrate in the dust; the parish churches were filled by ministers of various denominations; the different sects of Christians were at strife with each other; and the flames of persecution raged between them.

During these commotions, and in the year 1655, two of the friends, whose names were W. Caton and J. Stubbs, came to Dover. As was their usual custom, they visited the several places of worship, and embraced every opportunity to instruct the people.

On the following Sunday morning, they attended at the two parish churches, which were then in the hands of the Presbyterians and the Independents, and endeavoured to address the people; but were not allowed to proceed. They succeeded better in the church yards; and Luke Howard,[1] whom we have already mentioned in

---

[1] It may be interesting to our readers to peruse a short account of this man's life prior to this period. He was born at

our account of the Baptists, defended Caton from the violence of rude boys, and a furious rabble.

Dover in 1621; and, during his childhood, was thoughtful and attentive. His father-in-law was a butcher, and it was intended he should follow that business; but he disliked such a cruel trade, and was bound apprentice to a shoemaker, in 1635. His master admired him for his diligence and attention; and Howard was no less delighted with the kindness and pious conduct of his master. Five weeks after his apprenticeship he went to London, to obtain employment, at which time the parliament were erecting forts around the city, and raising a troop of cavalry to oppose the king. He took a horse to join them; but the volunteers were so numerous, that he was thrown out by casting lots. We are sorry to find that he drew his sword against his sovereign; but this kind of enthusiasm was prevalent in those days, and many of riper years than young Howard, were led away by the same spirit of revolt.

Hearing that they were raising a troop of horse at Dover, he hastened back to his native place, to join them; but here the volunteers were also in such numbers, that he was rejected. Thus disappointed, he and several young men of the town entered themselves as volunteers to defend Dover Castle; and during this period he spent much of his time in reading the Scriptures. He became convinced that singing psalms was improper, and a mockery to the Deity; and while others joined in this devotion at the castle, he sat silent. The minister observed his conduct; and his late master with whom he had served his apprenticeship, sent for the learned Samuel Fisher, minister of Lidd, to reason with him. So far from convincing him, Fisher, who afterwards joined the Baptists, and then the Friends, became of the same opinion, and would no more sing psalms in his church of Lidd.

Howard, after this, felt a disquietude in his mind, and consulted the Brownists, Independents, Presbyterians, and Baptists, into whose faith he was baptized in 1643, as related in

In the afternoon they attended the service of the Independents, in the castle, and the Baptists' meeting, in the town; and, in the evening, Howard found them at an inn, eating bread, with a small refreshment of beer. He took them to the Baptist minister, who assembled his neighbours; and a meeting was appointed to be held on the next day, at their place of worship. Baptists, Independents, Brownists, and the small remaining number of Episcopalians, attended. The Friends delivered their testimony; and all, with one voice, pronounced them deceivers: and they departed to the inn, followed by a multitude, whom curiosity had drawn together. The mayor sent to the innkeeper, commanding him to turn them out; and threatened, in case of refusal,

---

our account of that people. Finding himself still unhappy, he gave himself up to gaiety and diversion, which only increased his sorrow. In March, 1655, he went to London on business, and heard W. Caton preach in Lombard-street; but carelessly turned from him. He returned to Dover; and, on the following Sunday, he was informed that a quaker was preaching in the church-yard. Curiosity led him to the spot; and he was astonished to see the same young man whom he had disregarded on the preceding sabbath.

We refer to our history for a subsequent part of his life. He appears, from the testimony of many, to have been remarkable for his honesty, industry, and sobriety; and for his ready disposition to do good, either to his friends, or to those who cruelly oppressed or persecuted him. His death was tranquil and composed; and he yielded up his breath without a struggle in the seventy-eighth year of his age.

to take down his sign. Howard stepped forward, offering his assistance; and fearlessly took them to his residence. They continued with him till the following Thursday, when a numerous meeting took place at his house; and, at this time, he became a proselyte to their doctrine.

On Saturday, the corporation sent four constables to take them away by force, and to conduct them out of the town. Howard refused to give them up, relying on his right as an Englishman and as a freeman of the town; and the doors being shut, he kept the constables out, and sent them back to the magistrates. A court was convened, and Howard cited before it. He asked the magistrates if they had received any hue and cry after the two preachers? On their answering in the negative, he told them that the strangers were his friends; and, as they had not committed any crime, or used violence, he was certain that the magistrates could have no more right to molest his friends or his house, than he had to molest their friends or their houses. Such an answer disconcerted their measures; and they were content to receive a promise from Howard, that his friends should not attend the parish churches on the next day.

On Sunday, another large meeting was held at Howard's house; and, in the evening, he accompanied his two friends, three miles out of the town, towards Folkstone, and then returned.

The Friends proceeded to Maidstone, where they were put in the Bridewell, confined three days without food, and were afterwards cruelly whipped by order of one Lambert Godfrey, for declaring their testimony. When taken from prison, the constables separated them, and they were conducted, in opposite directions, out of the town; but they returned again, and proclaimed their doctrine in the streets. From Maidstone they returned to Dover, where they abode a few days.

After their departure, Howard and Daniel Beane, who was a custom house officer, provided a meeting house for the society; and it probably was the same which was afterwards used by them, and which is still remaining at the lower part of St. James's-street, opposite the stone masons' yard.

The Baptists were jealous of these new brethren; and, towards the close of the year 1655, the pastor of that elder society, J. Feetness, said he had a word from the Lord to speak to them. By these means he gained admission, for himself and flock, to the Friends' meeting house; but, contrary to expectation, this word of the Lord was a sermon from the text, "Try the spirits." But Howard put such difficult questions to Feetness, and to his father in law, Joseph Templeman, that they could not readily answer them; and Templeman afterwards joined the society of Friends, and became a minister among them.

After this, the Friends continued to frequent their meeting house, and adopted the plain deportment of the society, both in speech and dress. This was a new thing at Dover; and Howard says, "That he became a mock to the drunkard, and a taunt to fools, as he passed through the streets." He was sometimes moved to attend the churches, and to reprove the ministers; and, in one instance, he was taken from St. Mary's church by force, and the doors were shut to prevent him from returning. He also reproved the errors of the priests, and the licentiousness of the people, when opportunity offered in the town. Sometimes they received him with kindness and respect; and sometimes he was cruelly treated, and his clothes torn from his back, by the infuriated mob.

Before the beginning of the year 1666, Howard converted one of Cromwell's state prisoners, lieutenant colonel Lilburn, who was confined in the old dilapidated tower, just without king's gate and bridge, and which forms an entrance into the Saxon fortifications, in Dover castle.

On the 10th of February, 1659, he attended St. Mary's church to hear Mr. Barrow preach; and published a list of errors, which he had discovered in his sermon.

The Friends purchased their burying ground, adjoining Woolcomber-street, in 1660. It had previously been a garden, which was bought for

£15. 8*s*. 6*d*. and the wall cost £5. Some of the members belonging to the society continue to bury their dead in this ground at the present day.

During the first three years after the king was restored, in 1660, several of the Friends[2] were imprisoned in Peverell or Marshal's Tower, where the marshal usually confined his prisoners in Dover castle; but the name, at that time, appears to have been Bell Tower. The place of their confinement was a narrow filthy hole, without either beds[3] or a fire-place; and their friends, for six months at a time, have been debarred from coming near them. Their refusing to take an oath, to bear arms, and to refrain from their religious meetings, subjected them to this severe treatment.

At one time Howard was taken from his shop, and confined sixteen months; in consequence of which, he was obliged to discharge his six men and a boy, and his wife was reduced to the necessity of selling milk to support the family. His warnings from the Lord, written on behalf of himself and his fellow prisoners, from his bed of chaff and straw, in Dover castle, to the mayor,

---

[2] Among them were Luke Howard, Thomas Tunbridge, John Harrison, Thomas Coull, John Edwards, Laurence Knott, and John Hogben.

[3] They offered eight pence a night for two beds, and requested that their friends might be allowed to approach the gratings of their prison, but both these favors were refused.

to the town clerk, to the rulers of Dover, to the inhabitants, and several individuals, breathe a spirit of frankness and resignation ; and though they denounce the heavy judgments that must be visited on cruelty and oppression, they express, at the same time, a tender regard for those who persecuted them. And yet the antipathy against these people was carried· to a strange excess of severity.

Two quakers and a thief were brought before the mayor at the same time ; and he committed the quakers, but, because he was going to church, he could not find time to commit the thief. When the wives and children of the prisoners surrounded the court hall, soliciting the release of their husbands and fathers, the women were admitted and severely rebuked by J. Golder, the mayor, and by J. Slowman, who was marshal of Dover castle.

The only indulgence they could obtain, was permission to approach the gratings, where their husbands and fathers were confined; and to supply them with such trifles, as their extreme poverty could afford. These scanty refreshments were drawn up to the gratings with a string; but the marshal was offended, and additional iron bars were put on these gratings, and so close, that the light and air were almost excluded.

Under such an accumulation of sufferings, and deprived of every earthly comfort, they appealed to all who knew them, to produce a charge of any crime, or defect in their moral conduct; and their expressions of inward peace, joy, and consolation, are striking and impressive. One would suppose that their apologies[4] had been written by men who reposed on beds of roses, and not on beds of straw; and that they were surrounded by the sunshine of prosperity, and not by the horrors of so doleful a prison.

A sharp controversy took place in 1672, between Howard and Richard Hobbs, pastor of the Baptists, respecting some unfortunate members of each society, who had done credit neither to themselves, nor to the party to whom they belonged. Hobbs wrote a narrative to accuse the Friends; and Howard wrote, in reply, his Looking Glass for the Baptists, and his Seat of the Scorner thrown down; and some hard names passed between them. But although controversy ran high in those days, we are ready to hope, that both were actuated by a love of truth; and although their differences might continue till the end of their pilgrimage, they were certainly then ready to lay them down, and to enter, like fellow worshippers, into the temple of their everlasting peace.

---

4 These apologies or warnings, were written to the rulers of Dover; to the inhabitants of Dover; to John Golder, the mayor; to William Stoaks, a ruler of Dover; to John Pepper, town-clerk; to Robert Wickenden; to John Matson; to Elizabeth Vincent, the governor's wife; and to William Pepper.

In 1684, Howard, who was then three score years of age, and some others, were committed to Dover castle, for refusing to take an oath; and their confinement continued fifty-one weeks. Their apologies at this time, are written in terms of kindness and friendship towards those to whom they are addressed.[5]

During this imprisonment, two men, Fosten and Bayly, at midnight, took down the wall of the Friends' burying ground, adjoining Wool-comber-street. Howard, and two of his fellow prisoners, E. Coxere and J. Ginion, wrote to Thomas Stratford, town clerk, on the subject. He received their letter very kindly, and candidly confessed, that Abraham Jacob, who then resided in the mansion that was afterwards taken down and rebuilt, and is now occupied by Mrs. Rice, had given him two half crowns, to give to Fosten and Bayly, to take down the wall, that he might have a coach road through the premises. The prisoners then wrote to A. Jacob, reminding him of Naboth's vineyard, and requesting that he would rebuild the wall; but it should seem that he refused; and it cost the Friends £9. 7s. 6d. to erect a new enclosure, to secure the bodies of their deceased relatives.

On Christmas day, 1685, the Friends, as usual,

---

[5] These apologies were written to their neighbours, in Dover; to Thomas Tiddeman, mayor, and to the jurats; to Edward Roberts, jurat; to Robert Jacob, jurat; and to T. Russel, town-clerk.

S

took down their shutters; and the mayor, Robert Jacob, sent the constables, who not only put them up again, but wantonly secured them with long nails. Four of the Friends[6] were also sent to the prison, over Butchery-gate,[7] and confined till the evening. During their imprisonment, they wrote an exposition on Christmas day, and sent it to the mayor, who received it very kindly, and was deeply impressed by its mild forbearance, and by the weighty truths which it contained.

From this period, the persecutions against these people have been comparatively small; and they have been at liberty to worship according to the dictates of their conscience. May they and future generations, for ever enjoy this inestimable blessing.

About thirty years since, they left their former meeting house in St. James's-street, and erected a commodious chapel, in Queen-street. This chapel has also an adjoining burying ground, and a high wall surrounds the premises.

All unpleasant feelings towards these people, have happily subsided; and they now hold an equal and respectable rank, in society. Many of them are resident here; and several of the Friends visit Dover during the summer season.

---

6 Luke Howard, William Robinson, Edward Warry, and Thomas Chapin.

7 See page 149.

Zion Chapel, *(Last Lane.)*

Soon after the restoration of king Charles the Second, (which, in the course of two years, was followed by the Bartholomew act, passed in 1662,) the Presbyterians and Independents were, in their turn, driven from the parish churches, and the Episcopalians once more obtained the ascendency.

The Rev. John Davis, who was a Presbyterian, and who seems to have been a favourite preacher, was, at this time, ejected from St. James's church, Dover; but whether his immediate followers were dispersed, or whether they had, during the next forty years, any stated place of public worship, or were obliged, as was usual in those times, to assemble in secret, does not appear.

But in the year 1703, a spot of ground in Last Lane, on part of which stood a malt house, was purchased by Philip Papillon, esq. M. P. for the use of a Presbyterian congregation. In 1758, his son, David Papillon, esq. added greatly to his father's bounty, by remitting both the principal and the interest of the debt, owing to his family by the congregation.

It is stated in a document, dated Dover, July the 4th, 1706, that the congregation in Last Lane meeting house, (since called Zion Chapel,) was brought into regular order and discipline, at that time; and about eighty persons are named as " Members of a church, meeting now at Dover

" aforesaid, and gathered by the blessing of God,
" by the ministry of Samuel Pryce.—James Holes
" and Michael Russel, elders." [1]

Mr. Pryce was succeeded, in 1710, by the
Rev. John Bellingsly, who remained with them
upwards of twenty years; and was successively
followed by the Rev. James Worsfold and
D. W. Evans.

The Rev. Richard Holt, who united the profession of schoolmaster with the ministerial office,
took the pastoral charge in 1745; and, from the
testimony of respectable individuals, yet living,
who were his pupils, appears to have been a
learned and an excellent man: he died in 1769,
and was buried under the pulpit, from which he
had preached twenty-four years.   Mr. Holt's
death is said to have been hastened by the
general defection of the more opulent members
of his congregation, who, during the latter years
of his ministry, had conformed to the established
church.

The congregation being thus diminished, the
place was shut up till the year 1771.   At this
time, a few individuals who were attached to the
doctrines so long preached by their late pastor,
despairing of being able to support a successor,
sent a deputation to Margate, to invite the
preachers in the countess of Huntingdon's connexion, to pay them a visit.

---

[1] Church Book.

This request was complied with; and on the following Sunday Mr. William Aldridge, accompanied by Mr. Joseph Cook, arrived. The invitation sent to them had not, we conclude, proceeded officially from the trustees; since it appears that when they came, permission had not been obtained for them to make use of the chapel; and this may be the cause of their attempting to preach in the market place, from a chair supplied out of a neighbouring shop.

The people who were returning from St. Mary's church, were attracted by the novelty, and a large concourse assembled. Among these were several who shewed their hostility to the preacher and his companion, by an attack with every kind of missile they could procure. In the mean time leave had been obtained for the use of the deserted meeting house. Mr. Aldridge, therefore, prudently desisted, and concluded by requesting the attendance of his auditory, at the Presbyterian chapel in the evening.

At the time appointed the place was crowded to excess; and the preacher resumed his subject with all the energetic eloquence that characterized his style of address. Nor were his arguments without effect; for it appears, that some "Who came to mock remained to pray:" among whom were the ringleaders of the mob, who a few hours before had so furiously assaulted him.   One of them subsequently became the minister of a dissenting congregation; and died much respected, after continuing his office upwards of thirty years.

An arrangement was soon entered into with the trustees, who agreed to give possession for a term of seven years, on condition that ten pounds should be laid out annually in repairs, which were then much needed. This sum being found inadequate to insure the safety of the building, it was determined, in 1786, to rebuild it, with the exception of the north wall, at an expense of £500; and the surviving trustees, now reduced to two, testified their approbation by executing a new trust deed, and thereby secured quiet possession to the congregation, but still retained their own rights as trustees.

As the itinerary plan of the countess did not admit of a permanent residence for the preachers, the chapel was supplied by various ministers in succession till the year 1802, when the Rev. William Mather, who had just completed his term of study at her ladyship's college, at Cheshunt, received a general invitation from the members of this chapel; and having obtained the consent of the connexion, was appointed pastor of the congregation towards the end of that year.

It was discovered in 1814, that the chapel had been erected on an insecure foundation, and it was again resolved to rebuild the edifice in a substantial manner; and to erect two additional galleries for the accommodation of the increasing congregation. It is now sufficiently large to contain five hundred persons; and has a vestry and a house for the minister attached to it, and an adjoining burying ground. Several respectable families of Dover have burial places in this chapel, which are pointed out by numerous grave stones in the aisles.

For the late improvements in their chapel, the congregation are principally indebted to the exertions of Mr. Mather, who sacrificed much of his time, and a considerable portion of his emolument, to promote the object.

About the year 1818, Mr. Mather was seized with a painful affliction, that totally incapacitated him for his duties in the pulpit; but he continued to exercise his other pastoral engagements till the year 1823, when his increasing infirmities (which confined him entirely to his room) induced him to resign the charge, which he had exercised more than twenty years with credit and respectability. He died on the 20th of May, 1825, and was buried in a vault under the pulpit. The congregation have testified their esteem for him, by erecting, in the chapel, a handsome tablet to his memory.

Mr. Mather was succeeded by the Rev. Thomas Anderson, late of Kidderminster, who was chosen pastor in 1827.

A Sunday school, gratuitously conducted by members of the congregation, was established fifteen years since; and the present number of children is about 150.

The Wesleyan Methodist Chapel,

(Queen Elizabeth Square.)

The first appearance of these people, at Dover, was about the year 1760, when the Rev. Charles Wesley addressed the people, from a chair, near the Victualling Office; and was received in that riotous and disorderly manner, which this novel mode of preaching frequently met with from a thoughtless and enraged multitude.

On the following year, a place which had been previously used as a cooperage, was taken, in Queen-street, for a place of worship; and the late Mr. Peter Jaco occasionally officiated as minister.

After this, they removed to Limekiln-street, where two dwelling houses were converted into a chapel; and they continued here till the present chapel was erected, by the late Mr. Richard Cowley, in Queen Elizabeth Square. The premises were conveyed, on the 5th of April, 1790, to the Rev. John Wesley, and Messrs. Henry Moore, Joseph Bradford, John Broadbent, and John Pritchad, who were ministers in connexion with him, and were made joint trustees.

It is a commodious building, and can seat

about 500 persons.   The Sunday school, which
was established in 1813, is attended at present
by 260 children.   The present minister is the
Rev. Philip Jameson.

These people erected a new chapel at Buckland, about a mile from Dover, in 1808.   It is
a neat little building, and can seat 200 persons.
The Sunday school instructs about 130 children.

The Particular Baptists' Chapel,
(Pent Side.)

The Particular Baptists, as we have before
observed,[1] obtained their first converts at Canterbury and Dover, in the year 1543.   Though
they had places of worship in the neighbouring
villages, particularly at Eythorne,[2] we cannot
find that they had any place of worship in this

---

[1] See page 248.

[2] The parish of Eythorne is about six miles from Dover,
and the Baptists are supposed to have settled here at a very
early period.   At first they held the doctrine of the General
Baptists, and used to hold their devotional meetings in private
houses, at first in Upper Eythorne, and afterwards in Lower
Eythorne.   In the latter place they were much annoyed and
opposed.   The neighbouring farmers and their men would go
in among them, when assembled for worship, and smoke,
talk, and laugh, ridiculing and abusing them, and endeavouring
to prevent the service.

It is remarkable that pastors of the name of Knott presided
over this congregation more than 180 years.   One of them,
in the reign of king Charles the Second, being a zealous
preacher, attracted, in those days of persecution, the notice of

town prior to the year 1822, when they hired a private room for that purpose; and, on the following year, 1823, built a commodious chapel on Pent Side.

This edifice is sufficiently spacious to accommodate 500 persons; and has a Sunday school in the basement. At present, the school consists of about 80 children; and the present minister is the Rev. Daniel Crambrook.

---

informers; and was one day apprised, that an officer and a company of men were coming over Eythorne down, with a design to apprehend him. He had just time to escape by a back door, and to descend into an old sawpit, overgrown with weeds and nettles. The officer and his party found Mrs. Knott with a child in her arms, and the little prattler immediately said, " Daddy is gone out"——and was proceeding; but she shook the child to make it silent. While the party were searching for her husband, the good woman was preparing for dinner. They insisted on partaking of it, and she instantly offered them the best she had, waiting on them with the utmost complaisance and alacrity. This hospitality softened the hearts of these men, and they left the house without making any further search, declaring they would not do any thing to distress so good a woman. On another occasion Mr. Knott's goods were seized and offered for sale. A number of persons attended at the time appointed for sale; but his character stood so high that no one would make a bidding, and the goods remained in the possession of the owner.

Singing in public worship was not approved of by this congregation, and it was not introduced till the year 1750. In 1765, Mr. Knott of Barfreston was ordained pastor, and a small place of worship, capable of accommodating sixty persons, was erected in the same year. The meeting house was enlarged to double its former size, in 1770 The number was then thirty-six; and when Mr. Knott removed, in 1780,

SAINT JOHN'S CHAPEL.

This chapel was erected in Middle Row, at the Pier, in 1823, for a congregation of Independents; but the service ceased in 1827, and the chapel is now closed.

---

it had increased to forty-eight. The Calvinistic sentiments were introduced during his ministry, and the congregation united to the Particular Baptist denomination. Mr. Thomas Ranger succeeded Mr. Knott; and at the close of his ministry, in 1792, the members amounted to ninety-three. In 1804, they erected a neat commodious chapel, at a short distance from the former one, sufficiently large to accommodate 350 persons, and a large burying ground is attached to it. Mr. Ranger was succeeded by Mr. Giles, who died in 1827, and was much respected by all who knew him.

HISTORY

OF

DOVER HARBOUR.

In all parts of the world a process appears to have been, and is still going on, the result of which is a gradual change in the boundaries of the sea. The rains wash down from the hills a considerable portion of the soil; mountains are lowered, so that distant objects can now be discerned from points at which they were formerly invisible. Buildings long since erected in valleys, appear to have their entrances sunk into the ground. Rivers become charged with mud, banks form when they meet the ocean, and their waters, as in the case of the Nile and the Rhine, are divided into several streams. The land on the shore rises, and the sea recedes.

At what period of our history the ancient haven which flowed in between the hills, at Dover, became filled up with sand, beach, and the descending soil from the mountains, or what depth of water it might contain, cannot be accurately ascertained.

It is certain, however, that the loose earth is perceptible to a considerable depth below the present surface. A few years since, in sinking a well near Dolphin-lane, after descending twenty-one feet, a bed or layer of mud, such as we now find in the present harbour, was discovered.[1] This layer of mud, intermixed with leaves and fibres of roots, was three feet thick, and must, at some remote period, have formed the bed of the haven or harbour: and other layers of the same kind, may possibly exist still deeper. Similar layers, and large masses of sand and beach, have been found in several parts of the valley.

The surface of the ground where this well was dug, is only a few feet above the level of the sea, at spring tides; and should the valley be cleared of its accumulated soil to the depth of this layer of mud, it would, at the present time, form a haven between the hills, as it did nearly nineteen hundred years ago, when the writer of the Commentaries saw the armed inhabitants of the island marshalled on each side of it, as we have before observed.[2]

That the haven should have remained open more than two thousand years, from the era of the deluge till the time of Julius Cæsar, is more difficult to be accounted for, than the cause of

---

1 This well was excavated by Mr. Willson Gates, sen. in 1826.
2 See pages 137 and 138.

its filling up during the 1108 years which elapsed from the latter of those periods, till the reign of Edward the Confessor. If the quantity of beach which now flows round from the westward, had been equally copious in those ancient times, it must have had a natural tendency to form a bar, or ridge, at the entrance of the haven; and the soil descending from the hills, and brought down by the river and the tide, and meeting with such an obstruction, would necessarily accumulate behind it. The valley, by these means, would be continually filling up, and rising higher; and the depth of soil still increases, at the present day.

A traditionary account, said to have been taken from an ancient manuscript at Sandwich, informs us that Arviragus, who was contemporary with Claudius Cæsar, filled up the entrance of the haven, to prevent the Roman fleet from entering; but this relation is not well authenticated.

Though the haven was certainly frequented both by the Romans and Saxons, we have no description of it from the time when Cæsar wrote his Commentaries, till the reign of Edward the Confessor. At this time, and when William the conqueror extended the town wall more towards the east, the harbour occupied the ground on the lower part of Woolcomber-street; and the fishermen drew their boats on shore, and dried their nets, on a large open space between the town wall and the cliff, which is now covered with houses. The deep cavity of the harbour, which was filled and raised to form a level with the houses lately built towards the sea, was clearly discernable till the beginning of this century; and extended from the back of Liverpool Terrace, in a direct line to the gasometer.

This harbour was constantly in use from the time of the conquest till the reign of Henry the Seventh, yet no documents remain to point out the various changes and vicissitudes, that must have taken place in it, during a period of four hundred years.

In 1500, the harbour at Woolcomber-street was become useless, and the mariners were obliged to seek shelter for their vessels on the other side of the bay, under the projecting point of land, on which Archcliff fort was afterwards built. The sea, at that time, covered the whole extent of the bay, washed the bases of the cliffs where Snargate-street is now built,[3] and nearly approached the town wall.

---

[3] Mr. Hight, a few months since, in constructing the wine vaults for Mr. Worthington, in Snargate Street, and in excavating the ground for a bonded vault, at about ten feet from their entrance, discovered in the fissures of the rock, the beach that had been washed in by the force of the waves; and, at a few feet farther from the entrance, masses of beach were clearly discernable. This is a convincing proof, that the sea formerly washed against the base of these cliffs.

John Clark, who was master of the Maison Dieu, being provided with funds by Henry the Seventh, constructed a wall of chalk and earth, from Archcliff fort, in a line to the present south pier head, as far as the floodgates, or little basin, which have been lately constructed, where the culverts branch off in three directions, and here he built a round tower.[4]   Another round tower[5] was also built, in the intermediate space, in Round Tower-street.   Each of these towers was supplied with iron bolts and rings; and these works not only secured the mariners from danger, but the whole space within them was rendered so delightfully pleasant, that it was called Little Paradise.

The two towers built by Clark, are distinctly delineated in the paintings which represent the embarkation of Henry the Eighth, at Dover, when he sailed to Calais, in 1520, to have an interview with the king of France, on the plain between Guisnes and Ardres.   At this period, a road extended from Above Wall down the side of the cliff, on the western side of the present Snargate-street; and the king's attendants are seen passing in this direction.   One of these

---

[4] The foundations were discovered in constructing these flood gates, in 1813.

[5] The foundations of this tower remain in Round Tower-street, under three houses built by Mr. Church, in 1798, and under a storehouse belonging to Mr. Reynolds.

paintings still remains in Windsor castle, and another in the grand jury room, at Dover.

Prior to the year 1530, the eastern tower was washed down by the surges, and the wall broken in several places. Sir John Thompson, master of the Maison Dieu, observing the distress of the mariners, drew a plan of a more substantial and extensive work, which was much approved of by the inhabitants of the town, and they requested that he would present it to king Henry the Eighth, and collected £4. 10s. to pay his expenses to London.

The plan was highly approved of by the king, who advanced £500 to begin the work, which was commenced in 1533. Thompson, with four assistants, was appointed superintendent; and his majesty frequently attended to view its progress.

The first works, which enclosed a small basin of water with a quay for shipping goods, were confined to a narrow compass in Paradise pent. It was intended, however, in order to secure this small harbour and the bay, to extend a main pier, from Archcliff fort, 131 rods eastward into the sea, or about 20 rods farther out than the present south pier head. Two rows of piles, or pieces of timber, each pile being twenty-six feet long, and some of them shod with iron, were driven into holes cut in the solid rock, and fastened together with large beams, bolts, and bars of iron. Immense blocks of stone (some say of twenty tons weight) were placed between the rows of piles, and the interstices filled with chalk and beach. By the contrivance of one John Young, whom the king rewarded with a yearly stipend, during life, for his ingenuity, these stones were brought from Folkstone, on rafts or frames of timber, supported by empty casks.

Two projectures, one called Chapel, and the other Stoneham's groin, were built on the south side of the pier, and secured with blocks of chalk. The work was extended nearly to the site of the present south head, to a place called the Black Bulwark, on which it was intended to erect a platform for cannon. The foundation was extended about twenty rods farther, and may still be seen at low water, and is called the Mole Rock.

After expending £50,000[6] on these works, the king died in 1547, and left them in an unfinished state; and no provision being made to keep them in repair, the sea soon made several breaches in the wall, and accumulating banks of beach were forming in the bay.

Nothing appears to have been done during the short reign of Edward the Sixth; and though queen Mary granted letters patent to collect money throughout England, to repair Dover

---

[6] The Dering Manuscript says £80,000.

harbour, the sums were inadequate for the purpose. The banks of beach increased to such an alarming degree, that a boat drawing only four feet of water, could not enter, and the timber and iron work of the dilapidated ruins, were stolen by the distressed mariners.

Pressing applications were made to queen Elizabeth on the subject; and Sir Walter Raleigh considered the harbour to be of such importance that he presented the following memorial to her majesty respecting it.

" No promontary, town, or haven," says he, "in Christendom, is so placed by nature and situation, both to gratify friends and annoy enemies, as this town of Dover. No place is so settled to receive and deliver intelligence for all matters and actions in Europe, from time to time. No town is by nature so settled, either to allure intercourse by sea, or to train inhabitants by land, to make it great, fair, rich, and populous: nor is there in the whole circuit of this famous island, any port, either in respect of security and defence, or of traffic or intercourse, more convenient, needful, or rather of necessity to be regarded, than this of Dover; situated on a promontory next fronting a puissant nation, and in the very strait, passage, and intercourse of almost all the shipping in Christendom. And if that our renowned king Henry the Eighth, your majesty's father, found how necessary it was to make a haven at Dover, (when Sandwich, Rye, Camber, and others, were good havens, and Calais was also in his possession,) and yet spared not to bestow of his treasure so great a mass, in building that pier, that then secured a probable means to perform the same, how much more is the same now needful, or rather of necessity, (those good havens being extremely decayed,) no safe harbour being left in all the coast almost between Portsmouth and Yarmouth. Seeing, then, it hath pleased God to give unto this realm such a situation for a port and town, as all Christendom hath not the like, and endowed the same with all commodities by land and sea, that can be wished, to make the harbour allure intercourse, and maintain inhabitants; and that the same once performed must be advantageous to the revenue, and augment the welfare and riches of the realm in general; and both needful and necessary, as well for the succouring and protecting friends, as annoying and offending enemies, both in war and peace; methinks there remaineth no other deliberation in this case, but how most sufficiently and with greatest perfection possible most speedily the same may be accomplished."

The corporation, to second this memorial, assured her majesty that her houses, then built on the ground which the sea had left, and let on lease in her majesty's name, would be washed away, and the harbour be entirely ruined, unless speedy repairs were granted. The queen listened to their representations, and granted to the town the free exportation of 30,000 quarters of wheat, 10,000 quarters of barley or malt, and 4,000 tuns of beer. The patent was sold to John Bird and Thomas Watts, who gave £8,666. 13*s*. 4*d*. for it.

Commissioners[7] were appointed to superintend the work, and they chose a surveyor, whose name was John True. He was to build a wall of stone, 200 rods in length, from above the water gate, where the river now enters the pent, nearly to the black bulwark, or the present south pier head. A firm and compact ridge of beach had, at that time, been formed between those two points, and the wall was to stand behind it, inclosing, on the land side, the river, which, running along the ridge, issued at the mouth of the harbour.

True expended £1300 in squaring stones, which were brought from Folkstone; and being paid ten shillings a day, he was suspected of a desire to prolong the work, and was therefore discharged.

Ferdinand Poins, who had constructed works to fence against the sea, on the coasts of Flanders

---

7 The commissioners were lord Cobham, then lord warden; Sir Thomas Scott; Sir James Hales; the mayor of Dover; Richard Barry, lieutenant of Dover castle; Thomas Wotton; Edward Bois; Henry Palmer; Thomas Diggs; Thomas Wilford; and William Partridge, esquires, all gentlemen of Kent.

and Holland, and who had been employed in similar works at Woolwich and Erith, was next employed by the commissioners.

Poins repaired Thompson's works, which extended from Archcliff fort, and built a groin or pier opposite to the black bulwark, and nearly to the extent of the present north head, to confine the water to a narrow passage. He then intended to build the wall of 200 rods, which had been marked out by True, from the east of the water gate, to this new groin or pier; but he had expended £1200, and objections being made to his charges, he appears to have been dismissed from his office, and the works were discontinued a short time.

About this period, Thomas Diggs, an engineer and mathematician, who had studied the nature and construction of the ports in the Netherlands, having been consulted by the commissioners of the harbour, addressed a memorial to the queen, and presented three plans for her majesty's inspection.

One of these plans was to extend the pier to a considerable distance into the sea; another, was to enclose the whole bay from Archcliff fort to the castle cliff, with an entrance and fortified towers in the centre, at a considerable distance from the shore; and the third, was to excavate the ground, and to form a harbour in the meadows above the town.

The queen maturely inspected these plans, and an act was passed in 1580, granting three pence a ton on every vessel, loading or unloading in any port within the realm, for seven years;[8] and three half-pence for every chaldron of coals, and the same for every grindstone, landed for sale. These sums were to be applied to the use of Dover harbour.

An examination of the harbour took place before the lord high admiral, in 1581; and the old mariners could then remember, when the sea washed the cliffs in Snargate-street; and they informed his lordship, that no beach had collected in the bay, till the wall or pier was built on the west side of it, from Archcliff fort.

Before the end of this year, a violent storm drove the sea over Thompson's wall, and choaked up the entrance at the black bulwark; and the harbour in Paradise pent was filled with mud and beach.

It does not appear why the plans of Mr. Diggs were not adopted, but they probably were too expensive; and it was determined to pursue those of True and Poins, with such improvements, as might be suggested by Mr. Diggs.

Sir James Hales was made treasurer; John Smith, expenditor; and Mr. Diggs, surveyor

---

[8] This act was afterwards renewed by several later acts, and continued till the seventh year of king James the First.

general ;[9] and the work was begun in May, 1583.[10]   Instead of stone, it was resolved, at the suggestion of Sir Thomas Scott, to construct similar walls to those at Dymchurch, which prevent the sea from entering Romney marsh, from whence men came to assist. The sides were raised with mud, covered with faggots, fixed down with piles, and the middle filled up with chalk.[11]

Sir Thomas Scott superintended the men on the long wall, which extended 120 rods, from above the water gate, down what is now the rope walk, near to the present York Hotel; and this wall was 70 feet wide at the bottom, and 40 at the top.   Richard Barry, esq. superintended the men on the cross wall, which extended 40 rods, from near the present York Hotel, passing the present Union Hotel, and extending nearly to

[9] Sir James was to receive 5s. 8d. for every £50 received or disbursed, and his clerk £5 yearly. John Smith was to have a salary of £20 yearly, and his clerk £5. Mr. Diggs was to have 20 marks yearly, which he gave to his clerk, Alexander Mindge.—*Ancient Report of Dover Harbour*.

[10] The wages for a man, a horse, and a cart, were 1s. a day. The single cart, or tumbrel, was 14 feet in length, 2 feet wide, and 16 inches deep. The double cart, with two horses, and as many men, had 2s. a day. Trifling as this may now appear, it was at that time worth notice; and men with carts came to Dover, from Maidstone and Sevenoaks, to assist in the work.

[11] Two shipwrights, Baker and Pett, objected to this plan, and insisted that nothing but a fence made of wood, could answer. They produced a plan of this kind; but it was rejected.

the cliff. This wall was 90 feet wide at the bottom, and 50 at the top; and they were both finished in less than three months, and cost only £2700.

Having completed these walls the object was to make the back water useful in cleansing paradise pent,[12] which was still . the principal harbour, and to remove obstructions from .the entrance, at the black bulwark.

A small sluice was constructed near the present bridge, at the bottom of the great pent; but the only canal, by which vessels could .pass into this new pent, flowed round the western side of the present Union Hotel, and passing between what is now Strond-street and the cliff, entered paradise pent. From hence the canal passed on, occupying the site on which Mr. Ismay's premises have since been built, and emptying itself at the mouth of the present harbour.

At the upper part of this canal, by the Union Hotel, a lock, with flood gates, was constructed, to admit the vessels into the great pent, and to reserve the water. From hence a jetty, consisting of two rows of piles filled with blocks of chalk, was formed on the east side of the canal,

---

12 This pent or harbour was bounded, on the south-west, by the present Limekiln and Bulwark-streets , and, on the north-east, by the lower part of Strond-street, Mr. Ismay's buildings, and Roundtower-street.

where Strond-street has since been built, and continued down to paradise pent.   At the lower part of paradise pent, near the site of Mr. Ismay's present buildings, another lock and gates, twenty-four feet wide and seventeen high, were constructed, with a large stone sluice on the west side. The former of these locks and its appendages, were estimated at £795; and the latter, with a store house and the queen's effigy in front, at £1000.

Below the gates at the entrance of paradise pent, an angular jetty was constructed, which seems to have included the site of the houses, eastward of Mr. Minet's mansion, the angular point being near the present crane.

By an ancient plan, we perceive that Stoneham's groin was continued, with two angular turnings, to the gate we have just mentioned, at the entrance of paradise pent; but not being able to find any record when it was constructed, we suppose it might be about this time.   Nor can we find when Colebran's head, near the present boom house, was built; but are induced to place it near the same period.

The water, pent in by the gates which we have just mentioned, and guided by the jetties, was let out when the tide was down, and completely cleansed the beach from the entrance of the harbour; but the velocity was such, that it injured the foundation of the black bulwark and of Poins' groin, and both were soon in a ruinous state.

These breaches were repaired; and, in 1592, the long wall that had been built down the present rope walk, was extended from what is now the York Hotel, to Poins' groin, or the present north head. Jetties were also formed to enclose the site of the present Castle Inn, and the square of adjoining houses and store rooms, now called the Old Buildings. A large space below the cross wall that extended from the York to the Union Hotel, and where the basin has since been constructed, was also excavated at the same time. As the lower cross wall was not then built, this space formed a part of the outer harbour, at that period, and was called Great Paradise.

Several works were constructed in 1593, to defend the long wall from the fury of the ocean. Five rows of piles, having a space of twelve feet between them, and one foot between each pile in the rows, were placed in a line, at low water mark. The rows gradually rose above each other, and the space between them was filled with large stones. Above the rows of piles, was a frame of wood work, declining in an opposite direction, and strongly bound together with long cross beams.[13]

---

[13] Some of these foundations were laid open, since the begining of this century, by the force of the sea.

At the same time, a jetty, formed with piles twelve inches square and twenty-six feet high, with a space of six inches between them, and the whole strongly bound together with iron bolts, was constructed to secure the continuation of the long wall, from the York to the pier head.

In 1594, jetties were constructed from Colebran's head to paradise pent, and the two pier heads were repaired, and extended a short distance farther into the sea.

It was now intended occasionally to bring the whole weight of back water through great paradise, or the present basin, to act with greater force at the entrance of the harbour; and the small sluice at the bottom of the great pent, was taken up, in 1597, and another, 13 feet deep, 16 broad, and 80 long, substituted in the place of it. Lord Cobham was at that time warden of the ports; and he not only superintended the workmen, but kept an open table to encourage their exertions.

To defend these works against an enemy, Archcliff fort commanded the south-west; cannon on the black bulwark and from the round tower, secured the entrance of the harbour; a large battery on the long wall, another under the castle, and the castle itself, flanked the bay; and an open space was reserved near the pier, to assemble the forces, from whence they might march, to any point, on the shortest notice. Thus defended, Dover was considered to be as secure as Antwerp, Flushing, or any town on the coast of the Netherlands.

On the death of queen Elizabeth, in 1603, the corporation of the town had engrossed the whole affairs of the harbour; and laid claim to the waste land, left by the sea.

King James the First demanded a resignation of all their claims, and of all their power, relative to harbour affairs; and, in 1606, granted a charter of incorporation, by the title of the "Warden and Assistants of Dover Harbour." The lord warden, the lieutenant of Dover castle, and the mayor of Dover, are principals; and eight more are chosen to assist them.

They have power to fill up vacancies, to have a common seal,[14] to choose officers, appoint a house of council, make bye laws, inflict penalties, and other privileges. The land left by the sea, below Snargate, westward to Archcliff fort, and that eastward to Moat's battery, under the castle, was given to them by the same charter, for the use of the harbour; and they let it for a term of years, on what are called harbour leases.

The new commissioners[15] of the harbour, be-

---

[14] The seal of this corporation, which is used at present, was not made till 1646. It is of silver, and of an oval form, and has the ports' arms within a shield, with the inscription,—"*Dover Harbour, anno. Dom.* 1646."

[15] These commissioners were Sir F. Fane, Sir G. Fane, Sir Thomas Fane, Sir Thomas Waller, Sir Thomas Harfleet, and

gan their improvements, by rendering the sluice constructed by lord Cobham, at the bottom of the pent, more effective. The opening was enlarged, and the foundations sunk to the solid rock, by which means a greater quantity of water was delivered in a less space of time.

It was discovered, at the same period, that the jetty of square piles,[16] erected by Mr. Diggs, to defend the continuation of the long wall, was too low, and that the pebbles beat over it into the harbour. To remedy this defect, the commissioners ordered it to be raised considerably higher; after which nothing of importance appears to have been effected for some years.

A memorial was presented to king Charles the First, in 1635, and £2000 was requested for repairs. To meet this exigency, his majesty granted an additional impost on foreigners, who entered their goods at this port.

The harbour appears to have been kept in good repair till the year 1652, when a squadron of armed ships, being of the fourth rate, came in to clean and victual; and the depth of water was then twenty-two feet, at the pier head.

But, in 1661, a memorial was presented to king Charles the Second, which states, in glowing colors, the dilapidated state of the harbour; and

---

Sir George Perkins, knights; William Monins, Henry Finch, and George Byng, esquires; the mayor of Dover, Aaron Windebank, gent. and Edward Kemp, of Dover, jurat.

16 See page 292.

says that the whole would soon be involved in one common ruin, unless speedy repairs were granted. An act was therefore passed; but the whole of the money raised was not to exceed £30,000.[17]

Furnished with this supply, and desirous to increase the store of back water, the commissioners formed the present basin, by constructing the *lower* cross wall. An opening was left in this wall, 38 feet wide, in which were placed two massy gates, to retain the water, or to admit vessels. Sluices were constructed on each side of these gates, and it was intended to bring the whole force of back water this way, to operate more effectually in clearing the entrance of the harbour. The turnwater, between the pier heads, was also completed at the same time.

These improvements rendered the canal which passed through paradise pent, useless; and it was, in the course of time, filled up and covered with houses.[18]

---

17 It is reported that this act produced only £9000.

18 After the canal was filled up, the space occupied by the harbour in Little Paradise, or Paradise Pent, became a waste, useless, and unhealthy swamp, covered with reeds and bulrushes; and continued in this state more than a century. The ground was occasionally raised, and, as it became firm, houses were built on it; but the progress was by no means rapid, prior to the year 1798. At this period, in order to remedy the nuisance, the warden and commissioners of the harbour offered leases of ninety-nine years, to those who would raise the ground, and erect houses on it. This produced the desired

Several sail of merchantmen, worth at least £140,000, and unprovided with anchors or cables, were driven by a storm into this harbour, in 1689, most of which would probably have foundered at sea, or been taken by the enemy, if they had not availed themselves of this secure retreat. Several sail of transports, in 1693, were also saved by seeking shelter in this pier; and king Charles the Second ascribed a great part of the success gained in his maritime wars, to the convenience afforded by Dover harbour.

By a report made on the 12th of February, 1699, in the reign of William the Third, it appears that the harbour was again in danger of becoming useless. Even the packet boats, sailing between this place and the continent, could not enter in safety; and the captains petitioned for leave to land the mail at Deal.

It was estimated that the repairs would cost £30,000, and an act was obtained to raise the necessary supplies. The commissioners were allowed to borrow £6000 on this act; and, on the 1st of May, 1717, they had expended £20,136. 13s. 1d. The act, which expired at this time, had produced only £20,896. 5s. and

effect, and the water was soon confined to a narrow channel. To evacuate the back springs which run into this channel, it was necessary to leave open a communication under Mr. Ismay's premises, and the tide continues to flow in; but the whole was arched over, and nearly covered with houses, in 1823.

the harbour was still in a dilapidated state. On a report being presented to this effect, the act was continued ten years longer.

During this period captain Perry had been consulted. He advised that the south head should be carried out 150 feet beyond the north head; and that two or three jetties should be built on the west of the harbour, and five or six on the east of it. These works he estimated would cost £35,000, which was a sum greater than could be raised; and the only new works we can find, were the repairs of Cheeseman's head, on the west of the piers.

Though the rents of the houses built on the waste, had now much improved; though the lands left by will,[19] had much increased in value;

---

19 Henry Matson, late of Dover, merchant, by will, dated the 12th of October, 1720, left to the warden and assistants of Dover harbour, £150 a year, in lands, to be expended in repairs, on condition that they kept the trunnel holes stopped on the pier head. He appears to have dropped a favorite gold headed cane through one of these holes, and was never able to recover it. No particular lands belonging to his estates, are mentioned in the will; but Solton farm, and Diggs Place, were allotted to answer the purposes of it, by a decree of the court of Chancery, in 1722, which allowed to the relatives of Mr. Matson, a perpetual annuity of forty pounds, from Solton farm. In 1799, an act passed the legislature for the redemption and sale of the land tax, which empowered all corporate bodies to sell any part of their posses- sions, to redeem the tax on the remaining part of them; and Solton farm was sold for that purpose, subject to the forty pound annuity, to the late Mr. Thomas Hatton, of Buckland. Since that time, it has been sold to the late Mr. Coleman, of Dover

and though the tonnage duties[20] were at this time considerable; yet the expenditure very far exceeded the income.

To increase the difficulty, the government, after so many disappointments at this place, turned their attention to the town of Rye, and two thirds of the tonnage duty, in 1736, were transferred from Dover to that haven.[21]

From this period till 1737, nothing, except necessary repairs, was attempted; but in that and the following two years, the lower cross wall was faced, on both sides, with Portland stone, new gates built at the entrance of the basin, with additional sluices on each side, and a swing bridge erected over it, for foot passengers.

Soon after this, a pair of gates was erected in the upper cross wall, to admit vessels into the great pent, which had been useless, except as a reservoir for back water, since the canal that passed through paradise pent had been filled up.

---

priory, and still remains in that family. Diggs Place remains in the possession of the commissioners, and forms part of the present revenue of the harbour. The ceremony of stopping the trunnel holes was soon reduced to a farce. On a day appointed, the mayor and a few others assemble for this purpose; and, after viewing the premises, or driving a few pegs, retire and regale themselves with a supper.

[20] The average of the tonnage duty during twelve years of peace, was about £2526, per annum; and during twelve years of war, about £1300 per annum.

[21] The harbour of Rye afterwards received one half only, which was taken from that haven in 1797.

The pier heads appear to have been rebuilt about this time.

No new works of importance were undertaken till 1753, when a head, 176 feet in length, was constructed under the castle cliff, to prevent the pebbles from being driven out of the bay.

Complaints having been made of the large sums of money, expended on this harbour,[22] which was still very incomplete, the commissioners appointed Mr. Smeaton, in 1769, to inspect the works. He proposed to extend the south head sixty feet farther into the sea; and if that failed, and the pebbles still continued to collect at the entrance of the harbour, to erect sluices to drive them away.

As the commissioners had not funds sufficient to put these plans in execution, they were laid aside, and Mr. Nickalls was consulted in 1782. He complained that the harbour was not capable of receiving ships of war; that the water at the apron in the lower cross wall, was only ten feet six inches, at neap tides; that the sill of these gates was eighteen inches too high; that the declivity of the great pent, from the present new bridge, and from its sides, was too great; that the enclosed water, being only 47,160 tons, at neap tides, would not form a body more than

---

[22] The whole expenditure for repairs, from May the 1st, 1737, till May the 1st, 1757, was £22,226. 4s. 2d.

thirty inches deep, in the outer harbour, when let out in the shortest possible time; and that such a force was not sufficient to clear the obstructions from the entrance of the harbour.

To remedy these defects, he proposed to enlarge the space of the great pent to 13½ acres; to deepen the sill at the lower cross wall, and to sink the bed of the pent and basin to a level with it; to form a canal or reservoir above the new bridge, where a sluice of a peculiar construction should deliver the back water with sufficient force to cleanse the pent, basin, and outer harbour; and to extend the pier heads 200 feet, and to furnish each head with canals that should be sufficient to discharge 16,000 tons of water in a minute, and to drive all obstructions before it: but it does not appear by what means the back water was to have been conveyed to these canals.

With these improvements, the haven was to be capable of containing 300 sail of ships; frigates of the largest size might ride at anchor; and a sixty gun ship go into dock, near the new bridge, at spring tides. The estimate amounted to £60,000.

Mr. Nickalls was employed in the harbour several years; and though the revenues were not equal to such a plan as he had proposed, all his improvements had a tendency towards it. He enlarged the entrance into the pent, lowered the apron at the gates, laid two new sluices in the lower cross wall, cased it on both sides with stone, and built several feet of the wharfs with the same material, sinking the foundations eight feet below the surface, with a view of lowering the whole space to that depth.

Mr. Nickalls could not give general satisfaction; and he was dismissed, and his plans laid aside.

Mr. Oxenden, now Sir Henry, then undertook to direct the works; and, in 1791, rebuilt sixty-five feet of the eastern extremity of the north head. The harbour, at this time, was in a respectable state.[23]

The old part of the south head was in a dangerous state, in 1802, and Messrs. Walker and Rennie were employed to make a survey. They proposed to carry it 200 feet beyond the north pier; but their proposition was rejected.

The revenues of the harbour were much improved in 1807, by having the old tonnage duty restored. Three pence per ton was demanded of all shipping, from 20 to 300 tons, passing from, to, or by Dover, or coming into the

---

[23] In 1792, the Berkhout Dutch East Indiaman of 800 tons, formerly a fifty gun ship of war, sprung a leak in a storm, and was in danger of being wrecked on the coast of France. The intelligence no sooner reached Dover than a cutter immediately sailed to her assistance; and though she drew nearly twenty feet of water, she was brought safely into this harbour.

harbour, except ships in ballast, or those wholly laden with coals, grindstone, purbeck, or portland stones; from which only one half-penny was demanded for every chaldron of coals, and for every ton of grindstone, purbeck, or portland stones.

The old work on the inside of the north head, was beaten down by a violent storm, in January, 1808. Mr. Moon, the harbour master, gave great satisfaction to the commissioners, by rebuilding 195 feet of this head, in a masterly and substantial manner.

The harbour of Dover, unlike those that are formed by the mouths of large rivers, is, in its present state, an artificial construction, wherein those who are employed in its conservation, have to contend with the violence of the storm and the raging of the ocean. For these unremittingly combine their joint efforts to choak it up and destroy it, calling forth, at different periods, the talents and exertions of the best civil engineers, to counteract them.

The principal difficulty to contend with, has ever been and still is a shifting bar of beach or shingle which the wind, particularly from the south-west, brings before the harbour's mouth, preventing often, when its shelter is most needed by shipping, all ingress into it.

To remove this, the water, which at high tide fills the harbour and also the basins and pent, is, by means of gates, retained in the latter receptacles; and, when the tide is fallen in the former, the pent up water is suffered to issue through arches or sluices. The water proceeds with great velocity towards the mouth of the harbour, narrowed by means of a temporary work, called a turnwater, which is readily constructed or removed at pleasure. The current thus contracted, acquires additional force, and striking directly against the bar, makes a channel through it, and restores, in a greater or less degree, the opening.

This bar, having proved a constant source of perplexity, naturally engaged the attention of Mr. Moon, who, in the prosecution of the works entrusted to him, manifested no ordinary talent as an engineer.

For several years Mr. Moon occupied himself in managing or improving the means, already devised for clearing the entrance of the port. But observing with concern that they were still insufficient, he, in the year 1811, proposed to the board[24] a plan of a novel and extensive nature, from the adoption of which he hoped to obtain greater success. It was honored by decided

---

24 The commissioners were The Right Honorable the earl of Liverpool, warden of the cinque ports; George Dell, esq. mayor of Dover; Sir Henry Oxenden, bart. Sir Brook William Brydges, bart. William Deedes, Thomas Papillon, and William Hammond, esquires.

approbation ; and he was directed to proceed to its immediate execution.   We shall endeavour to describe it in the following account of its object, and of the mode in which it was carried into effect.

It had for its object to cause as great a body of water as possible to issue, not between the heads as formerly, (since he had observed that much of its power had been wasted by the stream diffusing itself,) but from within the southern head, whence it should discharge itself at three apertures, either of which might be made to operate as occasion should require.   Channels, within the heads, were to conduct it into the proposed directions; the channels themselves branching from a single one, beginning at a reservoir to be fed by a new basin near it.   This basin was to be formed by enclosing, with a wall, a corner of the harbour which had been hitherto nearly useless, and was to be supplied through another channel, running under ground, and con-conveying the water from the inner or old basin.

A collateral object, of considerable importance to the port, the construction of a Dry Dock, was proposed to be carried on at the same time.

In executing this grand project, the channels before mentioned were formed by means of cast iron culverts; those of the outer branches, which extend upwards of 200 feet, being seven feet in diameter, six feet six inches long, and weighing on an average four tons each; and those of the channel, which is 426 feet long, connecting the two basins, five feet in diameter.

The extremity of the south head, where two of the branches discharge, was built with large oaken piles, so placed as to have a space between them, in order that the waves striking against them, might have their force broken, and cause less agitation within the harbour.

The wall, 426 feet long, inclosing the new basin, extends from the custom house watch house, to the old crane opposite the council house.[25] An opening is left in it for ships to pass through, at which are built a pair of gates to confine the water or admit vessels, and a swing bridge for foot passengers.

In order to enlarge the basin, several houses on the east side of Crane, or King's Head-street, (now Clarence-place,) were taken down, and the work finished on that side, with a handsome stone quay.

At the south-west angle of the new basin is built the dry dock; and although the greatest care was taken, in constructing it, to secure the floor, yet the upward pressure, from the springs under the foundation, was so great, that fears were entertained of the possibility to counteract their force. The ablest engineers were consulted; and no means they could devise were deemed adequate. There are occasions in which acquired

---

25 The Commissioners hold their meetings here.

knowledge and previous study are rendered vain. Genius must devise new and untried methods, or the desired object must be relinquished. This was one of them. In an instant the needful expedient occurred to the mind of Mr. Moon; the plan was drawn; the models framed; and the board, confident of success, gave their sanction. The floor is now secured by iron bolts, two inches diameter, being fourteen feet six inches long, having a conical head, seven inches long and five inches diameter, at the base. This head being inverted, or the largest end downwards, is fastened, by four cast iron spreaders, each of which is connected by a hinge or joint, to a casing of fir in four parts, which surrounds the bolt, and which is five inches in diameter. The entire head of the bolt is left below the spreaders, in order to admit it into a hole, and the method of fixing is as follows:

A five inch hole is bored in the solid chalk, with a common auger, fourteen feet six inches down. At the bottom of this hole, a chamber is made with a cutting drill, in a conical form, nine inches at the bottom, five inches at the top, and nine inches in length. The bolt, with its fir casing and cast iron spreaders, is then let down into the hole, until the spreaders are exactly opposite the chamber, made in the rock to receive them. The bolt is then drawn up, and its conical head forcing out the spreaders, they become fixed. The casing is then caulked into the dock floor, in order to prevent leakage; and the end of the bolt, with a large nut and screw, stands a foot above the floor. A piece of oak timber, a foot square, is then introduced, crossing the beams at right angles, with holes bored four feet apart, to receive the bolts. On this timber the nuts are screwed, and the whole of the floor is kept down, which renders the dock perfectly secure. Several vessels have been repaired in it.[26]

During the progress of these works, in the year 1814, in addition to the many troops that had embarked or landed at this port at different periods of the war, the cavalry of the British army, whose victorious progress, after they had driven the enemy from Spain, and were proceeding in the South of France, was arrested by the cessation of hostilities, marched to Boulogne and Calais, and were mostly landed in Dover harbour, without difficulty or accident. More than thirty sail of large transports, some of them measuring upwards of five hundred tons, were sometimes lying in the harbour at the same time.

The immense works[27] carried on under the

---

26 See "Mechanics' Magazine," vol. iii. p. 313.

27 The foundations of the old wall, built by Clark and Thompson, in the reigns of Henry the Seventh and Henry the Eighth, and mentioned in pages 280 and 281 of this work, were discovered in making the necessary excavations for these improvements. From the foundations of Clark's eastern tower, discovered in

direction of Mr. Moon, were completed, with the exception of the third or inner branch of the culverts, in 1822; and their superior style of execution will remain a lasting testimony of the skill and abilities of the person, who projected and constructed them. The two outer branches of the culverts were tried on the 27th of January, 1722, and were found effectually to cut off the bar of beach close to the pier head.

The third or inner branch of the culverts, has been delayed in consequence of a reduction having taken place in the income of the harbour.[28]

---

forming the reservoir where the culverts branch off in three directions, the foundations of the wall were traced through the single arch which leads from thence to the new basin, and from hence to the head of the dry dock. From this point, forming an angle, the foundations proceeded in a line about five feet from the new quay, along Clarence-place; and from thence it undoubtedly continued on to the other round tower, which was situated in Roundtower-street. The old wall appears to have been constructed by putting whole elm trees, with the rind on, into holes dug three feet into the chalk rock, and placed in two rows, 26 feet apart at the bottom, and 20 feet at the top. The trees were fastened together with timbers crossing them; and the space between the rows, filled up with large blocks of chalk and lumps of clay. The parts of the trees which remained, were perfectly sound, and the rind was remaining on them.

[28] During the five years preceding 1822, the *permanent* annual income was, on an average, about £1700, the rates from vessels entering the harbour £1150, and from vessels passing the harbour £10,150, making the average annual income £13,000. During these five years, £23,500 had been borrowed, and £3000 prior to that time, making a sum total of £26,500, at an annual interest, (some being life annuities) of £1500. The total sum expended during that period, amounted to £81,500.

The committee on foreign trade, having examined witnesses respecting the works carrying on in Dover and Ramsgate harbours, and taking into consideration the falling off of trade, and the large sums paid by ships for the maintenance of these works, suggested to the commissioners the necessity of reducing the tonnage duty. In consequence of this representation, the board met at the council house, on the 11th of October, 1822, and came to the determination of reducing the duty one half, or to three half pence per ton, upon all ships passing, and of continuing the three pence per ton, upon all ships that entered the port.

In consequence of this reduction in the income, the works were suspended, and the number of men reduced, so as to leave only sufficient to keep up the ordinary repairs. The expenditure being thus lessened, the commissioners had, in October, 1827, a balance in hand of more than £13,000; and came to the determination of resuming the work, and gave directions to Mr. Moon to provide materials for that purpose.[29]

---

[29] The following is the number of ships, and their tonnage, which entered the harbour, from the 1st of January, 1808, till the 31st of December, 1827 :

Came in and consigned to Dover..	9743 Ships,	748320 Tons.
Came in for shelter, or in distress .	5448 Ships,	557332 Tons.
Total	15191 Ships,	1305652 Tons.

His Majesty's vessels, hired cruizers, victualling and ordnance, and all vessels belonging to Dover, are excepted.

The inner part of the south pier head, on each side of the place where the third branch of the culverts was to open, being very low and in a decayed state, so that the water frequently flowed over it and washed up the platform, he recommended to raise it to a level with the other part of the head, which he had lately constructed. This would require piles of thirty-two feet in length, which cannot be easily obtained; but he proposed to raise a foundation of stone ten feet high, which would reduce the length of the piles to twenty-two feet, and render it unnecessary, in any future repairs, to seek a new foundation, by working under water, which is very expensive in works of this kind. The extent of the decayed work, required to be rebuilt, is 465 feet.

These repairs are now in progress, and promise to be very substantial; and, independently of the advantage the harbour may derive from it, there will result a fine platform at this favorite resort, where numbers daily assemble to witness the arrival and sailing of shipping.

THE HARBOUR LEASES.

From the time of granting the charter,[30] in 1606, till the year 1812, the harbour leases, with a few exceptions, were renewable every twenty-one years; and though the whole rents, at 2.*s* 6*d*. in the pound, and at about one third of the actual valuation, amounted to nearly £700 annually,

---

[30] See page 293.

yet the property was considered to be nearly as good as freehold.

In 1812, the leases were called in, and new ones granted, at 3*s.* 6*d.* in the pound, on the fair annual value of the property, for sixty-one years, a remuneration being allowed to those whose leases were unexpired. This change caused a great ferment among the leaseholders, and apprehensions have been entertained, that eventually it might not only injure private individuals, but prove detrimental to the income of the harbour, by depressing a spirit of improvement. New houses, however, and improvements are still in progress ; and the ground is nearly covered with buildings. The new lodging houses, erected on the parade, have leases for ninety-nine years.

THE CORPORATION

AND

CIVIL JURISDICTION

OF

THE TOWN.

Nothing more can be expected from this Short Treatise, than a faint outline of the Jurisdiction of the town, and a mere transient glance at the changes that have taken place, from the time of its first incorporation, to the present day; the leading features of which will be collected from Mr. Lyon, Kilburne, Jeake, Hasted, &c.

We have already noticed, that Dover was the first of the cinque ports, incorporated by charter.[1] The town had, from time immemorial, enjoyed special privileges, which were confirmed by Edward the first, who, in his charter, acknowledged the corporation by the name of the mayor and commonalty.

---

[1] See page 156.

Choice of Mayor.

The mayor was formerly, by virtue of these privileges, chosen from the general body of the commonalty or freemen; and, when chosen, he proceeded to select, out of the same body, twelve assisstants for the year, who, on being sworn into office, were called jurats. The mayor, jurats, and freemen, then proceeded to elect their town clerk, and other officers; but the functions of each continued for one year only, at the expiration of which they proceeded to a new election, conducted in the same manner.

The freemen enjoyed these privileges till the sixteenth year of king Henry the Eighth, when, under the pretence that such popular elections were productive of riot and confusion; it was resolved in a court of brotherhood, held at Romney on the 3rd of August, 1526, that thirty-seven persons, to be named by a few individuals, in each of their ports, and twenty-four in each of their corporate towns, should assume the whole right of electing their mayors, jurats, and other officers. A penalty of fifty pence, or imprisonment, was also threatened against any freeman, not of this number, who should presume to vote.

This arbitrary proceeding met with opposition; but it continued till the fourth year of Edward the Sixth, 1550, when a meeting was convened between the contending parties, and the principle was recognized, that no bye law of a few individuals, nor even an act of a court of brotherhood, in opposition to the wishes, and injurious to the rights of the general body of freemen, could supercede a chartered right, or the law of the land; and the ancient method of electing a chief magistrate, was again adopted.

This method continued till the seventeenth year of queen Elizabeth, 1578, when some of the leading men of the town, being countenanced by the queen's council, succeeded a second time in restricting the franchise to themselves, in the following manner.

By the blowing of a horn on the seventh day of September, 1578, a public meeting was convened at the town hall; and it was there enacted that, in order to avoid future contentions in electing a chief magistrate, the mayor and jurats should assemble annually on the 8th of September, at nine o'clock in the morning, and nominate five persons from their own body, (the mayor whose functions ceased on the following noon to be always one of them,) out of which number, in order to retain the appearance of popular choice, the commons were to elect a chief magistrate for the year ensuing. It was also enacted, at the same time, that the mayor and jurats should fill up their number from the common council; that they should elect, from their own body, the bailiff to Yarmouth, the burgesses to parliament, and the bearers of the royal canopy; and that they should choose the several officers of the town, except the pounder and the mayor's sergeant, who were to be elected by the mayor.

The singular document that contains these enactments, characteristic of the despotic spirit of those times, is still in being; but is too voluminous to be inserted here. It was signed, says Mr. Lyon, neither by the mayor, a jurat, a single freeman, nor even by the town clerk; and yet it was permitted to carry all the authority of law, and it threatened fine and imprisonment to those who should attempt to violate it.

At that period, it appears that the queen governed the corporation with as much severity as the corporation could govern the town; and we find by a monument, in Hougham church, to the memory of William Hannington, that he was twice mayor of Dover, by the favour and command of her majesty.

The new system continued during a course of sixty-six years, till the twentieth of king Charles the First, 1644, when the freemen appear to have recovered their ancient privilege of nominating and electing their chief magistrate and other officers; and they were in possession of it during the Usurpation, and till the eleventh year of king Charles the Second, 1670.

The leading men of the town, at that time

made a final and successful effort to establish
their purpose, and nominated the late mayor,
John Matson, and four of the jurats. The freemen also nominated a candidate, who was elected
by a large majority of votes. Not satisfied with
such a result, the magistrates sent the state of
the poll to the king, who declared the election
to be void, and ordered them to proceed to a
new choice. It is evident, however, that he
favoured their wishes: and he advised them
to adopt the system which had succeeded in
1578; but to put the popular candidate in the
nomination.

The king afterwards granted them a charter,
on the same principle, reserving to himself the
power of displacing those who had been put in
authority. This was considered by the lawyers
to be unconstitutional; and his charters, on this
account, were deemed voidable, if controverted;
and they were uniformly reprobated in the courts
of judicature.[1]

This charter of king Charles the Second, says
Mr. Lyon, was disowned, either by those who

---

[1] Mr. Hasted says, "That this charter, as well as another
granted by king James the Second, and forced on the corporation, being made wholly subservient to the king's own
purposes, were annulled by proclamation, Oct. 17th, 1788."
And he further says, "That this proclamation was made, to
make null and void all charters, granted between the years
1670 and 1688; and for restoring all corporations to their
ancient rights and privileges." *Vol. IV, page* 89.

received it, or by their immediate successors; and it was not acknowledged when king William the Third came to the crown. The leading men of Dover, at that time, denominated themselves a corporation by prescription, having a power of making bye laws, for the better government of the town.

The term, Bye Laws, implying as it appears to do, the idea of imperium in imperio, is so vague, that we cannot understand it, nor do we know either their extent in affecting the liberty, property, or life of those who are subject to them, or how they can be enacted without the general consent of the freemen, for whose benefit they appear to have been intended.

The corporation[2] consists of a mayor, (who is

---

2 " The corporation seal is a large round seal of brass, and was engraved in 1305. On the obverse is an antique vessel, with a bowsprit, and a mast with a pennon of three tails; the sail furled; a forecastle, poop, and round top, all embattled; the steersman at the helm. Two men on the forecastle blowing trumpets, another climbing up the shrouds, and two below forward at a rope; a flag at the stern charged with the port arms, inscribed, Sigillvm commvne baronvm de Dovoria. *The common Seal of the barons of Dover.* On the reverse is Saint Martin on horseback, passing through the gate of Amiens, and dividing his cloak with his sword, to cover a person naked to the waist, and leaning on a crutch. The whole within an orle of lions passant gardant, in separate compartments respecting one another."

" The old seal of mayoralty is of silver, and represents the same legend of St. Martin within a quatrefoil, with four demi-ships conjoined with four demi-lions in orle. Sigillum maoratvs portvs Dovorr. *The seal of mayoralty of the port of Dover.*

also coroner by virtue of his office,) twelve jurats, and twenty-four common council men. Four of the jurats are nominated by the corporation, and out of this number the mayor is chosen, on the eighth of September, by the resident freemen, each of whom receives one shilling, on giving his vote; and the officers of the town are chosen by the corporation.

The seal of mayoralty in present use is of steel, and of elegant workmanship. It represents the same legend of St. Martin, and has nearly the same inscription."

" There are also two steel seals, the one somewhat larger than the other, used formerly in the ports' register office for seamen; engraved in 1696. They bear an anchor enfiled with a tower, and four more towers, forming with the other a quincunx, between the stock and flukes. The larger seal has likewise a ship of three masts under sail in chief; and is inscribed, *The Cinque Ports' register for seamen.*"

" The seal of the chancery and admiralty courts is of silver, and of good workmanship. It represents a man of war of two decks under sail, with an ensign, and with flags at the main and mizen masts heads, all charged with the cross of St. George, and a pendant at the foretopmast head, passing by a castle on a hill, with a union flag displayed, inscribed, Mag*num* sigil*lum* castri Dover et cvriarvm cancellar*æ* et admir*alitatis* quinq*ue* port*uum*. *The great seal of Dover castle, and of the courts of chancery and admiralty of the cinque ports.*"

" The register of the castle has two seals nearly alike, with a castle of three towers; without any inscription. These are used for sealing writs."

" Brown Willis gives a curious account of the device on the common seal. It is, he says, a highwayman robbing a man on foot." *Boys' Sandwich, page 797.*

CHOICE OF MEMBERS OF PARLIAMENT.

Dover sends two members to parliament, in the choice of whom every freeman, whether resident or non-resident, has a vote, unless disqualified by law.

We have already noticed, that the barons of the cinque ports held an exalted rank in the great council of the nation, at a very early period.[1] The writ or summons was sent to the barons and bailiffs, and the persons elected had a stipend[2] allowed them, to bear their expenses during the session; and they were expected to act in obedience to their constituents.

To avoid the expense, some of the towns omitted to make their returns: and the town of Dover, in the reign of Henry the Sixth, agreed to receive forty shillings a year of the mayor and jurats of Feversham; and for this trifling sum, that corporation was allowed to name a person, once in three or four years, to represent the town of Dover in parliament.

About the same time, 1443, the inhabitants of the cinque ports petitioned that their representatives might be permitted to return home, after an absence of four weeks; or that only a few of them might remain at court, according to ancient custom. Such was their supineness and neglect, and so remiss were they in returning

---

[1] See page 113.   [2] Boys' Sandwich, page 402.

the writs, that they were afterwards sent to the
governor of Dover castle, to ensure greater
regularity.

The freemen of Dover appear to have preserved their privilege of voting till the year 1561.
At this period, the mayor, jurats, and common
council, took upon themselves to return the members to the house of commons, without either
consulting their brethren, the freemen, or taking
their votes; and they continued this practice
during a period of sixty-two years.

In 1623, the freemen petitioned the house of
commons against the return of Sir Edward Cecil,
knt. and Sir Richard Young, knt. The house,
in answer to this petition, resolved, "That the
freemen and free burgesses, inhabitants of Dover,
ought to have voice in the election;" and the
election was declared void, and a new writ
ordered. This determination was sanctioned, in
1729, by act of parliament, which confirmed all
prior decisions of that house respecting controverted elections.[3]

After this decision, the resident freemen were
allowed to exercise their elective franchise; but
the votes of the non-residents appear to have
been received or rejected, at the pleasure of the
corporation.

On the elevation of the Right Honorable
Buffy Villiers to the peerage, in 1770, Sir Tho-

---

[3] Geo. II. Chap. 24, 1729.

mas Pym Hales, bart. and John Trevanion, esq.
were candidates for the vacant seat. The non-
residents were, at this time, allowed to give
their votes, and Sir Thomas obtained a majority;
but Mr. Trevanion had a majority of the resident
freemen. He petitioned the house of commons,
and pleaded that the non-residents had no right
to vote; but the house resolved, "That the
non-inhabitant freemen had voice in the election,
as well as the inhabitant freemen."

At the general election in 1826, Messrs. Wilbraham, Thomson, Halcomb, and Butterworth,
were candidates. Mr. Thomson stood second on
the poll, including the non-residents, and was
returned; but Mr. Halcomb stood second if only
the residents had voted. A petition was presented to the house of commons, who decided in
favour of Mr. Thomson.

A similar objection was made in 1828, when
Mr. Wilbraham, now lord Skelmersdale, was
elevated to the peerage. William Henry Trant,
esq. was returned on obtaining a majority of the
freemen generally; but the major part of the
resident freemen had voted for John Halcomb,
esq. Mr. Halcomb founded his objection to the
return, on the first determination of the house
in 1623, which was sanctioned by law in 1729,
and which stated that the freemen, *inhabitants
of Dover*, had a voice in the election. He con-
ceived from hence that the right was confined to

the *inhabitants* only, to the exclusion of the *non-inhabitants*, and that the determination of the house, in 1770, was not only contrary to law, but also founded in error. The house, however, confirmed the return of Mr. Trant; and concluded that the word, *inhabitants*, did not exclude the *non-inhabitants*, but that both had a right to vote.

Freedom is acquired by birth, servitude, marriage, purchase, and by burgage tenure: but the franchise, if by marriage, ceases with the death of the wife ; or, if by tenure, with the alienation of the freehold. The number of freemen is about 1400 resident, and 900 non-resident, making a total of about 2300.

The HUNDRED COURT, or GENERAL SESSIONS AND GAOL DELIVERY.

This court has cognizance of criminal actions, committed within the franchise, and inflicts the punishment of death on gross offenders. The mayor, who is assisted by the recorder, the jurats, and the town clerk, presides ; and has the sole right of pronouncing sentence.

The mayor usually holds a court, by adjournment, every fifteen days ; but capital offences are tried twice in the course of the year.

We must necessarily pass over the obsolete and minor courts, county rates, &c. and hope the conciseness of this publication will apologize for such an omission; nor would it prove a pleasing task to enter on the latter subjects.

GIFTS TO THE CORPORATION.

Mr. Jonathan Taylor, who under a severe indisposition, had visited Dover, and had found its salubrious air instrumental to his recovery, left to the corporation, by will, £100 to purchase a piece of plate, as a testimony of esteem, for the respect that had been paid to him, during his residence in the town. The plate was to be made in the form of a punch bowl, and was intended to grace the convivial meetings of the corporation; but the will being litigated, the expenses of the process, after the cause had lain in chancery ten years, reduced the £100 to about £75. To fulfil, however, the intention of the donor, the corporation agreed to supply the deficiency from their own funds, and the bowl was finished, as directed by the will. It cost £107. 6s. weighs 200 ounces, and is sufficiently large to contain six gallons. The arms of the town, and an inscription from Mr. Taylor's will, are placed on it; and, from its neat and elegant workmanship, and from its magnitude, it may fairly bear a competition with the first pieces of plate in the county.

The late John Minet Fector, esq. to fulfil the wishes of his deceased honored father, presented to the corporation, in 1814, three chests of plate, containing a handsome ladle for the large bowl above mentioned; two smaller bowls, with appropriate ladles; two large candelabres, with four branches to each; and four smaller ones, with three branches to each. The whole, which cost several hundred pounds, are of excellent workmanship, and weigh 1070 ounces. Suitable inscriptions, and the town arms, are placed on them; and their appearance is grand and superb.

ALMSHOUSES AND CHARITIES, VESTED IN THE CORPORATION.

Prior to the time when assessments were first levied to relieve the poor, an almshouse adjoining St. Michael's church, in Bench-street, was erected by some unknown person; but the date of its origin cannot be ascertained. This house, in 1522, was exchanged by the corporation, for the present almshouse, in Queen's-street, which belonged to one Oliver Lygs. By a will proved in 1552, it appears that Robert Justice gave six and eight pence towards repairing the house; but the repairs did not take place till fifty-nine years afterwards.

The mayor for the time being, is master of the charity; and two of the common council, are warden and treasurer.

The early accounts of the charity being lost, it is not possible to determine for what particular purpose it was intended. As no poor laws were then in being, it probably afforded general relief to the distressed and indigent; but some have supposed that it was intended for poor sailors and soldiers, who might be passing through the town. No records remain of receipts and disbursements earlier than the year 1588, leaving a period of sixty-six years from the time when the charity was removed from Bench-street. Distressed objects of every description were relieved during the first ninety years of the existing accounts; and such objects have been occasionally relieved to the present time.

Several persons have given and devised lands and money to this charity;[1] and, from the wording of these documents, it further appears that it was intended for general relief.

The corporation borrowed £50 of the fund, in 1607, and the town house was mortgaged for a security. They continued to pay interest at £5 per cent. during a period of 148 years, at the expiration of which it was continued at £4 per cent.

A terrier of the lands belonging to the charity, was taken during the mayoralty of Luke Pepper,

---

[1] Thomas Andrews gave a house, in 1597 ; Richard Toms, lands, in 1599 ; George Buzy, lands, in 1603 ; Thomas Ellwood, £14, and a piece of land, in 1612 ; and Thomas Badcock, £10, in 1616.

in 1629, at which time Valentine Tatnell and William Richards were wardens.[2]

Two cottages, near Cow-gate, having gone to decay in 1685, the materials were sold by the corporation; and the ground on which they had been situated, was also sold in 1693, to Kennett and Monins, for £3, which was applied to the fund of the charity.

In 1758, the corporation borrowed £100 more of the fund, at four per cent. and continued to invest the overplus of the receipts.

There are four old small adjoining houses in Black-ditch, which appear to have been appendages to this charity; and which have been let, these many years, to poor widows, at one pound per annum.

The visitors and guardians of St. Mary's parish, were directed by order of vestry, in 1800, to petition the corporation for leave to inspect the accounts of the charity, conceiving that the casual poor ought to have been relieved from its funds. The order was not put in execution till

---

[2] The terrier of the lands and tenements, taken in 1629, is as follows :

Thomas Broom, 12 acres, at Hougham..........	£12	0	0
John Westrope, half an acre, at Charlton........	1	10	0
J. White, messuage, garden & tenement, Biggin-st.	1	0	0
Thomas Brounger, two tenements..............	0	1	0
Margaret Marsh, piece of ground, St. James's-st.	1	0	0
John Randal, a meadow, Paul's Corner, Charlton	5	10	0
Total from lands and tenements................	21	1	0

enforced by a second order in 1802; and, after some objections on the part of the corporation, leave was given in 1803. After the accounts had been examined, considerable difficulty was experienced in forming adjustments; and no satisfactory result being obtained, the cause was submitted to the court of chancery, in 1818, by Messrs. Thomas Chester, William Elgar, John Hammond, Marchant Barry, and John Philpott, on behalf of the parish.

The lord chancellor gave his decision in 1820,[3]

---

3 The amount of income, in 1820, was as follows :

	£		
C. Baker, 11 acres, 10 poles, land at Tilmanstone	10	0	0
J. Going, 2 roods, pasture land, St. Mary's parish	12	0	0
W. Collins, 5ac. 1r. 27p. arable land, Charlton ...	21	0	0
W. Coleman, 2ac. 2r. 21p. arable land, Hougham..	7	7	0
Daniel Pain, 5ac. 3r. 17p. arable land, Hougham..	37	3	0
Jeken & Co. part of field, Paul's Corner, Charlton	3	18	0
Jonathan Osborn's Representatives, part of ditto..	2	6	10
Ditto, part of ditto	6	4	10
J. Shipdem, ditto	6	4	10
W. Brockman, ditto	1	12	0
Mathew Kennett, ditto	1	13	0
James Curling, ditto	1	12	0
George Stone, ditto	6	10	0
George Stone, ditto	1	2	6
Michael Kingsford, ditto	5	12	0
John Smith, ditto	3	10	0
Matthew Kennett, ditto........................	3	10	0
Js. Worsfold, ditto, (the whole contains 2 acres, 12p.)	7	4	6
K. Collins' heirs, ground rent, house in Biggin-st.	1	0	0
Gilbee's heirs, garden ground, St. James's parish..	0	15	0

Carried forward...... £140 5 6

and ordered that the accumulated fund should be laid out in erecting additional small houses, for aged men and women, who are to pay £1 per annum rent; and the casual poor are to be relieved from the surplus income, or a succession of new houses erected with it. The parish of St. Mary is to nominate to one half of the new houses; that of St. James, to one quarter; and those of Hougham and Charlton, each to one eighth. Two persons are to be nominated on each vacancy, and one of them is to be selected by the master and wardens, who are to make up their accounts annually, and to transmit copies of them to the respective parishes. Seventeen neat new houses are already built near the four old ones, in Black-ditch; and the annual income of the charity still amounts to upwards of £170.

Mr. Hugesson, who gave the Market-place to the corporation, is supposed to have ordered

	£	s.	d.
Brought forward	140	5	6
Widow Hopper, small house, St. Mary's parish	1	0	0
Widow Brett, ditto	1	0	0
Widow Collar	1	0	0
Widow Cavil	1	0	0
The Matron, almshouse in Queen-street, valued at	10	0	0
Parker Smithett, for cellar in ditto	2	0	0
Total annual value of real property	156	5	6
Annual interest of the corporation for £150	6	0	0
Annual interest on £1500, in the £5 per cents	75	0	0
Total annual income	£237	5	6

the sum of £3 yearly, to be paid out of the rents,
for the benefit of six poor widows, each to be
paid annually ten shillings.

Thomas Papillon, esq. by will, dated the 30th
of June, 1701, gave £400 to the mayor and
jurats, to be invested in lands, houses, quit-rents,
or annuities, the yearly produce of which to be
applied in apprenticing freemen's sons, setting
them up in trade, or in relieving aged and
necessitous freemen.

PUBLIC BUILDINGS,

AND

MISCELLANEOUS ARTICLES.

The Town Hall.

Anciently, there appears to have been in the
market place, a building called the cross, which
in an old plan of the town, has the appearance
of a mean structure, with a cross on it. On
the site of it was erected, on massy pillars, the
present town hall, under which the market is
held. The hall is spacious, and has another
room adjoining for the grand jury. There are
some good portraits, and, in the jury room, a fine
ancient print, representing the embarkation of

Y

Henry the Eighth, at Dover, May 31st, 1520, preparatory to his interview with Francis the First.

The grotesque figures on the pillars that support the building, bespeak its high antiquity; but it has undergone several alterations: and the sides are now covered with mathematical tiles, and adorned with fine large Venetian windows, which give it a modern appearance.

THE THEATRE.

This building was erected in 1790, by a company of gentlemen, who advanced the money in fifty pound transferable shares. It is situated in Snargate-street, and is usually open as a play-house, from September till nearly April. Subscription assemblies are also held monthly, during the winter; and occasional dancing and card assemblies, in the summer.

THE CUSTOM HOUSE.

When the old custom house, which was situated where the bank of Messrs. J. Minet Fector & Co. has since been built, was falling into ruins, a new and spacious edifice was erected for that purpose, near the harbour, in 1806. Goods imported, or intended for exportation, and all baggage from the passage or other vessels, are brought here to be examined. The towns of Folkstone and Romney are within its jurisdiction; and the business carried on here is very extensive.

THE NEW GAOL.

This building is situated in the market-place, and was erected on the site of the old gaol, and of an adjoining strongly built old house, formerly called Tinkers Hall, and afterwards used for a charity school and a private dwelling. The first stone of the new edifice was laid on the 8th of September, 1820, by Sir Thomas Mantell, knt. whose mayoralty ended on that day.

THE CIRCULATING LIBRARIES.

The Kings' Arms Library, No. 1, Snargate-street, near the Parade, was erected, in 1826, by W. Batcheller. It contains upwards of five thousand volumes, embracing every branch of English literature, and is continually increasing. A handsome room is fitted up for the accommodation of Subscribers, where the London and county papers, reviews, magazines, &c. are constantly on the table. An assembly room is also fitted up, over the shop and library, which commands a beautiful prospect of the sea and harbour; and where promenades are held during the season, and quadrille and card assemblies in the winter.

The Albion Library, 86, Snargate-street, was built by Mr. G. Ledger, in 1782, and is conducted

by Z. Warren.   Papers, reviews, magazines, &c.
are taken in for the use of subscribers, and a
handsome room is fitted up for their reception.

The Marine Library, pleasantly situated on
the Parade, was built by Mr. Bonython, in 1823,
and is now conducted by Z. Warren. It is a handsome shop, including a reading room and library,
which has a good selection of books.

FELLOWSHIP OF TRINITY PILOTS.

This Fellowship was established, under the
direction of the court of Loadmanage, in the year
1515; and their employment is to pilot ships
into the rivers, Thames and Medway. They
were established at Sandwich, in the early part
of their institution; and an order was made
by the fellowship, that no person, unless duly
licenced by them, should pilot any vessel into,
or out of the havens of Dover or Sandwich.

King William, in 1689, restored to the pilots
their ancient right, (which had been wrested from
them by the hand of power,) to choose a master
or warden from their own body; and appointed
the lord warden of the cinque ports, for the time
being; the mayors of Dover and Sandwich, for
the time being; and the captains of Deal, Walmer, and Sandown castles, for the time being,
commissioners of Load-manage.

The pilots, in 1699, obtained an order of
vestry, for leave to rebuild, for their own use,

the gallery, at the western extremity of the middle aisle, in St. Mary's church; and, in 1748, they gave £20 to the parish,[1] for leave to obtain a faculty, to hold the said gallery, so long as they should keep it in repair at their own cost.

In the third year of George the First, the pilots obtained an act, authorizing an establishment of fifty pilots at Dover, fifty at Deal, and twenty in the Isle of Thanet; since which time, the mayor of Sandwich has been left out of the commission, but the other commissioners continue to hold the office.

By an act passed in 1801, the number of pilots at Dover was increased to sixty-four. They are divided into two classes, viz. *Upper Book*, or those that have been longest on the list, from whom the wardens are chosen; and *Lower Book*, or those who were last appointed, and who advance to the upper book by seniority. The upper book formerly piloted all vessels that drew more than eleven feet six inches water; and the charge is regulated by the tonnage.

The lord warden, as admiral of the ports, holds courts of Load-manage, for regulating the fellow-ship, and for appointing pilots at Dover, Deal, Margate, and Ramsgate. The instrument by which a pilot is admitted, is called a *Branch*,

---

[1] The faculty is dated Oct. 20th, 1748 :—Edward Hobbs and Edward Goodwin, churchwardens. They purchased the chandelier, which is suspended before their gallery, in 1752.

and the seal of admiralty and chancery, is affixed
to it.

These valuable men are a credit to their profession, and are highly respected by their fellow
townsmen.   Many years since, they established
a fund, from which, in case of death, their widows
receive £12 annually during life, provided they
remain unmarried.

CHARITY SCHOOLS.

The gentlemen of Dover, in 1789, raised a
subscription for a charity school, which was to
contain forty boys and twenty girls, the latter of
whom were soon increased to thirty.   As the
master and mistress were then paid at the rate of
one pound for each child, the income was not
considered a sufficient remuneration for them;
and the number of children was progressively
increased to sixty-five boys and forty-five girls.

The school was continued on this establishment
till 1820, when the trust were enabled, by their
accumulated fund, and by additional donations
and subscriptions, to erect a spacious school, and
a contiguous dwelling for the master and mistress,
in Queen-street; and to remove the school from
the site of the present gaol, in the market-place.
The two lofty and commodious school rooms are
sufficiently large to contain 200 boys, and 200
girls; and the whole edifice is a credit and
ornament to the town.   This charity extends to

all poor children in the town and neighbouring villages. An annual sermon is preached in the two parish churches of Dover, in aid of its funds; and the whole is supported by voluntary contributions. The children regularly attend the established churches, twice a day, on Sundays.

A School of Industry, under the direction and superintendence of the ladies of Dover, was established in 1818, for the education of sixty girls. It was at first taught in a private house, in Queen-street; but a new building was erected for the purpose, above Cow-gate, in 1827. The children are required to attend some place of worship twice on each Sunday; and the greater part accompany the mistress to the established church.

An Infant and Sunday School was established in 1826, and was at first conducted in a house, at the upper end of Fivepost-lane; but is now removed to the private house in Queen-street, where the school of industry was formerly taught. Preparations are now making to erect a building for the purpose, in Abovewall-street, where the Sunday school will be taught on the Sabbath day, and the infants during the week. The advantages of such an institution, are not only great to the little innocents, who receive early impressions of virtue; but also to the parents, who are enabled to place their little charge in safety, while they pursue their daily avocations of honest industry.

DOVER HEIGHTS.

During the war which ended in the year 1783, fortifications were erected on this elevated and commanding situation. Four guard houses were constructed, and their positions strengthened by ramparts and lines of modern defence, which extended a considerable distance on the adjacent hills; and seventy-two pieces of cannon were mounted to protect them.

Immense sums were expended in strengthening this elevated position, during the eleven years preceding the general peace, in 1814. Whole regiments of soldiers, (on extra pay,) companies of miners and engineers, and a large train of masons, artificers, and labourers, were continually employed in forming excavations, lines, breast-works, batteries, and redoubts; and all the formidable constructions of military defence. This lofty eminence is more elevated than the castle, and overlooks the summit of Shakespeare's cliff; and the extensive batteries not only command the town and harbour, but the approaches from the surrounding country.

Handsome barracks are pleasantly situated above the town, and have a communication with it, by means of a military shaft. The entrance from the lower part of Snargate-street, is through an arched passage, at the extremity of which, three spiral flights of steps wind round a large shaft or tower, open at the top to admit light, and sunk in the solid rock. One hundred and forty steps ascend the shaft; and the whole forms an ingenious and substantial piece of masonry, such as cannot fail to attract the attention of the curious.

Above these barracks is situated the grand redoubt, surrounded by a deep ditch or fosse. The ditch is not perceptible at a distance; but, on approaching the battlements, it opens its deep aud wide cavern, and forbids all nearer access.

On the ridge of the mountain, at a considerable distance from the town, is the citadel, defended by deep ditches, and numerous flanking and masked batteries, besides those that surmount the parapet. Lines of communication, and subterraneous excavations, connect every part of these extensive fortifications, which are sufficiently capacious to enclose a numerous army. At the conclusion of the peace, most of the cannon was dismounted, and the works left in an unfinished state. Should they ever be completed, they will form the strongest position in the whole kingdom; and the garrison would be well supplied with excellent water, from deep wells and curiously contrived tanks.

A military road made during the time of these improvements, passes over the hill, from Archcliff fort, near the sea shore, to the entrance of

the town, near the Folkstone road. The military hospital, which was erected at the same
time, is a handsome building, and is delightfully
situated on the declivity of the mountain, facing
the sea.

THE PRESENT STATE OF DOVER.

At the time of the last census, in 1821, the
population of Dover, including the divisions of
Charlton and Hougham, amounted to 11,468.
Since that period, many elegant lodging houses
and private dwellings have been erected, and the
number of residents, has very much increased.
Including the garrison, the numerous visitors,
and the passengers who are often remaining in
the town, the uumber must frequently amount
to upwards of fourteen or sixteen thousand.

The town, by its south-eastern aspect, affords
all the advantages of a seaport, without the
inconvenience of that extreme cold, to which
many others are subject. Had its original
founders anticipated, that it would one day
become a favorite resort of the invalid, they
could not have selected, within a compass of
many miles, a better shelter from the northern
blast, than the lofty castle hill. The heights to
the west, and Shakespeare's cliff, at a distance,
to the south-west, afford a cover from the wind
in those directions. And, in order to secure
a free current to the wholesome breeze, a most

beautiful and shaded valley opens to the north-west.

A vast expanse of sea spreads before the town, enlivening the prospect from the balconies and windows; and those who have been charmed with the fixed beauties of rural scenery, look with no less delight on the moving panorama of boats and vessels gliding along before them.

The variety of the scenery is truly delightful. Mountain and valley, land and water, rural and marine beauties, conspire to shift the scene at every instant; and the eye only turns from an object of admiration of one kind, to fix on another of a different character.

But the sea bathing is, perhaps, one of the greatest attractions. The town is but a few hours' ride from London, and fewer hours' sail from Margate and Ramsgate. The cleanness of the pebbles on the shore, and the transparent clearness of the water, invite to the pleasing refreshment of the cooling wave.

The constant intercourse with the continent is another never failing source of amusement to the visitor at this place. Since the establishment of steam packets, the time of their arrival and departure may generally be estimated within a few minutes. As it draws near, hundreds are seen bending their way toward the harbour to witness, from the platform on the piers, or from the several quays, the bustling scene that is to ensue.

Then, horses, suspended from the gigantic cranes, are reluctantly swung from or to the vessel, while their heads, hung down, and their extended limbs, betray their terror, and present a striking contrast to the sprightly aspect they exhibited but a few minutes before. Heavy carriages, nicely poised, are removed in a similar manner. Passengers are seen taking a temporary farewell of their friends, while others stepping on shore, seem to forget the inconvenience of a sea voyage, in their joy to revisit the land that gave them birth. And foreigners pass in review, in every variety of costume, from the Italian image maker and Alsatian broom seller, to the Parisian dandy or the turbaned merchant of Morocco.

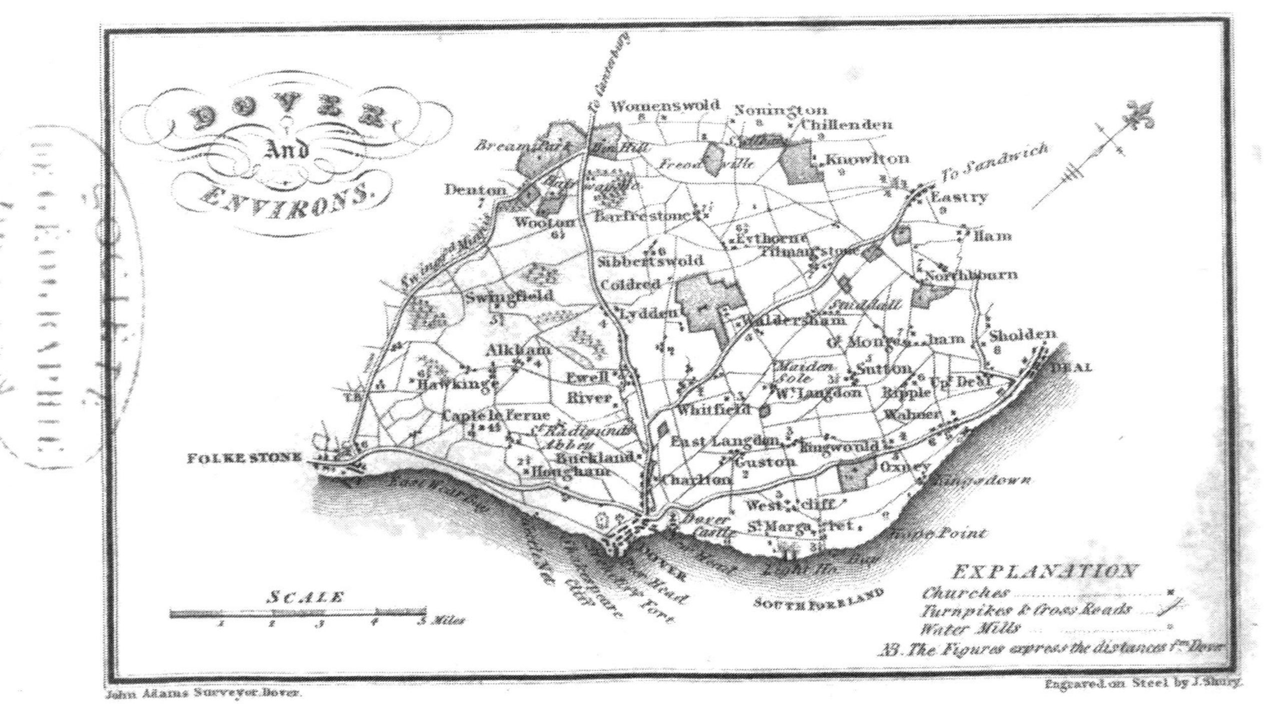

DOVER
And
ENVIRONS.
Womenswold
Nonington
Chillenden
Breamhill
Hill
Freodville
Knowlton
To Sandwich
Denton
Eastry
Wooton
Barfrestone
Ham
Eythorne
Pitman Store
Northbourn
Sibbertswold
Coldred
Tilmanstone
Lydden
Waldersham
Easthall
Swingfield
O. Monins
ham
Sholden
Alkham
DEAL
Maiden Fole
Sutton
Hawkinge
Ewell
River
W. Langdon
Ripple
Upr. Deal
Walmer
Capel le Ferne
Whitfield
St Radigonds Abbey
East Langdon
Ingwould
Buckland
Guston
Oxney
FOLKE STONE
Hougham
Charlton
Kingsdown
West Cliff
Hope Point
Dover Castle
St Margret.
SOUTH FORELAND
SCALE
1   2   3   4   5 Miles
EXPLANATION
Churches
Turnpikes & Cross Roads
Water Mills
N.B. The Figures express the distances frm Dover
John Adams Surveyor, Dover.
Engraved on Steel by J. Shury.

A

NEW DOVER GUIDE.

BANKERS, AND THEIR LONDON AGENTS.

John Minet Fector, & Co.—Minet and Stride, 21, Austin Friars, London.

Latham, & Co.—Barnetts & Co. 62, LombardStreet, and Herries & Co. St. James's Street, London.

THE PRINCIPAL INNS.

Wright's Hotel and Ship Inn, Strond-street, and on the Quay, fronting the harbour.   C. Wright.

York Hotel, fronting the sea, at the lower end of the Rope Walk.   Freeman Payn.

Union Hotel, Snargate-street, Pent-side.   John Jell.

New London Hotel, Council-house-street, near the harbour.   W. Chaplin.

City of Antwerp Hotel, Market-place. W. Huntley.

Shakespeare Hotel, Bench-street.   Charles Elvey.

Royal Oak Inn, Canon-street.   William Mowll.

King's Head Inn, Clarence-place, fronting the harbour.   A. Podevin.

Packet Boat Inn, Strond-street.   J. Hoad.

Gun Hotel, Strond-street and on the Quay, fronting the harbour.   G. Hipgrave.

Castle Hotel, fronting the harbour, near the north pier head.   T. Divers.

Cinque Ports' Arms Inn, Clarence-place, R. Eastes.

Flying Horse Inn, King's-street. Mrs. Chittenden.
Guildhall Tavern, Bench-street. Thomas Houghton.

BATHS, AND BATHING MACHINES.

Three new and commodious hot, cold, and shower
baths, comprising every accommodation for the infirm,
or healthy, are erected on the parade; and machines are
in constant readiness for sea-bathing. A handsome
room is attached to each of the baths, where the visitor
may sit and enjoy an extended view of the ocean, and
of the numerous vessels that are continually passing the
channel. The sea-bathing at Dover, on account of the
clearness of the water, and the convenience of the shore,
has obtained a decided preference to any other watering
place on the coast.

MUSICAL PROMENADES, &c.

Musical Evening Promenades and other fashionable
amusements, such as are usual at other watering places,
continue, during the season, at the Kings' Arms Assembly Rooms; and, in the winter months, balls are held
there, and at the Assembly Rooms, at the Theatre.

LAW.

William Knocker, John Shipdem, G. W. Gravener,
Thomas Pain, Matthew Kennett, Thomas Knocker,
Stephen Chalk, George W. Ledger, Edward Knocker,
John Hamilton, and Thomas Vincer.

PHYSIC.

Doctor Stolterfoth, Resident Physician. Stephen
Chalk, Philpot Elsted, Edward Norwood, Thomas Coleman, William Sankey, Edward Sibbett, William Cocke,
and William Robinson.

PASSAGE VESSELS.

The mail steam packets, two of which sail between
Dover and Calais, are under the direction of the general

post office, who have an agent resident in the town. Beside these, several steam and other vessels, belonging to private companies or individuals, and two French packets, are employed in the passage. They are all fitted up in an elegant and costly manner; and some of them are daily leaving, and entering the harbour.

TIDE TABLE FOR DOVER HARBOUR.

It may be desirable that we should add a tide table to the last article. The following has been of long standing at Dover; but we are fully aware, that no short table of this kind, can be calculated to any great degree of correctness, and that an error of half an hour or more may be frequently expected.

The first column contains the moon's age, and the second the time of high water, in hours and minutes.

Moon's Age			Hours.	Minutes.
1	and	16	11	47
2		17	12	35
3		18	1	23
4		19	2	11
5		20	2	59
6		21	3	47
7		22	4	35
8		23	5	23
9		24	6	11
10		25	6	59
11		26	7	47
12		27	8	35
13		28	9	23
14		29	10	11
15		30	10	59

The passage vessels can leave the harbour about two hours and a half before high water.—On a common spring tide, the water flows 18 feet over the apron, at the north head.

THE POST OFFICE.

Through the medium of this office, which is situated on the quay, near the custom house, a daily mail is established between London, Dover, and Romney. Foreign mails arrive and are despatched several times in the course of the week; but the precise period cannot be ascertained.

STAGE COACHES, &c. TO LONDON.

The Dover Royal Mail Coach leaves Wright's Ship Hotel daily, (Sundays excepted.) at eight in the evening, and returns at six in the morning.

Wright's Patent Safety Coaches from the Ship, Paris, Royal Oak, and Shakespeare Hotels, as follows:

The Courier, every morning at a quarter before eight, to the Golden Cross, Charing Cross, and to the George and Blue Boar, Holborn, in nine hours, without changing coach or coachman, and returns from the above places every morning, at a quarter before eleven.

The Sovereign, at ten in the morning, to the Golden Cross, Charing Cross.

The Regulator, at six in the evening, to the Golden Cross, Charing Cross, and to the Cross Keys, Wood-street.

The Union Safe Coaches, from the Union, Gun, and Packet Boat Hotels, the Antwerp and Castle Inns, and from their Coach Office, 45, Snargate-street, every morning at eight and ten, and every evening at six, to the White Bear Inn, Piccadilly; Bell and Crown, Holborn; Blossom's Inn, Cheapside; and 11, Grace-church-street; from whence they return every morning, at half past seven and eleven, and in the evening at a quarter before seven, in nine hours, without changing coaches or coachmen.

Chaplin's Safety Coaches from the Eagle Coach Office, Cross Wall; Chaplin's New London Hotel; York Hotel; and from the King's Head and Providence Inns, as follows:

The Mercury Fast Travelling Light Coach, every

morning, at seven, to the Spread Eagle Office, 220, Piccadilly, and to the Spread Eagle, Gracechurch-street, and returns every morning, at eight o'clock.

The Eagle patent Safety Coach, every morning at ten, in nine hours, to the above places, from whence it returns daily at ten, without changing coaches or coachmen.

The Swallow Superior Light Coach, every morning, at six, to the above places, from whence it returns every evening, at seven.

The Phœnix, every morning at half-past nine, from the York Hotel.

Rutley, Stanbury, and Young's Vans set out every day, from their warehouse in Snargate-street, to the White Hart Inn, Southwark, in seventeen hours; and return from thence every day in the same time.

COACHES AND CARAVANS

To the Neighbouring Towns and Watering Places.

The Union Coaches to Margate every day, and to Hastings every day during the summer, passing through Dover to Margate, at four in the afternoon, and to Hastings at twelve, where it meets the Brighton coach, and forms a communication between Margate and Brighton.

The Brilliant Safety coaches to Margate and Ramsgate, every morning at ten, and afternoon at four, from Chaplin's Eagle Coach Office, Cross Wall, and return daily at eight in the morning, and at four in the afternoon.

Ashtell's Coach from Hythe, every morning, and returns in the afternoon, (Sundays excepted.)

Bates's Coach to Margate, every morning at ten, and returns in the evening.

z

Williams and Johnson's Coaches from Margate, and return every afternoon, at four.

Kennett's and Hogben's Vans, to Ashford and Maidstone, every morning at eight.

Grant's Van to Canterbury, every morning at eight, and returns in the evening at seven.

Marshall's and Scarlett's Vans from Canterbury every day at twelve, and return at four.

Clement's Van through Waldershare to Sandwich, every Tuesday and Thursday.

Brace's Van from Eythorne, every Monday, Wednesday, and Saturday, at twelve, and returns at four.

Austen's Van from Deal, every morning at eleven and returns at six in the evening.

₊ Fly Chariots, Donkey Chaises, &c. are in constant attendance for short excursions, in the town and neighbourhood; and pleasure boats for excursions on the water.

THE DOVER PORTERS.

The employment of these porters is to carry parcels to any part of the town, to attend funerals, and to convey the baggage of passengers, either to, or from the custom house, or to embark or land their horses, carriages, &c. Each has a ticket, or number, and they form a regular establishment under the commissioners of the paving act, who have published the following rates of porterage:

	s.	d.
For shipping or unshipping any horse, mare, mule, or gelding	4	0
For shipping or unshipping of every carriage with two wheels	5	0
For shipping or unshipping of every carriage with four wheels	10	6
For every trunk, portmanteau, chest, box, bag, bundle, packet, or parcel, conveyed from any		

Inn to the custom house, and from thence to or
on board any boat, passage vessel, or packet
boat, or landed from any boat, passage vessel,
or packet boat, and conveyed to the custom
house, and from thence to any inn, or to the
custom house only, or direct to any inn, or to
any part of the town, not exceeding 28 lbs. wt.   0 6
Above 28 lbs. and not exceeding 56 lbs 1 0
Above 56 lbs. and not exceeding 1 cwt. 1 6
Above 1 cwt. and not exceeding 2 cwt. 2 0
Above 2 cwt. and not exceeding 3 cwt. 3 0
For every additional half-hundred cwt. 0 6

THE DISPENSARY.

A Dispensary was established here in 1823; but an
unfortunate dispute divided the subscribers in 1828, and
it was discontinued. In the course of a few months,
however, a new one was instituted, to supply its place,
and it is situated in the Market-place.

THE BIBLE SOCIETIES.

A Bible Society, called the Cinque Ports' Auxiliary
Society, of which the Right Honorable the Earl of Liverpool is President, was formed here in 1813. A Ladies'
Bible Association was also formed in 1819, of which Her
Royal Highness the Duchess of Kent is Patroness. The
exertions of the Gentlemen do not appear very conspicuous; but the perseverance of the Ladies does honor to
the cause they have so zealously undertaken.

THE SAVINGS BANK.

A Savings Bank was established here in 1825. It is
situated in the Market-place; and the deposits, on the
20th May, 1828, amounted to £ 23,794 : 7 : 6.

THE VILLAGES NEAR DOVER.

In describing the villages near Dover, our limits will not allow us to notice several of the ancient manor houses, or the great or noble families who have resided in them; but our remarks must be confined to the present appearance of the country, and to such particulars as may be most interesting at the present day.

CHARLTON.

This pleasant village was formerly near a mile from Dover, but now joins it by almost a continued line of buildings, many of which are within the liberties of the town. The church, dedicated to St. Peter, and which many years since had been reduced from its original size, was rebuilt and enlarged in 1827. Lofty hills and deep vallies diversify this parish; and the river Dour passes through the western part of it, and, in its course, turns a corn and oil mill, and two other corn mills after it enters the liberties of Dover.

BUCKLAND.

Almost a continued line of buildings, erected within the last twenty years, have united this village to that of Charlton, and to the town of Dover, from which it was situated more than a mile. The church, which is a neat small structure, is dedicated to St. Andrew; and Saint Bartholomew's hospital was situated in this parish, and is noticed in page 235. Hills and vallies, similar to those in the parish of Charlton, diversify the prospect: and the London road and the river Dour, pass through the centre of the parish, and the waters of the river turn two corn mills and two paper mills within its limits.

RIVER.

The rural and beautiful village of River, interspersed with cottages, gardens, and fertile meadows, is situated in the valley, about 2½ miles from Dover, on the west of the London road. The church, which is dedicated to St. Peter, is a small structure, and stands near the village; and not far from it, is seated the magnificent mansion of Kersney Abbey, built in the monastic style, by the late J. M. Fector, esq. in 1821; and which, with its rural scenery, engages the attention of every passing stranger. The river Dour passes through the valley; and, in its course, turns several corn and paper mills. On the other side of the London road, is Old Park, the residence of J. Every, esq. and more to the northward is Archers Court, the country retreat of G. Stringer, esq.

EWELL.

Farther up the valley, and about three miles from Dover, is the village of Ewell, with its church, an ancient structure, adjoining it; and the hills and vallies continue their romantic appearance on each side of the London road. The house of the Templars, once situated in this parish has been long since demolished.

LYDDEN.

This small village is situated between the hills, on each side of the London road; and the court lodge, and the church, dedicated to St. Mary, are at a short distance from it. It is four miles from Dover.

SWINGFIELD.

This parish, the church of which is small and dedicated to St. Peter, lies in a retired situation, on the south-west of the London road, and nearly six miles from Dover.

Swingfield minnis or common is two miles and a half long. The house of the Templars has been noticed in page 243.

ALKHAM.

On the same side of the London road, and about four miles from Dover, lies the parish of Alkham. High hills and deep vallies, with fields and clumps of coppice wood interspersed, give it a wild and romantic appearance. The church is a large handsome building, and is dedicated to St. Andrew the martyr; and the village adjoining it, is situated on a knoll, in the bottom of a valley, and is surrounded by lofty and spreading elms. We have mentioned the nailbourn, at Drelingore, in page 132.

POULTON.

This parish is no less wild and romantic than that of Alkham, and is situated on the same side of the London road, and nearly three miles from Dover. St. Radigund's abbey has been noticed in page 239. The church, which was dedicated to St. Mary, was appendent to the abbey, and was in use in 1523. There are now no remains of it; but a stone, with an inscription, about half a mile south of the abbey, points out the place where it was situated. The parish has had no church since the destruction of the abbey.

CAPELL le FERNE.

The parish of Capell (distinguished from Capell near Tunbridge by the addition of *le Ferne*) is more even and fertile than those of Poulton and Alkham, and extends to the cliffs that bound the ocean. Its small church, dedicated to St. Mary, is situated about a mile on the north side of the Folkstone road, and is nearly five miles from Dover. The farm houses and cottages do not form

a single village; but are promiscuously scattered at a
distance from each other. *13.*

HOUGHAM.

This parish also extends to the high cliffs on the sea
shore, and a part of it is comprehended within the town
of Dover.   The Folkstone road passes through it; and
the small church, dedicated to St. Laurence, and the
little village of East Hougham, are situated, at a short
distance, on the north of it, and nearly three miles from
Dover: and the village of West Hougham is still farther
to the north-west.   In the church lie buried several of
the Hougham, Malmaines, Fyneus, Nepeu, and other
great families; but their monuments are much defaced.
The ancient mansion of the Elms, built about the year
1640, but now in a ruinous state, is situated in this
parish.   Robert Lacy, esq. kept his shrivalty here in
1739.   Some grand views present themselves from the
tops of the mountains, and the air is healthy; but the
appearance, in many places, is rude and wild.   Dover
heights and Shakespeare's cliff, which we have already
described, are in this parish. *1317*

GUSTON.

Northward of the London road, on the high and level
ground, and about two miles from Dover, is the small
village of Guston, surrounded by extensive corn fields
and pastures.   The church is small and adjoins the
village, and is dedicated to St. Martin. *149*

WHITFIELD.

The parish of Whitfield lies on the north of the London
road, about three miles from Dover, and the new road
to Sandwich passes through it.   The situation is high,
level, and healthy; the fields large and well cultivated;

and some of the prospects, having the ocean in the distance, are charming and delightful. Near the eastern boundary is the little church, dedicated to St. Peter; and to the westward, on the turnpike road, the hamlet of West Whitfield.

COLDRED.

On the same high, but less level ground, and a little more than five miles from Dover, is the parish of Coldred, the prospects and appearance of the country being very similar to those of Whitfield. The small church, dedicated to St. Pancras, is situated within an ancient fortification, supposed to have been cast up by the Romans, who had a burying ground near it; and afterwards to have been repaired by Ceoldrid, (from whom the place probably took its name,) king of Mercia, who came to assist the Kentish men, in 715, against Ina, king of the West Saxons, and a severe battle was fought between these two monarchs, near Sandwich. The entrenchments, which in some places are nearly perfect, enclose more than two acres of ground; and a lofty mount was cast up towards the south-eastern part of them. A few years since, in making a new road through the centre of the enclosure, a well, more than 300 feet deep, was discovered, from whence the neighbouring farm house is now supplied with excellent water.

SIBERTSWOLD, or SHEPHERDSWELL.

The church of this parish, dedicated to St. Andrew, is situated near the London road, to the northward, and six miles from the town of Dover. Several Roman entrenchments are still visible in this neighbourhood. A boarding school has been lately established here by Mr. Gilbert, which has all the advantages of a healthy air, and a pleasant retirement.

BARFRESTON.

To the north of Shepherdswell, and more than seven miles fron Dover, is the parish of Barfreston, or Barson, whose little church, dedicated to St. Mary, affords a rare specimen of Anglo Saxon architecture, decorated with a profusion of sculptured uncouth heads, wreaths, and other devices. The delightful parks of Fredville, St Albans, and Knolton, are at a short distance to the north-east of this parish.

EYTHORNE.

This parish is divided into Upper and Lower Eythorne; and the church, dedicated to St. Peter and St. Paul, is situated in the latter division. The air is healthy, the prospects delightful from the gently rising hills, and the roads in excellent repair. Several Roman intrench-ments are visible in this parish. A boarding school for young gentlemen, under the care of Mr. White, and another for young ladies, under the care of Mrs. Rogers, are established in this healthy and delightful situation.

WALDERSHARE.

This rural parish is situated on the new road from Dover to Sandwich, and about six miles from the former. The noble family of Malmains resided here from the time of the conquest, 1066, till the year 1372; and their mansion, which was called after their own name, (now Marmage,) is at present a farm house. The Goldwells succeeded, and then the Monins, who were of Norman origin; and the first of this family who resided at Wal-dershare, about the year 1422, built a new mansion on the site where the baronial seat is at present situated. The Berties succeeded in 1663, of whose descendants Sir Henry Furnese purchased the estate, and rebuilt the mansion about the year 1700, and which continues at the present day. The noble family of Guilford succeeded in 1766, in whose title the estate still remains, and the present earl resides at Waldershare. The seat is built after a design of Inigo Jones, and is an elegant structure, surrounded by an extensive park, well stocked with deer, and adorned with groves, pleasure grounds, and delightful avenues, shaded by lofty trees, and enriched by a multiplicity of beautiful shrubs. Here might pleasure roam in sylvan scenes, or contemplation muse on nature's fairest features; or thence expand the enraptured thought to worlds of brighter glory, beyond the verge of this terrestrial orb. The belvidere tower, erected by Sir Henry Furnese on the higher ground in the park, lifts its majestic head above the trees. The view from the summit of it, is grand and sublime, and extends over the surrounding country, to the Nore, and to the coast of France. Sumptuous monuments adorn the little church, which is dedicated to All Saints.

WEST LANGDON.

This parish lies at an equal distance between the London and Deal roads, and is three and a half miles from Dover. The church, dedicated to St. Mary, has been in ruins since the year 1660. Langdon abbey has been mentioned in page 238.

EAST LANGDON.

The church of this parish, dedicated to St. Augustine, is situated near the Deal road, and is three miles from Dover. This, and the parishes we have already mentioned, on the high ground, north of the London road, are not only pleasant, but so remarkably healthy, that many of the inhabitants live to a very advanced age.

WEST CLIFFE.

This parish and its small church, dedicated to St. Peter, and in which there is service only once a month, is situated in a dry healthy situation, near the sea, and about three miles north-east of Dover.

SAINT MARGARETS, at CLIFFE.

At a short distance from West Cliffe, and three and a half miles from Dover, is the village of St. Margarets, with its adjoining church, dedicated to the titular saint of the parish. This sacred edifice is strongly built and rather spacious, and the features of antiquity are visibly impressed on several parts of it. A large and respectable boarding school for young gentlemen, conducted by Messrs. Temple and Son, is established in this retired and healthy situation; and being contiguous to the shore, the advantage of sea-bathing very highly recommends it. On the lofty cliffs, at a short distance from the village, are the South Foreland lighthouses, and a signal house not far from them. The views from these towering and almost perpendicular cliffs, with the sea nearly four hundred feet below their summit, and sometimes dashing against their bases, are truly grand and impressive. As the stranger passes along the footpath that sweeps this verge of the island, and leads from hence to the town of Dover, with the white walls of Albion under his feet, and the venerable castle just before him, he cannot fail to feel emotions, such as his own language can hardly express.

We must now take leave of our courteous reader; and should our endeavours to gratify him prove successful, we shall feel truly happy, and amply repaid, in having made the attempt.

INDEX.

FINIS.

W. Batcheller, Printer, Dover.

𝔓𝔯𝔬𝔭𝔬𝔰𝔞𝔩𝔰

FOR PUBLISHING A NEW
HISTORY OF DOVER,
AND OF
DOVER CASTLE.

IT has frequently furnished matter of regret, that among all the Histories, and Historical Sketches that have been given of Dover, of its venerable Castle, and of its picturesque environs, no description of those subjects has hitherto been published which combines utility with moderate expence, and the advantages of correct information with the principles of good taste. The professed Histories, published at a very high price, though composed with a great deal of elaborate detail, have been loaded with treatises upon things of comparative insignificance, and have been no less deficient in statements of importance. On the other hand, the " Sketches," having been hastily got up, have presented to the purchaser little more than some few disjointed portions, that have been extracted from more extensive works. Hence the complaint has arisen, that both publications are, in their kind, equally dry and uninteresting.

To obviate these objections, and remedy the defects too apparent in former publications, we have, in the work now offered to the consideration of the Public, endeavoured to take a middle course. Such another effort seemed to be absolutely necessary from some friend to Dover, and we have made it in our new History. In this we aim to give a local Description and History of the Town, so far as relates to statements worth knowing, divested of repetitions and petty particulars. We have endeavoured to describe the Port with as much clearness as may consist with brevity; and the Castle, without enumerating all the punctilios of military ordinances. On the other hand, we shall amplify as well as retrench; and consider the productions and appearances of nature, with no less veneration than the relics of antiquity, and speak of what our predecessors disregarded. In short, to strip detail of its wearisome excess by condensing the materials of preceding histories, to collect the anecdotes and descriptive matter, relative to our localities, from a variety of books of travels, and to illustrate the whole with a series of engravings, for the entertainment and information of the candid visitor, has been the design of this undertaking.

CONDITIONS OF PUBLICATION.

The manuscript shall go to the press as soon as 300 Subscribers are obtained.

It shall be printed on a fine wove paper, with a type entirely new, and comprised in Two handsome Volumes, post octavo, and embellished with numerous engravings.

Price, in extra boards, One Guinea.

A List of Subscribers' Names will be added.

Subscriptions to be paid on delivery of the work.

₊ As the publisher of the work, now offered to the Public, has been at a very considerable expence in endeavouring to make it every way worthy of a liberal patronage, he respectfully solicits the early delivery of names from those who may honor him with their subscriptions.

PRINTED AND PUBLISHED BY W. BATCHELLER,

King's Arms Library, Dover,

Where Subscribers' Names are received.